THEIR
RESTING
PLACE

BOOKS BY B.R. SPANGLER

DETECTIVE CASEY WHITE SERIES

Where Lost Girls Go

The Innocent Girls

Saltwater Graves

The Crying House

The Memory Bones

The Lighthouse Girls

Taken Before Dawn

THEIR RESTING PLACE

B.R. SPANGLER

bookouture

Published by Bookouture in 2023

An imprint of Storyfire Ltd.
Carmelite House
50 Victoria Embankment
London EC4Y 0DZ

www.bookouture.com

ISBN: 978-1-83790-115-9
eBook ISBN: 978-1-83790-114-2

This book is dedicated to my friends and family.
With much love, thank you for your support.

ONE

Charlie Robson didn't want to die today. She'd gone into the sunflower field when she'd heard her name called by someone. But it hadn't been by anyone she knew. It had turned out to be a nightmare. She ducked below the blooms now, her fingers clutching her phone, her muscles quaking as a cry became stuck in her throat. She stared at an arrow, the tip of it burrowed in the ground, the end brightly colored with green and orange neon fins. Its shaft was as black as coal, a dark blur when it had skinned her leg a moment ago. She touched the wound, fingers trembling, her blood horribly bright. Charlie swallowed a scream and searched desperately for a phone signal. No bars.

"This was a trap," she said, her heart beating wildly, terror clouding her head. How could she have thought the invitation was anything but sinister? With a gut-wrenching revelation, Charlie understood what it had really meant. "He's hunting me."

She should never have come alone. She should have thrown it away instead. Crumpled the note and tossed it in the trash. Wasn't it from the girls? The team? A get-together to talk about him? It wasn't. The writing was though, her name on the front, the folded paper sitting alone in her mailbox. There was no postage or return address. It wasn't junk mail or one of those fliers. Someone had been to where she lived and had placed it there for her. Charlie slipped the letter from her pocket, seeing it as she'd first seen it earlier that day. She read it again. Read the word, *guilty*, the writing done in cursive with tall looping letters.

Panic felt like a wildfire, kindled to burn through and all-consuming. To survive, Charlie had to escape. Her screen showed no bars. To escape, she'd have to get to her car. Foot-steps approaching. Heart shuddering. Heavy soled shoes stomped the ground, crunching the stalks with movement across the field. Beads of sweat teemed on her face with a sting. She crouched further and shuffled to a new spot behind heavily seeded blooms that were large enough to eclipse the sun. They were big enough to keep a secret, to keep her alive. A cold gust. A pending storm. The giant stalks swayed gently and spoke in delicate voices that hid her breathing. She peered up enough to see her car parked nearby. Stay hidden, and she'd stay alive.

The wound in her leg pulsed, dressing her leg red from the knee to her ankle. Cautiously, she held her phone to the sky, thinking that'd help. No signal bars. Charlie startled with the arrival of a bird. Flower petals circled a bed of seed, a chickadee swiftly flying from one to the next. The bird gave her a curious look, wings flitting as it took off abruptly. The footsteps were closer. Charlie teetered softly on her toes, squatting until she was nearly on the ground. She didn't dare lose her balance, grabbing a slender stalk to prop herself, the weight enough to break the stem and give up the secret of her hiding place. She sipped at the air as plump raindrops began to fall and join the tears on her face. She had to move again, chance a sound to get to her car.

Thirty feet, she thought, lifting enough to see the rusted yellow Mazda. It had been a gift from her cousin to help her get back and forth from classes. Emanuel was always good to her, watching out for her since his parents were lost in the accident. He was a cop and would be the first person she'd call for help. She eyed the phone's screen, a single bar blinking, a signal coming and going. Charlie's heart swelled as she swayed like the sunflowers, easing north and then south, honing onto a solid bar. A bar! She anchored herself, planting her bare knees into the field, the phone's cell service holding on to one bar. *Emanuel.*

The hair on the back of her neck rose like the bristly flower stems still in her grip, before an arrow struck sharply. She froze in the moment, her phone's screen shattering in an explosion. A red ribbon opened in her palm, splaying from her wrist to her fingers. Her phone tumbled onto the ground, pixels dancing violently as the battery wheezed out the last of its life. The punctured screen died then, turning black, an arrow stuck at the center of it. Pain rifled up her arm, but she ignored it and jumped into a run, the muscles in her legs telling her that they'd been sitting squat for too long. She ran lopsided, falling onto her side, panting frantically. She climbed over the sunflowers, their stems breaking with a snap, and was up again and running straight. Blood dripped from her fingertips, her view blurring. She didn't dare look back, staying in a straight run to where she'd seen her car.

Her lungs burning, Charlie reached an opening, her shoes clopping over lifeless sunflowers. An arrow whizzed by her head, the wind it carried touching her cheek with a cold kiss. "Please," she begged, a stifled scream rattling her teeth. But there was no mercy. Not when being hunted. Another arrow found her when her gaze landed on her car. She was less than fifty yards from it as the arrowhead bit into the back of her thigh.

She tumbled forward, chin striking the ground, chest crashing, her shoes flying into the air in an awkward somersault. Dizzied and confused, she'd fallen at the edge of an opening that didn't make sense, that wasn't supposed to exist. There was no time to understand it though, fire raging in her legs, an arrow grotesquely jutting from her flesh. A seedy bloom turned to her as if it was going to speak, as if it was going to warn her. She was in a crop circle, the sunflowers trampled to the ground in a perfect circular pattern. She clutched her chest when she recognized it for what it was. A kill zone. Her hunter had driven her to the spot in the open to finish what he'd started. The next arrow dug even deeper than the last, entering from behind, piercing her lower back. She clutched her middle where it stuck, where it protruded through her shirt, the metal tip dripping.

"Dark blood," she mumbled errantly, her body turning cold from the shock as she recalled the instructor calling it deoxygenated. It was venous blood; she'd learned that in her training to be an ER nurse. Her words wandered crazily with instructions as she crawled toward her car. "Care should be taken, or bleeding could be substantial."

Footsteps approaching at a steady pace. Charlie labored forward on her knees and elbows, her crawl turning clumsy when a fresh arrow plunged through her ribs. It was like glass being driven into her soul, the arrow stealing her air, collapsing a lung while she slipped back into the cover of the sunflowers. She stared aimlessly, finding the sunflower blooms above. The giant beauties peacefully danced with the wind of the oncoming storm while she slowly began to die. Gray clouds lumbered overhead, turning the day's twilight into a green seance. The sunflowers were good at keeping secrets, but he'd found her. There was no hiding.

"The body will experience cold and extreme pain," she rambled in short breaths, her instructor telling them about shock following a major accident. There was a cry deep inside her. The kind that turned her insides loose and made her sick. But the damage was done. She chewed on her upper lip, tasting the blood as it rose into her mouth. A chill rushed over her skin, adrenaline washing through her. A splash of color. A female cardinal landed on a sunflower and turned a beady eye on her, a witness to the last moments of her life. "Cold, clammy skin. Rapid pulse—"

A tune. Humming. The killer was at her feet. Charlie lifted her head to see them, finding a face hidden in silhouette instead. Charlie gasped when the shadows lifted.

"You?" she asked in disbelief, her voice gurgling. She spat the metal taste on her tongue. "Why?"

There was no answer, the view of her killer drifting with her focus. She almost thought she heard more footsteps. Or did they move? Someone new? Her killer loaded a new arrow, the bow hoisted shoulder-high into position, its string drawn taut and then released with a cracking whoosh. Charlie's eyelids peeled open with a start, her chest seeming to cave inward, the cardinal's wings flitting as it darted to another flower.

The killer was like a statue, watching her writhe. She tried to look away and not give her murderer the satisfaction. Emanuel might find her. Hadn't she seen a signal bar on her phone? Did the text message reach him? There was a cell tower near here someplace. Charlie's last thoughts were of the girl she'd seen in the news, a name from her past, the one who was killed in a sunflower field like this. Charlie would be number two today.

TWO

Five Years Earlier

The bow creaked as Charlie pulled the line into position. She firmed her foot against the soft ground, the field damp from the days of rain that had fallen. It was their first practice in almost a week and the strain crawling into her shoulder said that she'd be sore later. The pain in her fingertips confirmed it. A gust of wind carried a chill and the smell of autumn, strong enough to make the line sing and her hair fly around her head. Some of her team took to wrapping themselves in their jackets, but Charlie let the gooseflesh rise as she narrowed her focus. She sipped at the air, concentrating on the target, the meet with their rivals in less than a week.

"Now," she said with a whisper, letting go, the arrow flying straight and piercing the target with a thwack.

"Missed again, Charlie," Patti chided with a sly grin. Their team was good. One of the best in the state. And of them, Patti was a big reason why. But Charlie was sure she could beat her. She knew she could.

"One more," Charlie told her, gripping the insides of her

shoes, *fists with her toes*, her cousin Emanuel would joke. It was part of her setup, her form, and she did it without thinking. She pulled back until the bow creaked again and the line sang, straining to gain another inch and give the arrow some speed. "Just one more."

"Miss, miss, miss," Patti teased loud enough for some of the girls to hear. It stole Charlie's concentration, a frown forming. Patti's freckled face was bright in the dim light. She held her bow like a dance partner and pranced and sang, "Charlie Charlie, you can't win. You'll miss the target because you st—"

"Knock it off!" Jessie yelled. "Patti, do you really think that helps?"

Patti looked at them wide-eyed as though she'd done nothing wrong. "Sure, it does. The other team is going to razz us."

"No, they won't. And you know it," Jessie scolded. She approached, standing behind, hands on Charlie's hips, encouraging her form. Jessie's blonde hair flowed over her shoulders as she bumped Charlie's elbow and said, "Don't let your arm drop. Not even a little. It's why that last shot went high."

"Like this?" Charlie asked, her gaze drifting to Jessie. She was taller than Charlie, stronger too. *And pretty*, Charlie thought with a flutter of butterflies. She smiled nervously as Jessie looked over her form again.

"That's tight." Jessie returned the smile, pupils growing. "You want to draw the string to the same spot every time. Never deviate. Train your muscles to do it without thinking."

"Okay," Charlie said, her insides warming with the help. She peered at the target, inhaling deep, and then holding her breath, the bowstring tight near her face. She exhaled and released, the arrow flying straight and fast with a whoosh. It struck the target, missing the center by a few inches. "That's better!"

"It is," Jessie said with a wide smile. She rocked her head to

Patti who'd gone quiet while fidgeting with the neon-colored feathers on the end of an arrow. "Better give her a few shots too."

"Right." Charlie stepped out, blades of glass rising where her feet had been planted.

Patti took the position and went into form, her body firm and in perfect placement like something from the cover of the *Archery Today* magazine. She looked over at Charlie and gave her a wink before releasing the bowline.

"Bang," she said and blew a kiss, the arrow striking perfectly center, donning a smile filled with smugness. "That's how you do it."

"Come on, Patti," Jessie said, shaking her head. "Knock it off."

"What?!" Patti answered. "I'm trying to help."

"You can help by fetching some arrows," Jessie said, the team having already spent their arrows in the first fifteen minutes of practice. Their practice field was next to the high school, a wall of hay bales making up a berm behind five targets. There were arrows sticking out of the hay, some sitting at odd angles, giving wonder to how it was possible. The better shooters stayed on target, their arrows grouping around the yellow center, striking the red and the baby-blue ribbons.

Charlie wished Patti would have missed. Just once. Feeling low, she stepped up to offer, "I'll get them."

"I can help," said another girl, Bernadette Pare. She entered the target field, Charlie joining. Short like her, Bernadette's rust-colored hair was pinned back today, her face free of makeup. There were circles beneath her eyes that carried a worrisome look. Bernadette gave her a nod, saying, "You start there?"

"Okay. Thanks," Charlie answered.

"Anyone come up with a name?" Jessie asked the team. A new name had been in question since the team had come together for the fall semester. When no answer was given now, Jessie raised her voice, "Come on, guys. We need a team name for the yearbook pictures."

For the first time in days, sunlight broke through the gray clouds, turning their practice field a bright green, the hay bales golden, the colorful targets glowing. A few girls instinctively turned toward the sun and tucked their hair behind their ears. Charlie did the same, the rays warm on her skin, helping to rid the cold dampness. She closed her eyelids, the sunlight bleeding through them enough to see red. "Doesn't that feel amazing!?" she asked Bernadette. No answer.

"I got an idea!" a voice shouted. "How about, the sunshine girls?"

"Nahh," a voice answered immediately. "That's already been used before."

Charlie opened her eyelids to see half the girls facing the sun, their heads tilted to drink it in. To her they looked like the spring flowers in her mama's garden. "What about the sunflower girls?"

Silence. Patti was first to lower her chin and look at her. Charlie braced for an insult but got none as Patti nodded with a smile. She turned to see what Charlie was seeing and answered, "Yeah, we're the sunflower girls."

"I like it! That's my vote," Jessie said, holding up three fingers. "Who else?"

"Sunflower girls," Deanne Somer said, raising her hand. "You can count me in."

"Bern," Charlie asked as she returned to their chore, pulling an arrow free.

"Sunflower girls," Bernadette answered without a change in expression. She ducked behind a target, freeing arrows from a hay bale.

"Sunflower girls it is!" Jessie announced.

Charlie glowed with the contribution and tried to pry a

smile from Bernadette. "Got more in the hay than in the targets," she joked and yanked an arrow free.

"We're gonna get creamed in the next meet," Bernadette commented, holding a fistful, tugging on a stubborn one, the foam squelching. She stopped what she was doing, the motion abrupt. She gave Charlie a serious look as though she had to say something. The angst in her eyes went deep, unsettling, and hinted to a kind of trouble that made Charlie stop and pay attention.

"Bern, what is it?" she asked. Bernadette covered her front, hand drifting to her middle. Charlie's gaze followed her hands. "Are... are you pregnant?"

The team was waiting for them to rejoin them before resuming, a soft chatter continuing about their new name. They were still far enough for the two girls to speak candidly and Charlie fixed Bernadette a look that told her it was okay to talk. Bernadette shook her head and held up a broken arrow, joking instead, "We're sure to lose, unless they're as bad as we are!?"

"Bern?" Charlie asked, ignoring the humor. "What's going on—"

"Watch out!" Patti shouted, an arrow flying by Charlie's face, a hot rush of air touching her like a flame. The arrow landed in the target with a thud, Patti yelling, "Hold!"

"Yo!" Charlie yelled, her guts rising in her throat. Up field, Cara Palto, Karen Walter and Chrissy Jensen, the junior varsity squad, were just arriving, their bows in hand, arrows in place, except for Karen. "What the hell, Karen!?"

"No practicing when someone is downfield!" Jessie said, voice commanding.

"Hey, JV!" Bernadette yelled, coming to Charlie's side, concern furrowing her brow. She knew the rules, having been stung by a practice arrow once before, a ragged scar above her ankle. "Your practice doesn't start for another fifteen minutes."

"I wasn't even close," Karen answered snidely, silvery hair

pinned back, a piercing in her nose glinting sharply. Charlie shot Karen a disapproving look. It wasn't like she was new. This was her second year on the junior varsity squad, a sophomore, and might be added to the varsity squad soon. She knew better than to shoot, which meant she probably did it on purpose.

Chrissy Jensen, on the other hand, was a freshman. She was new to the JV squad. She looked downfield, wide-eyed and scared. She placed her bow onto the ground, shaking her head and answered, "I... We didn't see you back there."

"Sorry, Charlie," Karen said, the apology without merit. Charlie braced for what was coming. Girls could be the best of friends. They could be like sisters. But they could be mean too. Brutal even. "Maybe I was just showing you where the target was. Seeing how you've been missing it at the meets."

A sharp laugh. A hush fell over the girls as Charlie reared back, heat rising on her face. She needed to return a bite, the other girls watching. She could give as good as she got, but the words weren't coming, her tongue sitting fat in her mouth. Bernadette yanked the arrow and sniffed it and made a funny face, acting repulsed by a smell that wasn't there. "Yep, this one is Karen's. Marking the arrows again, are you?"

Karen cocked her head with a smirk. "Aren't you funny! I bet that you are—"

"Listen up!" the coach yelled, arriving from around the corner. Bernadette seemed to shrink in response. Her shoulders dropped and she lowered her head, ducking behind one of the targets. The coach waved his hand above his head, circling his finger. "Gather up!"

"Coach," Karen said while the girls made a circle around him, his eyes shaded by sunglasses, gum snapping, jaw clenching. He wore gym shorts and a tight shirt, unbothered by the cooler temperature.

Karen jabbed his bicep playfully, asking, "Are there any JV

moves for the upcoming meet? Ya know, since Christine quit varsity."

"We'll talk," he answered, glasses sliding down his nose as he peered over them. He shoved them back and addressed the team. "Big meet. I want you to relax your arms today and don't overdo it. Understood!"

"Understood!" the team chanted.

He lowered his glasses once more, searching their faces. "Charlie?" he asked, surprising her. She touched her chest, questioning. He shook his head, thumb hung over his shoulder. "My office."

"Coming," she said while the team disbanded, returning to their places, and resuming practice. The coach was already on his way and Charlie rushed to gather her gear, certain she was being kicked off the team. What would her mother think? Emanuel? The disappointment played in her like a fuel. It fed a fire she couldn't douse. She only needed more time. A few more practices.

A hand. Soft, but warning. "Don't." Charlie spun around, grass tearing beneath her shoes. It was Bernadette, her face pale and firm with concern. "Don't go."

"What are you talking about?" Charlie said, ignoring the warning and slinging her bag over her shoulder. "He's kicking me off the team."

"Oh," Bernadette said with a shake, the concern lifting. "How do you know?"

"You've seen how I've been shooting," Charlie said, a tear stinging, spinning back to leave the field.

The office was only twenty yards from the practice field, but it might as well have been a mile. Each step was heavier than the last, Charlie's insides soured with thoughts of having to tell her family she'd been cut from the team. She knocked on the coach's door, rapping her knuckles gentle, hoping she'd miss him. "Coach?"

"Come in, come in," he said, brow bouncing as he smiled. Shelves of equipment lined the walls, filled from floor to ceiling with footballs and basketballs, and every type of sports gear there was. The tight fit of the room smelled musty, the air stale. A metal desk sat at the center, daylight washing across two classroom chairs in front of it. Coach closed the door, latch hammering with a clack, the office suddenly dim, a single bulb hanging above the desk providing the only light. "Take your bow out, I wanted to work with you on your stance."

"My bow?" Charlie asked, her eyes adjusting. That's when she saw him, the hair on the back of her neck rising. He'd moved closer, too close, and the look on his face was different somehow and gave her pause.

"Uh-huh," he answered with the snap of his fingers, biting his lower lip, eyes wandering. She'd seen the look before from the boys in gym class. That didn't bother her though. Not like this. "Here, let me help you with that."

"I can get it." The first touch came as he retrieved the bow from her bag, handing it to her, his finger on her hand a moment longer than it should have been.

"It's okay," he said, shoes scraping the concrete as he shifted and moved behind her. He held her arms up, her bow in hand, instructing, "I want you to draw the bowstring and hold it."

"Okay," she said, relieved and feeling foolish for having assumed he wanted something else. Her confidence returned. Charlie fixed her posture as she'd done a thousand times, drawing the bowstring until it reached her face. "Like this?"

"Lift," he said, bumping her arm the way Jessie had done earlier. "You can't let your elbow drift. That's why you're hitting the targets high."

"Jessie said that too," Charlie commented and fixed her

form. Another touch. Gentle, fingers gliding across her middle.
Trust shattered. Fright squeezed her heart. When his breathing
quickened, she asked in a shaky voice, "Coach!?"

"Just hold still," he said, swallowing dryly, his mouth near
her ear.

"Coach?" Karen asked, metal on metal clanking, the door
opening wide. Daylight spilled into the office, the coach
jumping back, heat leaving Charlie's body. "Can I talk to you
about the varsity spot?"

"I have to go!" Charlie said, repulsed, her stomach twisting
and threatening to gush. It got worse when she thought of
Bernadette. Thought of how she'd changed in recent weeks.
Was coach getting at her? Who else?

The coach wiped his mouth and adjusted his pants as he sat
against the edge of his desk. He coughed to clear his voice,
saying, "That's enough for now, Charlie. Keep that elbow fixed
in place. Don't let it drift."

"Uh-huh," Charlie said, tears brimming, her insides rattled.
She had to get out of there. Had to run. Had to flee the office
and never go back. Heat rose in her like wildfire as she jumped
across the door's threshold, entering the daylight with a fresh
breath. She was free to run but couldn't. He'd get after Karen
too. The look on his face told her as much. She turned around
and grabbed hold of Karen's arm. "Karen?!"

"What do you want?" Karen asked, her expression twisting
with surprise. Charlie opened her eyelids wide with warning.
Confusion and annoyance cramped Karen's face. She looked
down at Charlie's hand and demanded, "Ya mind letting go of
my arm?"

"Come on in, Karen," the coach said. He put on a broad
smile, one of his front teeth a different color than the others.
Did she ever notice that before? Did it matter? He asked Karen,
"What can I do you for?"

"I need your help," Charlie pleaded, staring deep into

Karen's dark eyes, trying to warn her. She glanced at the coach and then back to Karen. When Karen didn't hear the warning in her voice or see it in her gaze, Charlie squeezed her arm hard enough to make Karen wince. "Come with me."

"Quit it!" Karen said, shaking off Charlie's hand. "Get outta here, ya freak."

"Whoa. Whoa, girls," coach said, intervening. He slipped his arm between them, slipping it around Karen's shoulders to urge her inside. Charlie shied away from his stare as he told her, "Charlie, time for you to get back to practice."

"Yeah, back to practice," Karen snapped. "You definitely need it."

A crack formed in Charlie's heart when the door clapped shut. There was no stitching that could fix it. No glue to mend it either. The crack widened and broke a piece of her innocence, stealing it forever as she shoved her gear into the nearby trash-can. It was the last time Charlie would ever play for the team. The last time she'd play for any team.

THREE

The curtains lifted with the smell of the sea, and the room filled with waves breaking and children laughing. A seagull's call rose while I watched beachgoers spread their blankets and test the water playfully, their happy sounds rising. Warm air hugged me in the open door of my apartment, the sun climbing into a fold of pink and red clouds. The swells were plenty, the surf tame, the ocean perfect for a morning swim. I loved everything about the Outer Banks, especially living on the beach. But as I slid my hand across the fourth of many cardboard boxes, I wondered if I really wanted to leave it all for a life in the city.

"That's one item off the list," Jericho said and closed his laptop with a click.

"What's that?" I asked, leaning into him, his arms wrapping around me.

"I finally sent in my resume," he answered with a short huff. I looked up, curious, to see his face cramped. "Honestly did not think it would take that long to update the thing."

"You do have a lot of experience to add," I said, excited by the prospect, turning back to face the ocean. "Whereabouts?"

"Some airport. The position is for a criminal investigation

job," he answered, cardboard rustling. "Not the international one. It's a small one."

"That would be Northeast airport," I answered, trying to think of the kind of work the position would entail. It didn't matter though. I was happy he was trying. On the outside, Jericho showed his excitement for the move, but I sensed a reservation too. When asked, he'd assured me he was fine. It was a big move, and considering he'd lived in the Outer Banks his entire life, I understood his doubt. "You'll find work. I'm sure of it."

A shrug. He dropped the box and approached. "If not, I'm sure I can find something to do," he said with a squeeze. "What are you looking at?"

"Just looking," I said, tipping my head for him to kiss me. I rubbed one of his hands. A scrape across the back of it had swelled, the scab weeping, after an unfortunate accident with a tape-gun. Our muscles were sore from a night of packing, the days counting down until the move north. "You should put some antiseptic on that."

"I will—" he sighed, nudging one of the empty boxes with his foot "—but probably best to keep moving." His warm touch leaving, my ears filled with scraping cardboard and the screech of packing tape unraveling. "By the way, what is this?"

I let out an embarrassed laugh when I saw what he'd dug out of a packed box. "What about it?" I asked, trying to defend the gallon-sized plastic kitchen bag filled with condiments. Collecting them had been a habit of mine for years. When he cocked his head with a frowning smile, I continued my defense. "I mean, you never know when you'll want some soy sauce."

"There must be a pint of it here—" He looked gobsmacked, or was it concern, fear perhaps, his questioning what he was getting into. "—along with mustards and mayo, and... and a small jar of brown goo."

"That's called Marmite," I said, trying not to laugh, the look on his face comical. "And by the way, it is delicious."

"Marmm-mite?"

"Better get used to some of my quirks," I warned and flashed my engagement ring. Daylight caught the pear-shaped stone and threw out sparkles, the brilliance warming my heart. "Like the vows say, for better or for worse."

"How about peculiarities?" he asked with a dry laugh. When I didn't respond, he put my collection back in the box, saying, "Fine, we'll bring it to Philadelphia."

"Thank you," I said, turning to watch a butterfly bounce on a breeze. It passed across swaying breach grass as a distant yell came from the children playing. There was a girl around three who resembled my daughter in a way that had me looking twice. The sight of her took me back to how I'd gotten here, and how I came upon this accidental miracle. That's what I called my life on the barrier islands, an accidental miracle.

Four years ago, I'd traveled from Philadelphia in search of my daughter. Her name was Hannah White, and she'd been stolen from me when she was only three years old. I was a cop, and later a detective, and had never stopped searching for my baby girl. Not once. Never. Some thought it mad that I'd chosen a life filled with despair, a refusal to accept her loss. What they didn't understand was that it was the angst that drove me. For fifteen years I had lived in purgatory, an endless cycle of hope and disappointment flowing like rolling waves. It had been heart wrenching. I'd abandoned my marriage, my home, and my family. But I had a career, which shined bright despite me. I solved murders and saved children, all the while continuing to search for Hannah. That was my life.

It had been an old clue that had brought me to the Outer Banks, a clue among clues I'd found tucked beneath a crop of thumbtacks and colorful yarn. A yellowed index card, its edges frayed, the corner of it bent and the ink faded. It had been one of a few hundred on a wall covered by more index cards, Post-it notes and articles from newspapers and blog posts I'd printed. There'd been an address and name and I'd accidentally lost the clue behind years of leads that had gone nowhere.

A short visit was the plan. That was all. A stopover at the address on the card, followed by my rehearsed script of questions before moving on to the next clue. On my way to the Outer Banks, I'd gotten lost on some backroads and had stumbled upon a young woman in dire need of a hospital. It was at the hospital's emergency room that I met Jericho Flynn, a ruggedly handsome man with wavy brown hair, a dimple on his chin and these blue-green eyes that reminded me of the sea that surrounded us. He'd been the sheriff at one time, and he knew everyone there was to know in the Outer Banks.

Some might think crime follows me like the rats followed the Pied Piper of Hamelin. Maybe it does? Maybe not. But that seemed to be the case when I'd arrived here. There'd been a murder and a crime scene that needed to be processed, and the investigating officer was without an active detective. The sheriff asked if I'd be willing to help, I agreed. But I told them that I'd do it in trade. With my credentials, and an afternoon without plans, I'd process the crime scene and then use Jericho as my personal tour guide to help chase down my lead. Before I knew it, I was temporarily employed as a lead detective in the Outer Banks.

That is when the accidental miracle happened. Investigating murder is what I do, and in the tragedy of this particular case, there'd been a karmic shine on my life that I will never be able to explain. It might have been coincidence, or the kind of timing seen once in a lifetime. I don't know what it was, or if I care. Whatever it was, it changed my life.

Along the beach the children squealed with laughter, the tide chasing them with a brim of foamy surf. A gull crossed our property, its dark beady eye on me briefly, the images from that first crime scene morbidly fresh in my mind like it was yesterday. I'd processed that murder, fulfilling my part of the bargain, but we hadn't found my daughter. That clue that had brought me to the barrier islands, it had turned out like the others. It had brought me two more clues, which brought me six more after that. It was like a bad boardwalk game of Whac-A-Mole. But we did discover that she could be somewhere in the area, and that was all I needed. Finding Hannah, that was a part of the miracle that would come later. I had decided to stay in the Outer Banks and continue in the temporary role of detective. I'd been told once that there was nothing more permanent than something temporary. For me, those words had never been so true.

"Morning guys," Nichelle Wilkinson said, her velvet-like voice carrying on the wind. She must have known we'd be in the back and come around to the ocean side of the apartment. She held her hair against a gust, tall poof leaning. Her complexion shone like bronze in the sun, her greeting with a smile. I waved her inside, the sight of her warming me. At one time, she'd been an IT technician at the station I worked and had been a part of my team. But those large brown eyes of hers had had big goals. Greater goals. And in just the few years I'd known her, I'd watched her career skyrocket. There was the move to becoming a crime-scene investigator. And then a huge move to working for the FBI, with their desire for her technical skills. They wanted her enough to request she move her life to their Philadelphia branch office on Arch Street.

"Food *and* coffee? You are a lifesaver," I said, mouth watering as I gripped the cups, the heat on them surprising. Our cheeks touched with an air kiss as she went inside and joined Jericho. Tracy Fields, Nichelle's partner, came around the corner, the sight of her giving me pause. She was a miracle. My miracle. Sometimes miracles are small, vague, a passing glimpse that is easily overlooked. That was true for me. Hannah had been in my life without my knowing who she was. If not for a case dating back decades, we might not have ever known that Tracy was Hannah, that she was the baby girl who I'd come to the Outer Banks to find.

Tracy stopped at the door to shake the sand from her sandals. She cringed at the touch of it on her feet, a trait I'm certain she'd picked up from me. Only, she wasn't a baby anymore. Not a toddler either. Fifteen years had passed since Hannah's kidnapping, and by the time I saw my daughter again, she was a grown woman. I gave her a hug, and jokingly told her, "It's just sand. It won't bite."

Her eyelids grew wide. "I've lived here most of my life, you'd think I would have gotten used to the way sand feels on my feet."

"Come on inside, you know where the towels are." Tracy was a crime-scene technician, and like her father, she had dimples buried in her cheeks. She was also tall and lean like me and shared my wavy brown hair and her father's baby-blue eyes. She'd accelerated through school, earned multiple degrees and had been introduced into my life as Tracy Fields. None of us had known she was my daughter. Not until a case exposed an illegal adoption ring. That was the first part of the miracle. Our miracle. She still goes by the name Tracy and continues to call me Casey, but that doesn't bother me. Maybe one day she'll call me mom. But if not, I think I'll be okay with that too. "Thanks for coming to help."

"Of course, we're going to help," she said, handing me a couple bags of food. She gave me a look that was filled with emotion, my hands closing on hers. "I can't tell you how much it means to me that you'll be in Philadelphia with us."

I grinned and told her, "You'll have to start calling it Philly." She flashed a smile, but like Jericho, I sensed the move might be bothering her. I wondered if she felt guilty, or maybe she wasn't ready? Tracy's relationship with Nichelle had risen like their careers. From a budding friendship, it had grown beautifully, and the two decided to make a life together, which included the move. I'd just found my daughter and wasn't willing to be apart from her any longer. A life back in Philadelphia. It was ironic considering we were moving to my hometown. I nudged Tracy's shoulder and tugged on her arm until the smile I knew she had appeared. "Don't worry about us. Philly will always be home."

Her eyes became glassy as she hugged the air out of me, saying, "Thank you."

I rested my head on her shoulder briefly, answering, "But you guys have to help us pack the rest of this stuff."

"That's what we're here for," Nichelle replied, holding a box as Jericho taped its bottom.

The second half of my accidental miracle was love. I had never expected to find love in my life again. Maybe it was the chip on my shoulder, the one that told me I wasn't deserving of anyone's love. It happened though. And I never saw it coming. Not even a hint of it. Side-by-side, Jericho and I had worked the case of a murdered woman discovered on an abandoned yacht. We'd also solved the puzzle of the young pregnant woman I'd found alongside the road. In the process, I'd fallen head over heels in love with the man. He had felt the same, and the two of us have been nearly inseparable since that day we first met.

It was time to get back to work and I turned around to find Tracy, Nichelle and Jericho huddled near the kitchen, talking about the coffee or pastries, or maybe the new boxes we'd need to buy. It didn't matter though, and I breathed in the ocean while sunlight beamed into the half-packed room. I was with my family and that's all I'd ever wanted. That was the miracle. But before I could pack another item, there came a knock at the back door. A shadow covered me, the sun eclipsed by the frame of a large man.

"Casey?" the shadow said, asking in a voice I recognized.

"Emanuel?" I said, questioning the familiar voice. There

was only one person I knew to be his size, tall enough to fill a doorway. Emanuel Wilson had been a professional basketball player a lifetime ago. And then had joined the police force and had worked for Jericho when Jericho was sheriff. For the first couple years of my time in the Outer Banks, Emanuel had worked for me. But that would never have lasted. He was good. Very good. A lead detective spot had opened on the mainland, and I'd pushed the promotion. But now the ex-basketball player was standing at my doorway, blotting out the sunlight, his face in silhouette. Even in the shadow, his features dimmed, I could see he'd been crying. My heart sank as I waved him inside. "What's happened?"

"Emanuel?" Jericho asked, extending his hand, dragging a kitchen chair into the room. "Sit. Can I get you a water?"

He nodded, chair legs groaning. "My wife and kids are at my mom's house."

"They're okay?" Nichelle asked as we gathered around him.

A tear dropped from his face with a nod, relief coming with a collective sigh. But it was news about someone he knew. "We came over for a visit, and I just got word about my cousin."

"What happened?" I asked while Jericho poured him a glass of water.

"Murdered," he answered, his voice barely with sound. He fixed a hard look on Jericho and then turned to me. "I need your help."

"Whatever you need," Jericho was quick to answer.

"Thanks—" he said. He swiped at his eyes aimlessly, words stuck, his mouth quivering while trying to dry his face.

"How can we help?" A hundred questions sprang to my mind. I didn't know his cousin, but I knew homicide and couldn't help myself. I wanted to know the details. The murder must have taken place in another district. Otherwise we'd have gotten word, a police report first, along with a notification for the medical examiner to join us at the crime scene. Then I realized why we hadn't heard anything. The murder was local to him, to his station and where he was the investigating detective. Although packing to move, I still had another week of work left. It was the same for Tracy too, our sharing the last day of the month on our resignation letters. I grabbed his arm, nodding. "On the mainland?"

"Yeah. At home," he said, trying to muster the words, the picture becoming clearer to me. He shook his head as a fresh mournful wave took him. He had no voice, saying, "I can't do it."

"We'll go for you," I told him, understanding the circumstance.

He pawed at his chin, which continued trembling. "Thanks, I'll need to call ahead so you can work the case."

"I know your captain well enough to make this happen," I said, feeling Emanuel's pain. "She'll understand—"

"Make her understand!" Emanuel said, his tone suddenly hot and giving me pause. Jericho tensed at the anger, body shifting, guarding. Emanuel flinched as if released of restraints, shaking his head until his expression turned soft. He quickly added, "Casey, I don't trust that anyone else can do it."

"I'll take care of it," I promised and wrapped my arms around him, the tenseness lifting. I'd investigated dozens of murdered girls, a hundred or more possibly, while I was searching for my daughter. Thinking back, I don't know how I'd been able to do it. How I could have stood in a morgue as a medical examiner pulled the drawer from a body refrigerator, all the while believing it might be my daughter I was providing an identification for. I braced Emanuel's shoulder to assure him. "We're here for you."

FOUR

I took to the phone during the drive, hoping to establish a chain of command and bend protocols just enough to help a colleague. My conference call began with three, but quickly ballooned into a growing list of who's who, their all jumping on to support Emanuel. At one point we had the mayor and Emanuel's captain, as well as the sheriff, all speaking at the same time, talking over one another while essentially saying the same thing.

By the time I'd reached the mainland, it had been decided that our station would work the case. This meant that Emanuel was out, which was probably the healthiest thing we could do for him. With the loss of a loved one, and he was past the initial shock and sadness, the anger was going to rage. We'd seen a hint of it already and needed to keep it at bay out of concern he could compromise the case. While everyone exited the call feeling good about their contribution, the only thing I could think of was finding the killer to fulfill a promise I know Emanuel would hold close to his heart.

The wind whispered through the sunflowers as if telling me

a secret, telling me there'd been the murder of a young woman named Charlie Robson. We arrived on site within the hour of hearing the news from her cousin, a string of patrol cars guarding the entrance to the sunflower farm, their lights flashing with silent brilliance. The body of Emanuel's cousin wasn't visible from the road, but I could smell the secret the field kept: the stench of death and blood mixing with the sweet earthy loam where the plants found life.

I helped Tracy with her gear as she followed me up the stony driveway. When the eyes of civilians found us, I positioned my badge around my neck, making it clearly visible. We passed the farmhouse, the farmer and her family standing on their wood porch, their carrying a hard look of worry. We'd speak with them soon enough, but I was certain I'd have no words to ease their concerns. There'd been a murder near their home, a fresh stain on their lives like the blood that was spread across their farm.

The yellow and black flowers were tall and plentiful, larger than expected, the field measuring in acres. Vegetation crunched beneath our shoes, each of us dressed in protective suits—plastic coveralls, I called them. We each had booties and gloves and a cap. The medical examiner from the area was on site and had insisted on the extra precaution. I knew why with the first glimpse of the crime scene. There was blood on the flowers, a trail of it that measured over twenty yards. We could see where the attack began and then where she had succumbed to injury and died. My heart ached understanding that Emanuel's cousin had suffered, that she'd been tortured repeatedly.

I stopped and commented, "With this much distance, there should be evidence left by the killer."

Tracy raised her knee and searched beneath her foot. "The soil is soft enough." She checked beneath her other foot. "But I only see one set of footsteps."

"I know," I said as we took care to maneuver around the path where Charlie Robson had walked. "That's what is bothering me."

I passed a sunflower plant that had been trampled, stripped of its leaves, and imagined the victim taking hold of it and holding on as if it would save her. Others were bent awkwardly, the stalks snapped in half by her hand as she bled profusely, which had turned dark in the hours following the murder.

I lifted one of the bent plants, saying, "She was trying to stay upright." The path was parallel to the road, making me think she could have been lost. "If she was trying to get back to her car, I don't think she knew the direction."

"What led her here?" Tracy asked, her camera flashing with a blink that turned green to white and colored the blood like charcoal. "She wouldn't have just walked into the field."

"She was called?" I answered, uncertain of it. Tracy frowned, looking far and wide where there was nothing but sunflowers. "It's one explanation."

"Yeah," she replied, her voice blocked by the back of her camera as she focused and snapped another picture. It was a footprint in the soil, the dirt smooth, the print without any tread. Tracy placed a marker next to it, along with a crime-scene ruler for measurement. We'd use the measure to conclude the print was Charlie Robson's, but from the collection of them, the blood spatter, I was already sure of it. "Something had to have brought her here."

"Agreed. A young girl isn't going to drive to the middle of nowhere and enter a sunflower field by themselves." We knew the secret this sunflower field kept, but it was keeping some of the truth from us too. We'd have to recreate Charlie's steps, one at a time, if we were going to understand what happened to her. It would take us most of today to process the crime scene, possibly the next morning to finish. "See how the footprints are equally spaced over there?"

"You think that's where she entered?" Tracy asked.

"Correct. Footprints are equally spaced and there's no disturbance to the plants." I carefully moved to the first broken plant, the footprints clumped together, the dirt stirred. "This is where the attack began, causing her to stumble."

Tracy took another picture while I placed markers. She pointed toward the road, saying, "Her car is over there, away from the farmhouse, which means they probably had no idea someone was out here."

I spun around, commenting, "It's isolated. Even from the road, nobody would know you were in here." A cluster of trees lined the property, their height towering the farm. "The only visibility is from the farmhouse rooftop, or those trees over there."

"The killer knew he'd have the privacy he'd need." Tracy shook herself, the comment frightening.

"Never thought of sunflowers as being scary." I turned back to face her, feeling vulnerable like Charlie must have felt. "The killer was here, hiding, waiting. She pulled up, got out of her car, and then what? The killer called her name?"

Tracy's eyelids opened wide. "Would you enter a field like this if you heard your name?"

"I would if I knew the voice." I knelt next to the first sunflower, its body leaning derelict, its bed of seed lying in a pile. "See the blood?"

"Let me get that," Tracy said, taking a picture while I shielded my eyes from the flash. "Stand there."

I carefully placed my feet where Tracy asked, placing a marker behind a small puddle of blood. "I think these are the first drops. He waited until she walked a couple yards deep into the field and then attacked her."

"By what?" Tracy asked. Rapid camera shutters filled my ears. "There's drops of blood in front of you."

I twisted around, searching behind me. "And blood spatter behind me." I stepped away from the path Charlie had taken, motioning for Tracy to join me. Her coveralls clung to her skin, the air growing thick with humidity, the sweat teeming on my back and chest. Pointing to the direction I thought the attack took place, I said, "Whatever it was, it would have been through and through. The weapon entered her from the front and exited the back."

Tracy acted out the scene, facing the direction the blood traveled, mimicking a strike. "That caused her to double over and take hold of this sunflower," she added. She framed the blood drops on the broken sunflower's stalk. We shifted to concentrate on the spray, spatter of blood blown across a patch of plants. Nodding, looking for agreement from me. "The weapon would be faster than a knife?"

"We have spatter on the plants, which would have come from an exit wound." I nodded with Tracy. "Agree. Faster than a knife wound."

"What about a gun?" she questioned.

"A small caliber bullet would do it, but patrol said the farmer and her family didn't hear anything." The breeze stopped, the slender plants becoming motionless. The sky threatened with darkening clouds that'd wash away the evidence and steal the story we were trying to build. "Let's take a look at the injuries."

We followed the bloody path to the body, careful where we stepped, taking pictures of the sunflowers Charlie hung on to while she tried to escape. "Marking a footprint," I announced, placing another marker, this once numbered 12, the black print shadowed by the growth around it. If not for the trampled plants, it would get lost in the field. My heart jumped and I waved Tracy over, saying, "This print is different. Look at the faint tread."

"Gotcha," she said, framing the picture, flash strobing, the electronic wheezing as it cycled. "They weren't as careful as they thought."

I glanced over to the farmer's house, eyeing her family, the faces of the sunflowers waving between us as I measured the children's ages and thought of their shoe sizes. Indistinctly, I told Tracy, "Or might be that it was one of the kids who'd discovered the body."

She looked over her shoulder at the medical examiner, Charlie Robson's arm visible. Her skin color was once the same golden bronze as Nichelle's, but in death it was like ash, a contrast to the sunflower plants' sunshine yellow petals and their green stalks. "What a horrible thing to see." She knelt and placed the crime-scene ruler, taking three more pictures. "We'll get the family's shoe sizes and some pictures for comparison."

When we reached Charlie's body, the medical examiner looked up. Her skin was like alabaster, and her eyes a light hazel color. They were gentle and unguarding, and welcoming as she gave us a nod. She spoke from behind a mask that muffled her voice. "I understand you are an acquaintance of Detective Wilson?"

"Emanuel, yes," I said, my focus on his cousin. Her body was in a crumpled pile, her legs folded beneath. Arms were splayed, as though she was a knot for us to undo to be able to understand her last moments of life. The lividity was heavy, a bluish-purple discoloration in her legs and arms and where her back lay against the ground. "He was on my team a couple years before moving here."

"Doctor Foster," she said, ground crunching. Around her the area was trampled.

"Detective Casey White," I replied, getting the cursory introductions out of the way. "This is Tracy Fields, an investigator working with me. She'll be handling the crime-scene photos."

"I understand you worked with Detective Wilson?" I nodded. Foster looked at Tracy and then the victim, their ages close, perhaps by a couple of years. "The victim is his cousin. Did either of you know her?"

Tracy shook her head while working her camera, carefully moving around Charlie's body while focusing and taking pictures. "We've never met."

"Sad thing," Foster said, a hint of emotion in her voice. "Murder is always bad, but when it's one of your own—"

"—it's personal," I continued for her, our eyes locking.

She clicked her tongue with a tsk-tsk under her breath, and then added, "There were more than a dozen injuries visible, and I suspect we'll find more during autopsy."

I nudged my head toward the beginning of the attack. "The blood patterns tell us the injuries were through and through."

Foster cocked her head. "There were no reports of gunfire. A gun with a silencer?" she asked.

"A silencer is a possibility." In my years as a detective, I'd never had a case where a silencer had been used. "That injury on her leg. It could be a bullet graze."

We knelt at the same time, Charlie's right thigh sleeved in dried blood which had cracked and begun to flake, a shallow cut the source. "At first, I thought this might have been from running. You know, injured while she was attempting to flee."

"Her fingers," I said, looking at the blood coating the tips of her hand. "She grabbed at the wound first, and then started her way in this direction."

"Definitely not a knife wound," Foster said as she made room for Tracy. "I don't think this is from a bullet."

"Why is that?" I asked, leaning over to view Tracy's camera, having her zoom the rear display so we could search the injury close-up. I rubbed my arm where a bullet had once grazed it, the scar wide and ugly, a divot showing the bullet's path. I was familiar with the injury, what it would look like.

"From the close-up, the surrounding tissue appears to be torn."

"Let's take a closer look," she said and pulled out a magnifying glass, a ring light mounted to the front of it. She shone it on the wound, the path of the injury clearly visible. "Concentrating on the abrasion rim, there appears to be a parallel abrasion with central sparing."

I didn't follow the medical language, and asked, "Then you believe the injury is consistent with a bullet wound?"

Foster said nothing as she tucked the magnifier away. She glanced around the field, saying, "Gunshot wounds are complex, and we generally have supporting evidence such as shell casings or a weapon."

She looked to Tracy and me as if asking the question. I answered, "None found."

"Hmm. For a gunshot wound, the pathology would generally exhibit a more violent and traumatic injury." She lifted Charlie Robson's blood-soaked shirt, revealing a wound to the left of the girl's belly button. The injury had a clean entry that was a quarter of an inch, possibly more. Foster felt around Charlie's back, saying, "I think we have our answer."

"No exit wound," I said, voice rising, knowing the question of a gun with silencer would be answered. Her eyebrows rose with confirmation. "If there was a gun involved, then the bullet is still inside her."

"Yes. If there's no exit wound, we'll find a bullet," Foster answered, and retreated to stand, waving her hand in the air, seeking guidance. Much of her face was covered with protective gear, but I could see she wasn't much older than me. There were faint lines on her brow and at the corners of her eyes. I gave her my hand, she must have noticed the look on my face, adding, "A herniated disc. Recovering from a spinal fusion."

"Sorry to hear that." When she was back to her feet, I asked, "You're good?"

"Once up, I am good to go. Thank you." There was a smile in her eyes. It faded as she continued. "Autopsy will confirm the caliber used if there was a gun involved."

I glanced at the diameter of the wound, and then at a sunflower plant. Its wide face was pocked, the seeds spilling from a hole. "It was a missed shot," Tracy suggested. Sunflower plants were leafy, some of them the size of a tablecloth. Tracy joined me in finding holes marking the plants. She held out her hands to show the direction and angle.

"Came from over there, entered this area, and then?" I turned toward the line of trees, the same direction she must have been facing. I frowned with the direction confirmed. "It can't be there."

From her bag, Tracy brought out a laser pointer, angling it behind a sunflower, pointing the light through the hole until it landed on my belly. "This angle says that the bullet that went through this plant came from those trees." I shook my head again, unconvinced. "Maybe they were up in the tree? You know, like a hunter's perch?"

"It's the caliber. And then there's also the addition of a silencer," I said, moving across the body to the other side of the small clearing. "Aim and caliber suggest a close proximity, and we haven't seen a single bullet casing."

"We'll test for gun residue," Foster commented. She shared in my doubt, adding, "Those trees are less than fifty yards."

"The bullet from a handgun can travel more than two thousand yards." The distance was plausible but lacked aiming accuracy. A large crow cawed, drawing our attention. We followed its flight, wings batting the air as a second bird joined it and they landed on the arms of a scarecrow. The figure towered over the field and wore a white and blue flannel shirt that was stuffed with hay. Its head was made of a weathered burlap sack, thick seams frayed, its face crudely sewn. The sight of the crows gave me an idea, a reminder of how farmers would deal with stolen crop. "The killer could have used a small gaming rifle." Brows slowly raised with agreement, encouraging the idea. "That would give the killer distance and accuracy."

"That does work," Foster said. She shook her head, clicking her tongue again with a tsk-tsk. "The number of wounds. What torture it must have been."

"Yes, it was." My chest cramped at the thought of it, at the thought of Emanuel reviewing the autopsy report. "Bullets?" I said with a shout, stirring the dirt with my booted shoe. "The angle from those trees."

Tracy recalled her comments from earlier. "Any missed shots are in the ground."

"Exactly. We need a metal detector."

"I'll get on it," she said, leaving in the direction Charlie Robson entered.

"Tracy, stop!" I shouted. She stopped at the entrance, white coveralls bright in the sea of yellow and green foliage. "Walk toward me, and carefully spin around."

"Like this?" she asked, carefully avoiding the markers placed where there was blood and evidence of missed shots.

"Yes, like that," I said with an understanding that made me sick.

"What do you see?" Foster asked.

"From up there, he could see everything," I said, pointing to the trees. "And he was shooting around her, sometimes missing."

"Yeah, the missed shots." Tracy wiped blindly at her face, sweat beading.

"What if he wasn't missing," I suggested, Tracy's eyes growing big. She spun around to face the opening, retracing her steps. "He was hunting her like an animal."

"You think so?" she asked, disgusted by the idea.

"Think what?" Foster asked, frowning as she tried to follow along.

"Charlie Robson entered the field, and then she was driven here, to this small opening."

"Like livestock," Foster added.

"She was slaughtered."

FIVE

A memory can breathe life into the dead. I believe that. The realness, the mourning, a cruelty felt until they pass. I glanced at my daughter as I thought of Charlie Robson's mother, my mind filling with the days and weeks after Tracy had been taken from me. It was impossible for us to ever recover the time we'd lost, but we had today and that meant everything to me. I felt a pinch in my heart, a breath stunted by a scar that'd never heal. Charlie Robson's mother would never have another day with her daughter. Her pain was deep. It was forever. All she had now were the memories. But those would never bring her daughter back.

A new day. Life resumed in the Outer Banks as though nothing had happened. People woke up with the growing daylight, they left the comfort of slumber, the warm sheets of their beds. They brushed their teeth, ate breakfast, and drank coffee, or tea perhaps, and then set out. But for Charlie Robson, she was on a bed made of cold steel, a tray in a body refrigerator, the effects of death slowed by temperature. Her blanket was made of blue plastic, a medium duty body bag with a J-shaped zipper down the center of it.

We placed her in the body bag near the end of yesterday. The rigor mortis that had already set in objected, meaning it took three of us to unfold her legs to inspect the wounds. We took samples from her shoes, and measured and then remeasured the wounds, determining which were entry and which were exit. The day was leaving us by the time we'd combed every inch of her dead body, finishing with the crime scene investigation before the sun was gone. Our timing was narrow, the evening clouds shedding heavy tears as we drove away from the sunflower farm, windshield wipers batting raindrops, a downpour washing the evidence from the field. The crime scene was done, but we weren't finished. We were far from finishing.

Tracy and Nichelle joined me on the drive to the mainland. The morgue was a mile and a half from the station where Emanuel was the lead detective. Jericho was with him this morning, the two having been friends for more than a decade. As tragic as the case was, it helped having Jericho involved. We'd need to speak with Charlie's mother, interview her and any family members to better understand how it was Charlie would end up dead in a sunflower field that was more than ten miles from her home.

We were on the latter half of the Wright Memorial Bridge, the hump of it in my rearview mirror, when the first brake lights bloomed and car horns shouted like gulls. I rolled my window down, needing a breath of fresh air, the car suddenly stuffy and uncomfortable with the smell of burnt coffee. Tracy mirrored the move, lowering her window enough for the air to blow across us, along with idling engines and boats motoring across the bay. Sunlight sparkled on the water's surface, rippling bright enough for me to lower my sunglasses.

"Crap," Nichelle said, her face appearing between the front seats. I followed her gaze to see brake lights going dark, extinguished as the stalled traffic shut their cars off. Her phone appeared, fingers tapping the screen. "I'll see if it was an accident?"

"Whatever it was, we're not moving," I said, taking my turn as I reluctantly shut off the car. I texted Doctor Foster, telling the medical examiner we'd be late.

She immediately replied, *Any objection to my starting the preliminary review? I have an idea about the entry and exit wounds.*

Nope. I texted back, sipping my coffee which had lost its heat.

No objections.

I'll see you in a few.

"Doctor Foster is going to get started," I said, chimes filling the car as they opened their laptops, making the best of the stalled moment. "The entry wounds. There were fifteen, and we counted twelve exit wounds."

I heard Nichelle comment with an "Uh-huh." And scanned my text messages.

"If the preliminary autopsy involves dissection, the doctor will find the bullets," Tracy added.

"The full autopsy is scheduled for later today," I said, finding nothing new in my messages. "Emanuel is bringing Charlie's mother to see her daughter and speak with Doctor Foster."

Nichelle's brow narrowed. "We'll have to wait on retrieving the three bullets?"

"Sounds like it," I answered, watching a boat inch across the bay, a Jet Ski buzzing by it. "Might be that's what Doctor Foster's idea was about. So we don't have to wait."

"It'd help to know so we can focus on the weapon used," Nichelle commented. She looked up from her laptop, finding me in the rearview mirror. She shook her head, asking, "There were no bullet casings found by the trees?"

"Not a single one," Tracy answered for me, her disappointment shared.

"That's part of the mystery. The caliber isn't right either. And what about the missing bullets?" I asked, the measurements bothering me. "To cover that distance with accuracy, the killer would have had to have used a small gaming rifle."

"The farmer and her family heard nothing?" Nichelle asked. We nodded as she flipped her laptop around to show suppressors for a 22-caliber rifle. "A silencer must have been used."

"That's what we were thinking," Tracy said, turning toward the center, asking me, "The caliber wasn't right."

"Not for a 22-caliber. They're close, but the wounds are bigger. They are closer to a 380-caliber bullet. Those rifles are semi-automatic, a different class."

"Could have used one of those," Nichelle said, brow raised while showing more suppressors, the gun silencer web page filled with a dozen types and sizes.

"We'll know the caliber soon," Tracy added, turning back around. "Once Doctor Foster recovers the bullets."

"Bigger mystery is how we could not find a single bullet. The metal detector didn't pick up anything."

"There were more than a few missed shots too," Tracy said, referring to the holes in the sunflower plants.

Impatience, especially when sitting in traffic, is a bad trigger for me. I wanted answers, wanted progress, but was unable to move. "Then we talk about what we do know."

"The victim," Nichelle answered.

"Correct." I faced her, the sunrise putting her in silhouette. She kept her laptop below the rear window to read the screen. "Anything about Charlie Robson we can investigate?"

A horn. The sound blaring. Motion resuming on the bridge.

I started my car and stomped the gas while Nichelle began to read her notes. "Charlie Robson, age twenty-three. A recent graduate of a local college and working as a waitress at a diner."

"Education?" I asked, wondering why the diner. "Job market isn't that bad? Is it?"

"There's not much demand for English majors," Tracy said. A click of a seat belt buckle. "Might be that she is applying for teaching positions."

"Nichelle, a diner you said?" A grin appeared on Tracy's face. When Nichelle nodded, I told them. "Yes, a diner trip is coming up. We'll want to talk to the staff. This murder wasn't random."

"Diner trip," Nichelle commented, holding a thumbs-up for me to see in the rearview mirror. They knew diners were one of my all-time favorite places.

"I see you grinning back there," I said, my hip buzzing with a text message. "Where else can you get breakfast any hour of the day?"

"I'm getting one too," Tracy said. The phone call coming in went to messages, but a text message followed, including Tracy's. "From Jericho."

Concern rose sharply, but then went still. "He's not on patrol today. Emanuel's mother?"

Tracy shook her head as she began to read it. "Stop by the farmhouse. Evidence."

"Evidence?" Nichelle asked, the car's rear thumping as it exited Wright's Bridge. She peered through the window, adding, "It's clear now, but that was a fierce rain."

"Windy too." Tracy texted back, speaking as she typed. "Thanks. We're still on the road. How is Emanuel?"

"Poor guy." Nichelle rolled down her window, wind buffeting in my ears. "Sorry."

Head shaking. "Casey, we didn't miss anything... did we?"

I hated feeling what I was feeling. That sense of error, of a mistake. "I can't imagine." I stuffed what I was feeling, adding, "But we got a call. We'll swing by before the morgue. Kit?"

"I've got everything in the trunk," Tracy answered as I spun the wheel left, crossing lanes of oncoming traffic and headed to the sunflower farm. "Hopefully this will be quick."

It wasn't long before the roads became gravel, some of them bare enough to see dirt and fill with rainwater. I steered clear of the puddles, avoiding any sharp stones. A flat tire wasn't in our plans, especially since I'd already delayed the morgue visit by a few hours. The farmhouse and sunflower field were as we'd left them the day before. With the farmer and her family outside, the scene looked like it had been sprung from a Norman Rockwell painting. The siding on the farmhouse needed fresh paint, peeling, the wood graying. The tin roof and gutters were faded too, but the windows appeared newer. The field was in good condition, the sunflowers standing tall, save for a few which appeared windswept.

"Ma'am," I said, the farmer approaching before we could step out of the car. She was makeup-free, hair combed back and braided. Her denim coveralls were clean, faded blue, a plaid shirt beneath it with an oval stain, a coffee spill perhaps. "I got a call—"

"I am so sorry about this," she began, a hard look of worry appearing. Before I could open the door, she leaned over, perching her elbows, her face a foot from mine. Freckles saddled her nose and dressed her cheeks, her eyes a light brown, which darted from me to Tracy and then Nichelle. "We had no idea until early this morning."

"What is it, ma'am?"

"Sue-Ellen, please," she said while reaching into a pocket. The farmer glanced over at her family, a young boy shying away. He was seven, maybe eight, with scraggly dirty-blond hair, his cheeks and hands shaded by the dirt he'd been playing in. "Our boy didn't know any better."

"Know any better?" I asked.

"I put it in a plastic baggy," she said and handed me a sandwich bag. There was a folded letter, a note with dried blood. "He didn't mean nothing. The boy likes to collect things he finds in the field."

"I appreciate your getting this to us, ma'am, Sue-Ellen." I flattened the plastic, the sound of latex snapping as Tracy put on a pair of gloves. I sensed the woman's worry. "Ma'am, there's no harm. Thank you."

"Again, we're really sorry about it." She stood up, knocked on the door, lips pressed tight. As she walked away, I could hear her saying, "Boy, don't you sulk."

"Let's see what this is," Tracy said, snapping a second glove into place. The baggy opened with plastic crinkling, Tracy carefully removing the paper. It was a thick stock, the kind used in formal invitations, the edges appearing freshly cut, one corner bent and covered in the farm's field dirt. There were bloody fingerprints on the front and back, the name *Charlie* handwritten elegantly across the center, the tall letters accented fancily.

"She was invited somewhere?" Nichelle said, asking, shifting forward until her arms were resting on the center console. "Usually don't see writing like that, except on an invitation."

"True, you don't," I replied while taking a picture of the larger fingerprint, the blood smeared over the letters of Charlie's name. "The killer invited her here."

"One more," Nichelle suggested. I nodded and photographed the front. There were smaller smudges from the farmer's son, but these were dirt, a partial print possible in one of them. I didn't hesitate, and sent the pictures to Doctor Foster, to confirm Charlie Robson's print. "Go ahead."

"And on the inside," Tracy exclaimed and opened the fold to show the same fancy writing. There were two rows of numbers, along with a date and a time. Her expression turned to surprise, the feeling shared. "Oh shit."

Beneath the numbers and the date and time, there was one word. The letters were large and capitalized, they were made bold with what might have been the rage and anger of the penman. I sat back and read what it said. "Guilty!"

SIX

Guilt can be a fault, an offense, a moral culpability. Or it can be a wrongdoing, maybe a shortcoming, a failure to do what's known to be right. What may have started with one lie, had maybe led to a second to cover the first. That might have been followed by a third, piling onto the previous two, the first of them festering and souring the intended outcome. Our job was to find out what it was that Charlie Robson had done or what it was someone believed her to have been guilty of doing. In the eyes of the law, she could be innocent. However, to the killer, Charlie must have done plenty, and made her pay. The fee was her life.

My throat closed tight, constricting with a tickle in my chest, the air suddenly cold. My breath turned white as it drifted between my lips, the thick doors closing behind me with a clap that reminded me of the morgue back home. Only this wasn't our morgue. We were two miles west of the station where Emanuel was the lead detective. The room was twice the size, the walls and ceiling painted white. There were six autopsy tables, each of them gleaming metal, held in place by a large pedestal which had tubes and wiring going to and from.

The table itself was made with a lip, forming a shallow pan, a large sink with instruments at the end of them, and used to collect the bodily fluids flushed during the procedures. Above each table were surgical lights, a handle at the center, the shape like a flower, the petals dimmed, save for the one with Charlie Robson's body.

Doctor Foster motioned toward the lights, a microphone hanging, a red light indicating she was recording. She waved us over, encouraging us to enter the morgue. Like the room, the body refrigerator had twice as many drawers as ours did. Its size had me wondering if this part of the mainland had that many more homicides, requiring they reserve so much space for their dead.

I brushed my arms, challenging the cold that was making me shiver. Tracy did the same, but her tolerance for it was better than mine. Nichelle was like me, her teeth chattering loud enough for Doctor Foster to hear. When she looked up, Nichelle covered her mouth, an apology in her eyes.

"Let's break," Doctor Foster said, her assistant flipping a switch, dousing the red recording light.

"Sorry about that," Nichelle said, her words made visible by a puff of cold.

Doctor Foster wrinkled her nose and waved a gloved hand. "Not at all," she said and took to a lean, stretching her back. Her attendant rolled a chair around the autopsy table and helped Foster sit. "I can't stand more than forty minutes at a time anyway."

"Would it be easier for us to sit?" I asked, lowering myself.

"This will work," she replied. "That way you can get close to the victim while I talk through the findings."

"You have something?" I asked, trying not to sound excited by the idea of findings. Even though this was Emanuel's cousin, the family member of a close friend, the detective in me hungered for answers.

"Please," Foster said, an arm extended for us to gather around the table. Charlie's clothes had been removed, her injuries cleaned and made clearer for the investigation. The attendant worked a spray hose called a washing gun, the dried blood made liquid again as it was cleaned from the table, trickling along the table's edge to the drain. "Fifteen entry wounds just as was counted in the field."

"And twelve exit wounds." I moved close to look at the gash in Charlie's leg, the open flesh pale, the edges ragged. "We've moved away from the ideas of a 22-caliber being used. A 380 is closer in size."

"Well, that might be a problem." Foster grunted as she struggled to get to her feet. Instinctively, Tracy made herself available, offering a hand. That wasn't something learned. It was who she was. Her father was quick like that, the kind of person to help without hesitation. When Foster reached the table, she pointed out the wounds. "This one, that one, and this. No exit wounds."

"Bullets would be recoverable," I said, unconvinced by the frown on Foster's face. "What is it?"

"When you got stuck in traffic, I thought of a non-invasive evaluation, expedite the preliminary autopsy." She nudged her chin to the wall behind us, two monitors flipping on, screens flashing. "I used our mobile X-ray machine."

"It can't be," I said, my jaw loose; Charlie Robson's body spanned the monitors, her posture and the position of her arms and legs the same as they were on the table. Only, the wounds were missing something. They were missing a cause. "I don't see any bullets."

"That's because they're not there." Doctor Foster went to the screens and pointed to a rib below Charlie's chest, the bone a light gray with a piece broken, the splinter floating in her tissue. "Not one bullet. But soft tissue injuries, and to vital organs, enough to sustain heavy blood loss."

"And death," I said, perplexed, unable to look away from the bone fragments. "The broken rib. What if it had been a bullet?"

"The damage would have been more substantial. Particularly if fired from a rifle." Foster tapped the screen, another set of X-rays appearing. I searched the X-ray for any bullets, but found none.

She flipped to a photograph, tracing an injury. "An abrasion as noted in the field," Foster said. "Note the similarity to a bullet graze wound, but less significant."

"Less significant," I repeated. "What can cause injuries similar to a bullet wound, but is less damaging?"

"It's like a riddle," Tracy said, voice soft as she regarded the image of Charlie's leg. "What travels like a bullet, leaves an injury like a bullet? But isn't a bullet?"

Our voices were replaced by the low hum of the body refrigerator. I thought through the hundreds of cases I'd reviewed, the thousands of coroner reports and remembered one case in Philadelphia. "An arrow!?" I answered, my voice curving with uncertainty. It was enough to draw their eyes. "Back in Philly, I was on patrol and responded to a shooting. Only, there was no gun. It was a belly wound, and could've been mistaken for a small caliber gun."

"Yes!" Foster said, voice rising. "A bow and arrow could do this."

I rubbed my gut, pointing to its side. "The victim had an arrow that went through him, an entry and exit wound."

Doctor Foster returned to her chair, fingers pinching her chin while she considered the weapon used. "The velocity, the shaft on the arrow, heat, tearing—" as she spoke, her eyelids widened. "Yes, these injuries are consistent with the damage an arrow can inflict."

"Easy to collect too," Nichelle said, showing us her phone's screen. "Thirty-inch shaft made of highly visible colors. The killer didn't have to spend any time searching for them."

"It's sickening to think it, but most of the arrows would have been sticking out of her body while she was trying to escape." Tracy centered on one of the wounds that had touched bone, asking, "Wouldn't there be a lot of damage when the killer pulled them out?"

"Barbless?" I suggested. It was a good question, the thought of sharply angled barbs on the arrowhead. The same used on fishing hooks to prevent them from sliding out of the mouth. "Take that as an action. How many kinds of arrowheads are there? There's a strong suggestion these are not the kind used to hunt game."

"We have twelve injuries with an entry and exit wound," Foster said, flipping through screens on her tablet. "We have forensic techniques for close-up imagery to perform an analysis of the tissue. A technique used with stab wound victims."

"You'll be able to determine a type of arrow?" I asked, excited by the idea. "Barbed or no barbs."

A nod. "But mostly for confirmation," she agreed, returning to the table. "Even without the analysis, we can see the edges of the wounds are smooth."

"There's something else about the arrows we know too," I began to say, following the doctor to Charlie's body, the mystery of the bullets and caliber put to rest. "Arrows are silent. Deadly silent."

SEVEN

Who doesn't love a diner? The bell above the door rang, the hollow ding was deep and resonated through me. Jericho peered up at it with surprise on his face. This was the place where Charlie Robson had worked as a waitress. This is where she had waited tables to earn tips, her shifts taking place all hours of the day, sometimes seven days a week. We learned from Emanuel that his cousin's school debts were high. She had needed the job, and it was also one of the reasons she lived with her mother, her path to a career job stalled. It had been eight months since her graduation, her degree awarded in December, a full semester early. The college she went to was next on our list of locations to visit, Tracy researching it for us.

"Are you guys hungry?" Jericho asked as the warm smells reached us, his gaze following a tray of food. He rubbed his belly jokingly, Nichelle joining him. We were hungry and I was glad he could join us. Emanuel had escorted Charlie Robson's mother to the morgue to meet with Doctor Foster. It was only after their meeting that the full autopsy would begin. At that point it was a formality. The preliminary review was telling. Use of arrows as the murder weapon was at the top of our list.

Jericho nudged my arm to follow our hostess, commenting, "I think I could eat one of everything on the menu."

"I've got an appetite," I answered, my ears filling with the noise of flatware clanking against plates, staff calling out orders for pick up and the low murmur of lunch conversations. The diner was an old-style one. A dining car Jericho had called it, the outside of it plated in shiny metal with neon colors around the edges, the sight of it inviting like a carnival amusement. The floor was made up of black-and-white checkerboard tiles, with booths lining the windows and a counter across from them with pedestal seats bolted to the floor. Behind the counter, I could see clear through to the rear, the cooks working to the beat of a tune playing on a small radio, trading diner lingo as they prepared the orders. "It smells amazing in here."

"Your booth," the hostess instructed, placing a handful of menus on the table of an empty booth, the last of them that I could see. "Your waiter will be with you in a moment."

"Thank you," I said, sliding across the red vinyl. Jericho sat close to me in the short booth. Tracy and Nichelle took the seat across from us, a tabletop jukebox stealing their attention. Before the hostess was gone, I asked, "Ma'am?"

"Yes." She wasn't more than fifteen years old and had light brown freckles on her cheeks and nose. Her hair was a dirty blonde and frizzy at the ends. She snapped her gum and peered over her shoulder, the cowbell grabbing her attention.

"Did you work with Charlie Robson?" I asked quickly, the diner bustling with lunch hour traffic.

"Is she the one who died?" the hostess asked, shaking her head. She peered over at the counter, a pillow of steam rising as a cook poured a basket of fries onto a plate. "Not really. I only work weekends for my dad. He owns the place."

Before I could ask her another question, the hostess was gone, moving fast, her clothes smelling of the diner as the air followed her. She returned to the front and collected menus and then seated a pair of men at the counter.

"This is a busy place," Jericho commented, his eyes floating over the top of his menu.

"How is Emanuel doing?" I asked as a busboy poured water into our glasses, tipping a jug sideways, ice cubes striking. Jericho motioned to him, catching the young man staring. The hostess must have shared my questions with her co-workers. From the way he looked at me, I could see he knew Charlie. "You worked with Charlie Robson?"

The busboy gave me a nod, answering, "Most of us did."

"Would you have any reason to believe someone would have wanted to harm her?"

He grimaced, the question bothering him. While none of the details about her death had been released, the news had reported the cause of death as being suspicious. "So she was, like, murdered? Is that right?" He scratched at his jaw. "That's what we wondered, but there's not much on the news about it."

"I'm Detective Casey White, leading the investigation," I answered, careful to maintain focus. "We're looking to fill in some blanks. Who she worked with, last seen with? When was her last shift?"

"I mean, yeah, we all... like, we all worked with her," he said with a stammer. "Like, we went out as a group a few times, you know, to hang out."

"Was she working here Friday?" I wet my lips, stealing an ice chip from my glass.

"Friday?" he mumbled, his focus drifting toward the window as he thought back. He gave us a nod. "We both were. I was off from school, worked the morning, seven to three."

"She left here at three?" I asked, adding a note to my phone.

Another nod, followed by a shake. "Probably closer to four. We did prep for the dinner shift."

"Any boyfriends, girlfriends that would have come around

here?" Jericho asked. The busboy wore a face of concentration, thinking as he wiped drippy sweat from the jug of ice water. He shook his head, lips turned down. "How about any customers? Anyone she complained about? Made her uncomfortable?"

"No more than the usual." He continued shaking his head. "Nothing she couldn't handle."

"Jason," the cook behind the counter said sharply, twirling his hand above his head. "Make the rounds."

"Sorry, I gotta clear the tables," the busboy told us. I shoved a card into his hand, his glancing at it before stuffing it into a back pocket.

"Call us if you think of anything else," I said, insisting. "Anything at all. It doesn't matter how minor it is."

Laptop opening, Tracy said, "She seemed well liked. Had friends here."

"Anything on the college she went to?" I took another ice chip, wetting my mouth, stomach growling.

"Nothing that sticks out," Tracy answered, her face cased in the screen's blue light. "She had some online stuff for school, papers and projects, that sort of thing. But on the social media front, only a few things."

"Like what?" I asked, thinking about how many young people were documenting their every waking moment these days. Some, even documenting their sleep.

"I found one site where her profile was public, mostly cat pictures—"

"Lemme see!" Nichelle interrupted, Tracy turning the laptop. The first was a cat on an older woman's lap. "Is that Emanuel's aunt?"

"Camille," Jericho answered. "She raised Emanuel."

"What?" I asked, surprised that I didn't know. "His parents?"

Jericho cocked his head with a sad look. "They died when he was young. Car accident, I think it was."

A flutter of nerves woke in my belly, an understanding of how close Emanuel was with his cousin. "That means Charlie was like a sister to him."

"Close family," Jericho added.

"That's a lot of tragedy for one family," Nichelle said, voice quivering.

"Yes it is." Our waitress arrived, hair pinned back, pencil sticking out the side, her face made-up heavily. She held an order pad, white and green, another pencil at the ready in her hand. She looked to me first, nudging the pad. "I'll take an order of your breakfast special, number five, please."

"Breakfast for lunch. I like to do that too," she grinned. "And how would you like your eggs?"

"Staring at me," I answered. "A side of grits also."

"Sunny side up," she said, turning to Jericho. Tracy's fingers were still on the move, her brow furrowed. Nichelle was next, ordering a double cheeseburger and fries, and a strawberry milkshake to dip them in. I'd showed her that trick.

"And for you, ma'am," the waitress asked Tracy. But she was lost in her laptop, having found something.

"Tracy?"

"Huh?" Her head popped up, eyes darting from me to the waitress. "Oh sorry. Breakfast special. Sunny side up too. And rye toast, extra butter, please. Thank you."

When the waitress was gone, I asked her, "Found something?"

"Emanuel's cousin didn't have a lot of stuff posted on social media," Tracy began, pausing to drink her water. "I thought maybe I'd have more luck finding posts from her college."

"What did you find?" Nichelle asked. She got up on her elbows and turned the laptop, air hissing from the seat. On the screen there were photographs of a body with wounds similar to those on Charlie Robson. There was a second picture showing a sunflower field, blood staining the leafy plants, some bent over, others broken. To look at the sunflower field, I would have thought these were pictures from Charlie Robson's crime scene. Only, this was a different victim. She was a Caucasian woman with red hair, a grimace locked on her face, a death mask she'd wear forever. An older couple across from us saw the screen, the husband's alarmed eyes urging me to block it from their view. "Where did you find those? Better question is how?"

"Her name is Bernadette Pare. She was a student at the same college," Tracy answered, voice soft as she read aloud. "It's a fund-me page to raise money for legal fees, to support an appeal for another student named Jacob Wright."

"These don't look like crime-scene photographs," Jericho commented, dust shimmering in the late afternoon sunlight. "They were probably posted by whoever came across the body."

"A sunflower field, students from the same college. That's a big coincidence," I said, reaching the fund-me page for Jacob Wright on my phone. "Says here that Jacob Wright was convicted for the first-degree murder of Bernadette Pare."

"This is less than twenty miles from here," Nichelle added, phone in hand, reviewing the case details that were made public. "A couple since high school, the jury deliberation was less than three hours."

"How about a murder weapon?" I asked, staring at the pictures of the victim, lividity turning puncture wounds into black holes with a purple cloud around them. "A cause of death?"

Tracy raised her brow, turning her head. I knew the look, a question forming. "A murder weapon was never recovered."

"Jury trial? Short deliberation?" Jericho asked, the food arriving. We made room, Tracy moving her laptop, flatware clanking as dishes were placed. "What did the district attorney have?"

"A signed confession," Tracy answered.

"That'd be the single piece of evidence introduced to the

trial," Nichelle added. She shook her head. "Explains the quick deliberation. DA only needed to put a convincing story around it, like an argument or a breakup."

"Young man. Girlfriend murdered. No murder weapon." An image started coming to mind, and why there was a fund-me page to pay the legal fees for an appeal. "I'm thinking the signed confession is questionable."

"Another sunflower field." Jericho bit into his food, chewing fast, and then asked, "Assuming it's the same guy, it's been a year. Why a year?"

"Great question. Assuming this is the same killer, the same MO and targeting students from the same college. They take a year's hiatus before striking again. Why?" My eggs were perfectly round, golden-yellow and staring up at me just as I'd ordered. I broke one of the yolks, stabbing it with the tip of my toast and added a slice of bacon before devouring a bite. I noticed we'd all started eating fast, questions forming around Bernadette Pare's murder. "The trial?!"

"The trial," Jericho repeated with a nod. "What kind of killer would that make them? Serial killer?"

"Bernadette Pare's murder was a year ago," Tracy began to say, her laptop tucked below the table as she ate and researched at the same time. "Sunflower blooms are throughout the summer. Plenty of opportunities for another murder."

"If they were a serial killer, but this guy isn't." I stabbed the other egg yolk, swishing my fork around the insides, coating my last piece of bacon. "A serial killer would have stuck to their MO, picked another student and sent an invitation."

"The invitation?" Jericho said. "I didn't see it."

"It had the coordinates and Charlie's name," Tracy said, lifting her laptop, the screen showing the paper with fancy writing.

"It also had the word guilty." I sat back, wondering if

Bernadette Pare had gotten an invitation too. "What about revenge?"

Nichelle lowered her milkshake, two fries sticking out the top. "That fits the timeline of a trial. If it was a revenge murder, the killer would want them dead, but not the credit."

"They'd deflect any suspicions, and guilt," I said, warming to the idea.

Tracy held up her hand, asking, "You think they let Bernadette Pare's boyfriend take the blame?"

"Must have," I answered. "This is a killer with patience."

"It also means they don't think there's any merit in the boyfriend's appeal," Jericho added. "Signed confessions are almost impossible to overturn."

"That might be, but with Charlie's crime scene, the likeness of it to Bernadette Pare's murder, that's a strong coincidence for any judge to hear." I searched my phone for the name of the investigating detective, and any other details about Bernadette Pare's case. "There could be an appeal provided we find one thing."

"What's that?" Jericho asked, finishing his food, seeing I was eager to get a move on.

"A piece of evidence that connects the two murders," I answered, the last bite of toast disappearing. "That'd mean concrete, nothing circumstantial."

"But we don't have anything else," Nichelle said, dunking a fry. "Just similarities."

"There's one detail we didn't find reported online. It's something the investigating detective would have." I stood up to stretch my legs, waiting for one of them to reply. When they didn't, I answered, "What if Bernadette Pare got the same invitation? The word guilty written on it."

"That'd be enough for an appeal," Jericho said, his hand in mine as I helped him from the seat, air whooshing to fill the cushion. "An invitation is hard evidence."

"If we find an invitation, then that would mean there's a young man sitting in prison for a crime he did not commit." They looked at me, a sad understanding of the stakes. I held up two fingers, asking, "If this is the same killer, how many more will there be?"

EIGHT

Dreams make up some of my earliest memories. The ones where monsters lurked beneath my bed. Or waited in the dark corners of my bedroom. Sadly, I never grew out of them. They followed me into my later years, haunting my sleep, showing me lost loves and drifted friendships. A case that had gone unsolved, but unforgotten. The scariest nightmares were the ones that tricked me. Making me feel it, making me think that I was awake. This morning had been like that. It had me stuck, relentlessly trapped, unable to shake free.

Hot welts rose on my bare legs where I'd seemed to brush against the sunflower plants. My lungs were bursting, arms pinwheeling as I was chased down by an arrow that sliced open my side. A scarecrow stood tall against a red sky, calling out to me, his burlap head turning to face me, a sinister kiss waiting on its crooked smile. His eyelids popped open to show patches of black-striped sunflower seeds. Impossibly dark and frightening like a horror movie. But the scarecrow was only a distraction. He was a trick like the fright-filled real-feeling dream where he lived.

There was a second arrow, the air rushing by my face, its

flight swift like a sea bird's dive. A third found its target, plunging into the back of my neck, jutting from my throat to steal my voice and stifle my screams. Blood coated my teeth and ran thick like molasses across my tongue. I woke with a jump, panting hard, hands clutching my sweaty neck to search for an arrowhead that wasn't there. Jericho bolted upright, bleary eyed and confused. I swung my legs over the bed, the dream telling me to get moving. Telling me there was no time to lose. There were lives at stake.

Rain pelted my car as we drove across the bridge to the mainland. The clouds were sleeping in late this morning, lying in bed, blanketing us in a fog that stole our sight. It was a white-knuckle drive, my focus tensed on the cars ahead, unable to see more than a few of them, the speedometer needling twenty-five. The plan was to stop at Charlie Robson's home and meet with her mother. Jericho and Emanuel would meet us there, the family's last visits to the morgue complete. When Doctor Foster gave the okay, they'd receive Charlie's body at the funeral home, a date and time and plot picked for them to say goodbye.

The detective for the Bernadette Pare case agreed to see us and compare notes, brief us on her case and on the conviction of boyfriend Jacob Wright. From the phone call, his answers were short, gruff even, and I could tell he was reluctant to our introducing evidence that could help the upcoming appeal. It was a fine line we'd walk. We needed his help and would have to play a balancing act to get it.

Brake lights flashed ahead of us in the misty air. The thick traffic was a constant stop and go, tires thumping with each expansion joint like a countdown as we queued to reach the other side of the bridge.

"We almost there yet?" Tracy asked. Nichelle laughed.

"Don't you two start that," I snapped, a chuckle rising. "Ten minutes, children."

"The district attorney involved in Jacob Wright's case sent over the confession," Tracy said, the laughter gone with a reminder of the seriousness of the case. She tapped the keyboard, paging through, saying, "A lot of the details are redacted. Wonder why?"

"That'd be any person identifiers, like the victim's name or mention of an acquaintance." I turned the steering wheel, the weather clearing as we drove north. "Do you have the notes from the trial?"

"Uh-huh, looks like it," she answered, face pinched with concentration. "A signed confession entered as evidence is only admissible if a judge deems it was voluntary."

"True, to eliminate an argument about coercion," I said, unsure if Jacob Wright's confession was influenced in any way. "Alone, it isn't enough to convict. The DA would have had to supply corroborating evidence."

"What was it?" Nichelle asked, her arm resting on Tracy's, fingers sliding across the trackpad as the two reviewed the trial notes. "Must have had something else to sustain a conviction."

"Here it is," Tracy answered. "They provided a witness statement; Jacob Wright was last seen with Bernadette Pare the day of her murder. The witness saw them arguing at the school's courtyard."

"That could be anything," Nichelle said, shaking her head. "I mean, couples argue."

"It's thin," I commented, the fog clearing from the road, the drive becoming a climb uphill. We cleared the weather at the top, sunlight breaking through the clouds, the trees wet, the leaves and branches sparkling. "Couples do argue. Any mention of if it got physical?"

"No mention," Tracy answered.

Nichelle rubbed Tracy's shoulder, saying, "We don't argue, right?"

Tracy raised a brow. "Only when you hog the remote."

"Small stuff," she remarked, and shifted close enough to see my phone, the map, the destination highlighted with a star. "We almost there yet?"

"What did I say about that!" I said jokingly. We were almost there though. "Another minute. The detectives questioned Bernadette Pare's boyfriend after a witness saw them arguing. How long was Jacob Wright questioned? Did he have a lawyer? For a signed confession to be admissible, the judge must conclude that it was given freely."

"Guilty," Tracy said. But she wasn't speaking of the note we'd found with Charlie Robson. I glanced at my bag. Inside, that note was safe, secure, having signed it into our custody. "This says that there was a note, the word guilty written on it."

"There's the corroborating evidence," I said, thumping the steering wheel. "The story the DA told the jury would have involved Jacob Wright writing the note after the argument, luring his girlfriend to a remote location where he killed her."

"Guilty of what though?" Nichelle asked.

I shook my head. "Does it matter?"

"From a juror's perspective, it could have been anything," Tracy added.

"We need to see that note," I said, entering the police station's parking lot. There were two cars parked, the building a small red-brick box with telescoping antennas sprouting from the roof. "If it has the same fancy handwriting, it will eliminate Jacob Wright as the author of the note."

Wooden legs creaked, the detective forcing a lean, tipping himself, his shoes perched on his desk. The station was twenty miles north of where Bernadette Pare had been murdered. It was a one-room building made of brick and stone, with two desks and a holding cell which had been filled with supplies, some poking through the iron bars, piled ceiling high on the cot. We sat down, sliding chairs into place while Detective Tom Gardner sized us up. A heavyset man with thick graying hair, his eyes were beady, his chin covered in a week's growth. He wore his badge like a shield, a leather holder sleeved into his shirt pocket. There were cards and small gifts strewn across the top of his desk, some with racy cartoons and gag gifts that pointed to a recent celebration to poke fun at a retirement.

"Pardon the mess," he said and went to clean, shoving much of it into a drawer. "Retirement party this past Friday."

"I'll get that," a deputy said, clothes hanging loose from his shoulders, gaunt, all elbows and knees. He wasn't young, but he wasn't old. He took away the bigger items, dipping his head in my direction, focus on my badge, "Ma'am."

"Congratulations on the retirement," Jericho said, breaking the ice. "Thank you for your service."

The detective paused to look at the team, and then returned to Jericho. "Thanks. Appreciate it." He moved faster, shoveling the remains on his desk into a drawer. "Help me out here. You're investigating Jacob Wright's case?"

"Not exactly," I answered. He flipped on his monitor and poked at a keyboard with two fingers, the screen flashing with a list of case numbers. I slid to the edge of my chair, the beginnings of Charlie Robson's case minted in a new folder clutched in my fingers. The folder was new, the edges sharp. It'd grow fast and accompany the digital hosting where all of our cases lived an eternity. "There was a murder this past Friday. The victim's name is Charlie Robson?"

"This past Friday?" he asked, brow narrowing with a question. "Jacob Wright's case is a year old. There's an appeal coming up—his lawyers are looking to get a retrial."

"We believe there are similarities with our case." I opened the folder, his eyeballs bulged, the whites yellowed and veiny, darting from picture to picture. I covered his desk with the sunflower field and Charlie Robson's body. He cleared his throat, the resemblance to Bernadette Pare's crime scene obvious to him. "What do you think?"

"Yeah, well—" The corner of his mouth curled, the tips of his fingers digging through the scruff. "I mean there are multiple stab wounds. Then there's the field, and sunflowers."

"We came across some unofficial photographs of Bernadette Pare's case, the crime scene." I nudged a photograph, the one showing the tarnished blood pooled around Charlie's body. "We also learned that the victims went to the same college."

Taking my cue, he poked his keyboard, muttering annoyance. "Thought those pictures were taken down." His screen remained blank, his annoyance turning to confusion.

I began to feel concerned, worried he didn't have some of what we'd come for. "If there is anything you can share that could shed light on Charlie Robson's case?"

He thumped the keyboard, saying, "Like I told you, I've got retirement coming. It's in a couple days." He looked past us and searched the station. "My computer has been archived, anything that was on here isn't anymore."

"How about a hard copy?" I suggested, nudging Charlie Robson's folder.

"Might be," he answered, wagging a finger, chair legs threatening again with a creak. He stood and went to the jail cell, waving his hand over his shoulder. "Big guy, you wanna help an old man."

"That'd be you, big guy," Tracy said, her and Nichelle smiling. Jericho cringed. They'd razz him on the drive home.

"Yes, sir," Jericho answered, the iron gate sliding gracefully, metal on metal filling our ears. He looked at me, mouthing, "More boxes."

"We should have it here," the detective grumbled with a heave, lifting a box, handing it to Jericho, the two working to clear a pile and create a new one. "That's the one!"

"I'll carry it," Jericho offered, easing it from the detective's hands.

Excited, the detective began ripping the tape before the box was placed on the desk, his hands diving inside, sifting through the folders. "Was a time that all we had was paper and pen."

"I remember," I commented, standing to read the names of the files.

He motioned to the side of the station where the brick's color was less faded, preserved, hidden from the window's light, the patch in the shape of a rectangle. "They put the files online six months ago and told me to get rid of the filing cabinets." He leaned in and winked. "They'd been here since 1920. I got them in my garage now. Took 'em as a parting gift."

"They don't make them like that anymore," Jericho said, encouraging the conversation. "After they archived the files, they brought the files back?"

"Yep, marked for incineration," the detective said, lifting a folder with Bernadette Pare's name on it. "Lucky for you, I didn't get that far."

"Were you the investigating detective?" I asked, this being a small station.

He shook his head, answering, "That'd be Detective Tom Riley. Only, he passed a short time ago."

"Sorry for your loss," we said, our words slurring together.

"Detective Riley handled Jacob Wright's confession?" A nod. "Would you be able to walk us through the case, a high-level brief?"

The detective regarded the request, reluctance showing. After a moment's hesitation, he sighed. "I'm familiar with it. I'll give it a try seeing how you made the drive out this way." He grunted as he settled into the wooden chair, flipping open the case folder. The first crime scene photograph was a wide-angle view of Bernadette Pare's body, clothes dirtied, the blood stains dried black, the surrounding sunflowers leaning where they'd been broken. The quality of the photograph was superior to what had been posted. There was greater detail in her hair, the strands falling over her gray skin, the purple-blue area on the side of her face closest to the ground. There were bright yellow petals in her red hair, nested throughout, showing us the struggle as she tried to escape. "Caucasian woman, early twenties, Bernadette Pare. Her body was discovered in a sunflower field with multiple stab wounds—"

"How many?" I interrupted, palm itchy with a need to take hold of the folder. The detective frowned, uncertain of the count. "The stab wounds? Is there a summary from the autopsy report?"

"I'd think so, but let's see." He flipped a handful of pages, and then another pair, loose sheets fanning the air. He stopped when he got to the autopsy sheet, laying them in front of us. There were two diagrams, female, front and back, the injuries marked with red ink. There was no pattern, the victim sustaining multiple wounds like Charlie. "Looks to be more than sixteen. Ya know, I remember Riley talking about how none of them had been fatal."

"She died of blood loss?" I asked, his looking up from the autopsy sheets. "In our case, there was a path in the sunflower field, blood spilled around her shoes and on the plants. None of the injuries were meant to kill." His jaw went slack as I described the scene to him. "And there was a small clearing where the victim in our case succumbed to the injuries, bleeding to death."

"Yeah," he said, turning the page over, brow furrowed heavily, flipping to a photograph taken at a wider, elevated angle. The crime-scene photographer must have stood on a ladder. The sunflower plants had been flattened, Bernadette Pare driven to the center where the final blows would steal her life. His voice soft. "I remember when I saw this that I thought of one of them crop circles."

"That'd be why the DA asked for first-degree murder in the charges against Jacob Wright?" I asked. A slow nod. "Because it shows premeditation."

"Right," he said, continuing to nod while Tracy sifted through her crime-scene pictures, and presented to him a near identical one. As he gave it a hard look, he mumbled the word, "Premeditation."

I tapped my finger on the trampled sunflowers, the circle perfectly formed. "Was the detail of this ever released?"

He shook his head. "Uh-uh. The scene was plowed down by the farmer as soon as we lifted the crime-scene tape."

"That eliminates a copycat," Tracy said, reworking the pictures on the table. She organized her crime-scene photographs to pair with the ones taken of Bernadette Pare. "Other than their complexions, the location of the injuries—"

"—they're the same," he finished for her. His fingers returned to the scruff on his chin.

"What was the murder weapon?" I asked, already knowing there was none to be found.

"Never found it," he answered, abruptly sweeping the pages into a pile. He placed one page on top, the penmanship ragged, scrawled, the words barely legible. "In the confession, he said he'd tossed it, but didn't know where."

"And you believed him?" I asked, voice challenging.

The detective placed his hand over his heart, shaking his head. "I wasn't here when any of this happened."

"But do you believe his confession?" Jericho asked.

The detective sat forward, elbows perched, fingers clasped, and rested his head. "Off the record?" We didn't answer, his brow rising briefly before it settled above his eyelids. "Looking at your case, I don't know what to believe."

From my bag, I retrieved the note, the word guilty written inside it. "We know there was a note sent to the victim, another piece of evidence to show premeditation."

"That'd be in an evidence locker. We use an environmentally controlled storage facility now." He sifted through the pages, finding a picture. "But we got a picture of it which will help. This was taken at the scene."

Slipping latex over my fingers, I retrieved Charlie Robson's invitation and sat it next to the photograph. My heart raced when I saw them together, saw the identical fancy cursive writing. "Look at that."

A long sigh. The detective wiped his forehead. "Jacob Wright is going to win his appeal."

"It means more than that," I said, my breath short.

"What's that?" he asked.

"The killer is still out there."

NINE

It was the meeting that had my stomach tied in knots and put bumps of sweat on my upper lip. These only got worse when we pulled into the driveway of Charlie Robson's home. My years of being a cop and detective never seem to be enough to prepare for the difficulties when facing a victim's parent. It was made worse this time since this was the family of one of our own, sharing in their grief and mourning. With the formal autopsy underway, I hoped that the worst of this experience was over for Charlie Robson's mother but was surely wrong. As with almost every pain, time takes time.

The house was a craftsman style that was immaculately kept, the driveway swept clean, a curvy red-brick pathway from the drive to the patio. The property was edged with evergreen shrubs that were cleanly shaven, the tops and sides evenly shaped. The lawn was decorated with ceramic figurines, colorful stout mushrooms, some garden gnomes with one of them pushing a wheelbarrow. The grass was overgrown, blades thick and scraggly. The bird feeders stood empty with sparrows and a goldfinch pecking at the dusty seed tray. Understandably, the household's daily routines had been interrupted.

Jericho entered the drive, stopping behind a pair of cars. Emanuel appeared on the porch. He waved toward us, his body filling the doorframe. Car doors were opened and closed before Jericho finished parking the car, Tracy's shoes clopping the walkway. She reached Emanuel first, arms stretched around him, words replaced by the quiet sway of condolence. When I reached his side and took his hand, I saw the toll that mourning was taking upon him. He'd lost weight in the days since his cousin's murder. Grief must have stolen his appetite and made for restless evenings. His eyes were red and heavy-lidded, cradled by dark bags. A smile flashed in our direction for a moment, a contradiction to the days he'd been going through, but then was gone.

"Do you need me to move the car?" I asked, Jericho shaking the keys. Jericho pumped Emanuel's hand and clapped his shoulder, the two trading silent words.

"You're fine there," he answered, and shook a key ring of his own. "It's for the shed out back. My aunt has a push mower."

Jericho snapped the keys from Emanuel's grip, saying, "I'll fill the bird feeders too."

"You don't have to do that," Emanuel objected.

"Nonsense," Jericho told him. He looked to me, adding, "Besides, Casey may need your help."

"True," I told him, urging Emanuel to the door, Tracy getting behind him. As we stepped inside, I turned around, warmed by Jericho's help. "Thank you."

"This way," Emanuel told us.

Jericho grinned a half-smile before leaving the porch. He'd been a bit quiet and a little distant on the way over. I'd ask him later if he was okay, thinking maybe he'd gotten word about the resume he sent. When I entered Charlie Robson's home, I was plowed over by a large dog and taken to a knee by the size of him. My front was filled with brown and white fur, and the gush of a warm, panting breath, Emanuel scolding, "Zeus! Down!"

"Who are you?" I asked, touching the dog's collar. Its leather was chapped, with a metal dog-bone with the name Zeus printed on the tag. When I got my balance, I could see his face clearer, saw the one ear standing poker straight, while the other was floppy. He had chocolate eyes and graying fur around his face. He wagged his tail vigorously, waiting for my hand to greet him. Emanuel grunted the dog's name, Zeus's ears flattening. I assured him that I was fine. "It's good."

"You sure?" Emanuel asked. "I can put him in a room."

"I'm okay." I ran my fingers through the dog's fur, his tail becoming lively again, ears rising, the left one stuck in a permanent flop. He looked past me, to the door as if waiting for more to come. Was he waiting for Charlie? It hurt to think it, but I was sure he was. I leaned in and whispered, "I'm sorry, old boy, Charlie isn't coming home." He turned his head sideways the way dogs sometimes do, his tail stopping, the look on his face changing at the sound of her name.

"Come over here, Zeus!?" A voice called from the living room. At once, he retreated, nails ticking against the wood floor. I followed Tracy, passing a wall that was covered in pictures of Emanuel and Charlie. They were cousins but had grown up together like siblings. The resemblance between them was noticeable. I entered the living room, Emanuel's aunt next to him, standing tall, the family resemblance beginning with the height they shared. "Ms. White?"

"Casey, please," I said, taking her hand. "My sincerest condolences, ma'am."

"Thank you, Casey." She held on to my hand, covering it with hers, closing her eyelids, her lips moving silently. There was a cross above the couch and what might have been rosary beads on a corner table, candles lit in front of it. Emanuel closed his eyelids to pray with his aunt. She finished, saying, "May the good Lord keep you safe."

Like the outside, the home they kept was immaculate. While the furniture and decor hadn't changed in decades, the sofa, tables, and chairs looked brand new. Plastic covered the seat cushions, crinkling as we sat, my bottom sliding toward Tracy. There was a turntable on a shelf, the needle stuck at the end, a static hiss playing steadily in the background. Emanuel lifted it and turned the record player off before leaving the room, the kitchen soon sounding with the clank of glasses and ice. "Ma'am?" I asked, her eyelids closed, lips moving again.

"Constant prayer," she replied when opening them. She excused herself, "Sorry, it's the only thing that's helping."

"That's understandable," Tracy said. "We are sorry for your loss, ma'am."

"Thank you, dear," she replied, glancing at the two of us, her round face slowly rising with understanding. She looked to me, saying with a nod, "A miracle the Lord has given you."

A pinch of guilt found me, a sting deep inside as the woman congratulated me on finding my daughter while she mourned the loss of hers. "I appreciate it, ma'am," I said, gripping Tracy's hand briefly. "If you are up for it, could we ask a few questions about Charlie, her friends, school and work schedule—"

"Work and work and work," Charlie's mother answered, shifting her seat, the plastic crunching. "That is all my baby girl ever done. Work and work."

"Lemonade?" Emanuel offered, placing a metal TV tray in front of us. The colors were muted, its original flowery decoration faded and cracked. I poured two glasses while Emanuel sat across from us. When the bittersweet liquid touched my tongue, I lifted the glass with thanks. "Charlie was in debt and working every shift she could get to get ahead of the bills."

"Just the diner?" Tracy asked, confirming there was only the one place of employment.

"That's it," her mother answered, voice hollowed by the glass raised in front of her mouth. She winced and batted her eyes. Emanuel took the glass she handed him, her asking, "A touch more sugar for me."

He motioned to us, questioning. I shook my head, Tracy following, her lips puckering slightly. "It's good," she said politely. Tracy faced Charlie's mother, asking, "Did she meet with anyone she worked with, outside the diner?"

"You mean dating a boy?" Charlie's mother clarified. Her mouth turned downward with a pout while she shook her head. "None that I've ever seen."

"We have reason to believe your daughter was invited to the place where she was murdered," I told her, opening my bag to fetch the invitation.

Charlie's mother reeled back, questioning, "She was invited?" Emanuel sat next to her, holding the glass of sweetened lemonade, his eyes on my bag. "What makes you think that?"

"The sunflower farm was out of her way, accessible mostly by backroads." Tracy shifted while explaining, giving me time to cover the blood on the invitation, my palm sliding over the evidence sleeve, trying to lessen the shock of it. "It's not likely that your daughter would have come upon it accidentally."

"What's that you have?" Emanuel asked, a hard look on his face, his role as detective gone from his eyes. He was family of a victim, of someone who'd lost a loved one. His voice shaky, "Casey?"

"I'd like you to take a look at this and tell me if you recognize anything about it." I knelt in front of them and carefully removed the invitation from my bag, the evidence sleeves in place.

Emanuel extended his hand, curling his fingers, insisting, "Give it here." I held on to it, thinking it best, but he insisted again, "Casey, it's okay. The worst of it is past."

Reluctant, I handed him the evidence sleeve. He took care

in handling it properly, holding the edges and making the plastic taut so they could see the invitation. Charlie's mother took a sharp breath, her hand over her heart. "Is there anything familiar? The paper or the writing, anything at all?"

She ran her fingers over the writing, mumbling, "Pretty." She shook her head then, adding, "Nothing about this is familiar to me."

Emanuel handed it back, asking, "This was on her?"

"It was nearby," Tracy said. "It's like the other victim's, she had the same invitation."

"What?" Emanuel straightened his shoulders, alarmed by the mention of a second victim. Tracy glanced at me and bit her lip, the slip accidental. She was used to discussing cases with Emanuel since he was a part of much of her career. But that wasn't today. "When? Who was it?!"

"The circumstances are very similar," I answered, tucking the evidence away.

He eyed my bag, asking, "The same."

I nodded, adding, "And there was a sunflower field."

"Lord there was another," Charlie's mother said with a gasp.

Emanuel shook his head, rage rising with a hard frown. "I would have known—"

"You wouldn't!" I said, my voice rising to get his attention. He looked up at me. "Emanuel, you wouldn't have known because it happened a year ago."

"You were still working with us," Tracy commented, trying to lift whatever guilt he might have been feeling. "Plus, the DA brought charges against the victim's boyfriend. It was an open and shut case. He's in prison."

The frown returned, his asking, "But the circumstance?"

"The boyfriend's lawyers have an appeal." I tapped my bag. "They'll get a retrial, introducing new evidence, handwriting analysis, anything to generate doubt."

"What was her name?" Charlie's mother asked, weepy.

Tracy began to answer, but then looked at me. I gave her a nod. "Bernadette Pare, ma'am. She went to the same school as your daughter."

"Bernadette Pare," Charlie's mother said, voice a dry whisper, the color in her face fading.

"Ma'am?" I asked, leaning forward.

Without a word she stood up. Emanuel took her arm to help, her steps heavy as she walked across the room to the table with the rosary beads. Stacked behind the candle and a picture of her daughter were photo albums and scrapbooks. From the middle of the pile, she pulled out a book. The outside cover read, Sherman High School. "I've seen that name." She turned to Emanuel, asking, "Bring the chairs closer."

He did as requested, moving their chairs directly across from the couch, an oval coffee table with a glass top between us.

"May I?" I asked. She handed me the yearbook, the spine creased and the pages browsed more than a few times. I fanned the pages until I got to the student portraits, scanning the names alphabetically until I reached the name Bernadette Pare, her hairstyle made up for a graduation cap and gown. "Did your daughter know Bernadette Pare?"

Charlie's mother put on a hard scowl. Did my question stir a troubling memory? "Flip to the pages with the team pictures." I did as she said, continuing to fan the pages, stopping when she pressed her finger against the page. "There. Charlie was on that team, but only for a year."

Beneath her finger was a team photograph, each of the girls holding a bow, a white and blue and red bullseye target standing in the middle with arrows jutting from its center. Emanuel sat back hard enough to make the chair creak. "I remember her being on the archery team. Didn't she quit after that thing with the coach? He was fired, wasn't he?"

"The coach?" Tracy asked.

"Mm! More than fired," Charlie's mother said with a disapproving tone. "What ugliness that was with their coach."

"I was already gone, playing ball," Emanuel said, his voice thick as he focused on the team picture and the connection of his cousin to the first victim. He touched his aunt's arm, voice softening. "What happened?"

Her brow lifted and her gaze drifted toward the foyer. "Police come one evening. Said there'd been some reports from the other girls about the coach." She cupped her mouth and shook her head with a frown, the stare turning hard as if the ghosts of that evening were there. She turned back to us, pointing her finger at the black-and-white picture. "That man went to prison for molesting some of them girls."

"She didn't quit? There was no team after that," Emanuel said, hurt on his face. "Why... why didn't you tell me what really happened?"

"Oh, baby," she began, gripping his arm, fresh tears falling. "I couldn't put that on you."

"I would have come home," he said, the hurt deepening with disappointment. "I would have done something."

"Which is why I didn't tell you."

Emanuel sat back, his shoulder slumped, his aunt protecting his career to weather the storm without him.

"Archery," Tracy commented. She shook her head, asking, "Never after this? College maybe?"

"Not once, and it was such a terrible shame too," Emanuel's mother said. "She was good enough for a scholarship too but could never bring herself to pick up the sport again."

"I wish I'd known," Emanuel said, still reeling from the news. "With a scholarship, she wouldn't have had any school tuition to pay back."

"Ma'am, was your daughter a victim too?" I asked, keeping my voice soft.

"Such ugliness," she repeated and closed her eyelids with a

slow nod. "But not like the others. It never went beyond the inappropriate touching."

"I'm sorry that she went through that," I said.

Tracy nudged my arm, pointing to the signatures around the team pictures. Charlie had had her teammates sign her yearbook despite what had happened to them. When I saw what Tracy was pointing at, I read it aloud. *"To one of the best, we'll always have that special bond. With hugs and kisses, never forget, we are the sunflower girls!"*

"That's what they called themselves," her mother said, the memory warming her face. "The sunflower girls."

TEN

We left the Robson home late in the afternoon. The sun was setting, fireflies appearing in the dark brush of their walkway. Zeus followed us out the door, chasing our legs while Emanuel caught up to him, thanking Jericho for the help. We had made a connection with the first victim, Charlie and Bernadette belonging to the same sports team. But not just any sporting team. It was archery. We'd not only discovered a connection between the victims but tied it to the suspected murder weapon as well.

"I'll drive," I offered, seeing the tired look on Jericho's face. His hair was flat and there were sweat stains on his shirt. The bottom of his shoes was dyed green from the lawn work. He dropped into the passenger seat, filling the car with the smell of cut grass. "That was really nice of you to do."

"Anything to help them," he answered, grunting when the seat belt clicked. He rubbed his shoulder, cringing. "Feeling sore. Thanks for driving."

His shirt was wet where I caressed his arm, asking, "I can rub in some cream when we get home?"

He chuckled. "I think I packed it."

"I'll find it." I turned to Tracy sitting behind us while she slipped her laptop from her backpack. "What's first, Tracy?"

"We'd have to investigate the coach, right?" she answered, her face made bright by the blue light of her screen.

"That's where I'd go." The car lurched when I dropped the shifter into reverse. "His name is Benjamin Palto."

"I started pulling up information on him while we were talking." We backed out of the driveway, waving to Emanuel and Zeus. Zeus wagged his tail briefly, one ear pointed while he searched up the street. How long before he stopped looking for Charlie? From the looks of it, I thought it would be a while. "Okay, what it says here is that he taught chemistry and was the coach of the varsity archery team."

"Benjamin Palto," I said, repeating the name, looking to Jericho for recognition. He shook his head while wiping his brow.

"I don't know the name. You think the coach had something to do with it?" Jericho asked as I spun the wheel to take us east toward the ocean, to home. "Emanuel never said anything about problems with a coach."

"He didn't know," Tracy said, voice replaced by the click-clack of her typing. "Charlie's mom didn't want him worrying."

"What happened?" Jericho asked, his face growing rigid with concern.

"Emanuel's cousin belonged to an archery team in high school," I began to explain, taillights of the traffic ahead turning our faces red.

"Some of the girls complained that the coach was inappropriate with them," Tracy continued.

"What?!" he asked, staring blankly at the stopped traffic. "And Emanuel didn't know?"

"Uh-uh," Tracy answered, tapping the keyboard. "Casey, I just sent you the police reports from the team."

"What became of Benjamin Palto?" Cars parted to show an

opening. I gunned the motor and switched lanes, eager to be home. "It's probably safe to assume that he never taught school again?"

"Well, actually, it turns out that he was a teacher again." Tracy sat up, her face appearing between us. "He taught at the state level."

"You mean at a penitentiary?" Jericho asked. "Teacher for the inmates."

"Uh-huh." The drive was silent then, the tires ticking against the road, the tempo broken by Tracy's typing. "Found more. Sending it now. The trial transcript, including some of the girls' testimony too."

"How about Charlie?" I asked as a distant thought of a motive was born. That's how they start sometimes. With a thought, an idea framed around one of the oldest questions in history. *What if?*

"Umm, one sec," she said, returning to her laptop, a reflection shining on the rear window. "Nope. No court. She didn't take the stand at the trial. But the police report her mother mentioned was entered into evidence."

"Shit, Emanuel must be feeling terrible," Jericho commented, his stare continuing. "That family has been through so much."

"What was his sentence?"

Tracy returned, sitting closer and answering, "Looks like the trial ended with a plea bargain. Benjamin Palto pleaded guilty in return for a seven-year sentence."

"If Charlie was a junior when this occurred, then add a half a year or so for a trial," I said, counting the time. I gripped the wheel, confidence rising to confirm the earlier passing thought as a possible motive. "That'd mean Benjamin Palto was paroled in four years?"

"Yeah, wow!" Tracy answered, finding my eyes in the rearview mirror. "That's a really good guess."

"Time for us to have a talk with Benjamin Palto." I exited
the bridge, tires thumping before I spun the wheel to go south,
signs for Kitty Hawk shinning bright in my headlights. We were
back on the barrier islands, a sense of home warming us. "Benjamin Palto was a free man around the time Bernadette Pare
was murdered."

~

I woke up to the cold touch of a sheet and pillow, Jericho's side
of the bed empty. The clock's numbers said 5:45, the window
filling with breaking daylight. I knew he wasn't out on patrol
since he'd been off work this week to pack. And he'd already
resigned his position in the Marine Patrol. He wouldn't have
gone out either. Not this early. We'd made plans. An hour was
all I'd asked for, so that we could review a new lease. While
there was urgency to stick to a move date, we had a month
remaining in the Outer Banks. The extra time gave us a helpful
window.

The kitchen was silent, the rest of the apartment the same. I
sat up to the sound of a faucet dripping steadily, listened for
running water, the shower perhaps. The pipes were silent. It
was cool enough for the windows to stay open, the first light of
the day mixed with the sound of the shore birds calling. There
was the whir of a sand cleaning machine passing the apartment
too, and waves breaking. I swung my legs over the bed and went
to the patio door, shading my eyes against the sunrise as it broke
the horizon.

Near the ocean's edge where the waves churned a rumble of
white foam, I saw Jericho standing close to the water, a gusty
wind tossing his hair, his hands at rest in his pockets. The morning's weather was brisk, turning the air crisp, a welcome respite
from the sweltering heat we'd endured this month. I grabbed a
pale-green cardigan from the back of a chair, a gift from

Nichelle and Tracy, and covered my shoulders. Outside the back door, I found the sandy path Jericho had walked, the touch instantly turning my toes cold, a chill giving me goosebumps. The ocean sat at low tide, the salt air strong enough to taste, its smell wrapping cozily around me. When I reached Jericho, his feet were buried in the sand, ankle deep, and when I saw his face, saw the look on it, the chill turned to concern.

This wasn't about the case, or about Emanuel. This was about the move, about us. I snuggled up to him, breaking his stare briefly, and asked hesitantly, "You've been quiet." In the morning light, his face glowed the color of honey and the wet in his eyes was striking. He lifted his chin, looking up and down the beach, and then to the ocean, his home. The only home he'd ever known. He shrugged and crossed his arms, lips pressed tight, afraid the wrong words would come out. For a day, I'd known there was something that bothered him, but had hoped he was just tired from the planning and the packing. "Babe, what's going on?"

"This—" he began to say, his voice hollow, catching in his throat, a sea breeze blowing through his wavy hair. He pawed at his chin, biting his upper lip while struggling with what to say.

"What is it?" I asked, finding the same struggles, nervously spinning my engagement ring around my finger. I jumped on the only thing I could think of and asked about his search for a new job. "Did you get a call from the airport?"

"They emailed me right after I sent my resume," he answered with a nod, his stare remaining fixed on the ocean. "I have a phone interview this morning."

"Oh, you didn't mention it," I said, voice fading with a feeling of hurt. That would have been news to share, but he had kept it to himself. He wasn't excited by it. Not like I was. I think he also knew that he'd get the job, which meant that our move to Philadelphia was becoming real. My chest grew tight. Tighter than it'd ever been. "You don't want it?"

"I thought I could leave here," he said, shaking his head. "I thought I could go with you."

"You don't want to get married?" I asked, the words burning my insides, the sound of them alien.

He looked at me, answering, "I do, but—" but his eyes retreated to the sea, indecision on his face.

"Jericho—" His chin trembled while I stood there frozen, my feet sinking deeper into the cold. My heart was doing the same and I searched far into the ocean for the right words. But I had none. Less than fifty yards away, we'd floated in the warm waters, swells lifting us as he had proposed. On my finger, I wore a ring that lovingly marked our engagement. It was what we'd done after that meant more to me than anything. In the private company of the sea, we exchanged vows, sharing a moment that was more loving and intimate than any I'd ever shared before. He was the love of my life. But Tracy was my daughter, my baby, and I'd just found her.

He glanced at me, voice breaking. "Casey, I'm just really feeling torn about leaving."

"Jericho, I love you," I said, my voice raspy, tears stinging. I faced the sunshine and blinked them away before he took notice. Clutching his arm to press my head against his shoulder, I said nothing more about the move.

"I love you too." He pulled me close to him while we watched a school of dolphins break the surface, their bottled noses jutting from the sea, their steel-colored humps shaping the water. Torn between the Outer Banks and being with Jericho, or moving to Philly with Tracy, something else was breaking as I watched the wonders of the Atlantic Ocean. It was my heart.

ELEVEN

The paper was thick between her fingers, the invitation a surprise. Jessie Smith's idea of what she held lifted her heart, making it swell with thoughts of their taking the next step. Wasn't it just the other night that Steven mentioned a surprise, that he was planning something she would never forget? He knew her too. He knew how much she loved puzzles and riddles. The fun of them, the mystery they held, their begging to be solved. That's what the invitation was. It was a puzzle that'd lead to his proposal. A magnificent one. An excited laugh slipped from her lips as her feet touched the gravel road, heat from the sun blanketing her legs. Jessie peered at the invitation's numbers, the GPS in her car showing the same. This was the right place. She was here. But where was here?

A frown. A hint of disappointment. The road was empty, the invitation bringing her to the top of a shallow hill. The sun was dropping and painting long shadows on the road. A breeze spun up a dust devil, a whirlwind forming, gyrating, and dancing across the road. Behind her was a field with rows of green leafy plants. Lettuce, she wondered, or was it tobacco? She recognized the crop grown in front of her, the tall and slender plants that had the most brilliant yellow flower petals she'd ever seen. The sunflowers stared back at her, their brown faces empty of expression. The sight of them put a thought in her head. She'd create a new ice-cream flavor for her shop and call it Sunflower-Blast, a mix of ice cream and sorbet. Deep in the field, there was a scarecrow watching, his hat crooked like his eyes and mouth, his arms wide as if waiting for a hug that'd never come.

Jessie glanced down at the numbers on the invitation again, impatience brewing. Her brother, Jonathon, had helped identify what they were when she first looked at them. He'd seen the invitation first, found it in the mailbox at her shop, and explained to her that they were coordinates. He'd questioned what was inside too, the word *guilty* written in the same fancy letters. It was Steven, she'd explained to him. It was her boyfriend's corny way of saying they were guilty of love. Jonathon had shrugged and rolled his eyes, saying it was sappy, but what did he know.

"What if you were wrong?" she said, speaking to the breeze as it lifted her blonde hair and stirred it around her face. She pegged the top of her shoe into the dirt, annoyed, the time on her phone telling her she'd need to leave soon. She was the owner of the ice-cream shop in Duck, and other than her brother, she was the only one who could open it for business. He was out for the afternoon, leaving it to her. "Okay, Steven, where the fuck are you?"

"Jessie," she thought she heard, the wind playing with her ears, tricking her into a spin, seeking a voice that wasn't there. A text message. She'd send one to Steven, tell him the puzzle was solved and he could come out now.

No signal. No bars, the phone's reception dead. "Of course, there isn't any," she said, eyeing the telephone poles along the road, the wires, the irony of being close to them, but not having any signal. A pair of crows sat on the wire nearest her, one catching her stare, its beady eye shifting, cawing loudly. Annoyed by the game, she shoved her phone into her back pocket and shooed the birds. They leapt briefly, returning to their perch and ruffled their thick feathered coats before resuming to ignore the world.

"Jessie!" the low voice called again, startlingly stronger.

"What!" she called with a spin, her feet grinding the gravel, her stare frozen with silent anticipation. Steven's game was about to begin. She mumbled to herself then, "Follow the voice."

And that's what she did, her gaze fixed on the scarecrow, the voice coming from that direction, or so she thought. There were trees and hedges lining the sunflower field. And there was a beat-up trailer too. A single-wide with broken windows, the siding stained by rust and bullet holes from years of target practice.

"Not in there?" she whispered, grimacing at the thought. Steven had more class than that. "At least I hope you do."

"Over here," the voice told her, stopping her dead when she walked past the first row of sunflowers. She didn't know the voice, didn't recognize it. It was deep enough to be his but wasn't. "In here."

Gently, Jessie shoved a pair of sunflowers aside, the touch prickly with fine hair, their faces striking and in full bloom. Her hair lifted suddenly, straight up in a blur, a sharp whoosh passing, breaking the sunflower stalk in two. She jumped to the side, a reflex, confused by the motion. She heard the next one, air whistling, pain rifling from her arm before she could react, the end of an arrow sticking out of her. The image of it was surreal, making her stare while she tried to understand what it was she was seeing.

The shaft was black, the feathers bright, her pale skin turning blue around the entrance with blood seeping. Errant thoughts of archery came to mind. How long had it been since she'd seen an arrow up close? Years maybe? When she was back in high school and on the team. It was the arrow's feathers that broke the shock of what was happening. It broke her daze, scattering the confusion. The team always used plastic vanes. They never used feathers. Nothing like this one. It was Bernadette who'd asked about the feathers once, the coach explaining feathers were used when the arrow's shaft might bump a branch during a hunt, their soft touch letting the arrow slip past effortlessly, keeping the archer's aim true. She peered up at the flowery blooms, the hunter aiming at her through the sunflower stalks.

Jessie lurched to the left, crying out, "Please—", but the archer's aim did stay true as the coach had said, an arrow finding her again, slicing open that space above her heel, the tendon snapping in half, the end of it retreating into her calf. She fell forward with a scream, taking a sunflower with her, and immediately got to her hands and knees in a fast crawl, the pain making her cry out, "What do you want?"

"Guilty," she heard, the word carried on the snap of a bow. She braced herself, tensing her muscles, an arrow peeling through the sunflowers and landing in front of her. It missed.

She said nothing then and stood, her left foot dangling like a broken flower, before breaking into a clumsy run and bleeding on the plants she touched. Another arrow missed her, the shaft brushing her thigh with intense coldness, its friction quickly turning to a burn. The sunflowers gave way to an opening, hundreds of the plants leveled to form a circle, sunlight blinding her. Jessie shielded her eyes, an arrow opening her belly, the force driving through her, causing her to fall over.

Her breath came in short gasps while she tried to retreat, tried to escape back the way she'd come. The opening showed her like a dirty secret, the hunter volleying three more arrows in quick succession. Her mouth hung open, jaw slack, lungs collapsing, pierced by the arrows. When she turned to face the

sunlight, face the abandoned trailer, she saw the archer's silhouette, a monstrous shadow figure drawn across the field, the top
of the bow marking the opening where she'd die.

The last arrow came in a blink, piercing her neck, exiting
the other side, zapping whatever strength and will there had
been to fight. Jessie collapsed onto her front, face sweaty, the
field's earthy taste mixing with the blood in her mouth. Dirt
covered her lips, coating her damp skin. Death was slow and
painless, her body paralyzed from the neck down. She moved
her eyes, moved her ears, listened to the approaching footsteps.

"Guilty," the shadow said, appearing above her, a bow held
across their front. When she saw who it was, who was standing
and waiting for her death, there was a faint and distant sense of
regret that came for what they'd done. The invitation she'd
received was a reckoning, and the cost was her life.

"I'm sorry," she tried to say, tried to lie, her lips moving, her
breath absent. She could never be sorry for coming forward, but
she'd also never thought what happened would have ever led to
this.

When Jessie's heart fluttered and skipped a beat, she
wanted to think of Steven and Jonathon, wanted to think of the
time she'd lose with them. But strangely, her dying thoughts
were fondly for a flavor she'd never taste, her Sunflower-Blast
ice cream and sorbet mix. She was certain it would have been a
summer surprise for many, and a hit for her little ice-cream shop
on the banks of Currituck Sound. If only she'd had the time to
create it.

TWELVE

I felt full of numbness and confusion. I'd made the shower purposely cold, the water beating on my head and shoulders creating goosebumps in paths that the icy drops traveled. The temperature was turned down to help rid me of the restless feelings, to clear my head of the early morning beach walk that had ended with the news I hadn't wanted to hear. Jericho was already gone for the day, but before leaving, he'd told me that he'd take the interview with the airport since he'd committed to doing it. He passed me with a brief touch of his hand and showed me his phone with the number before he closed the front door. I'd wanted to ask if the interview mattered, ask him why bother if he'd already made a decision to stay in the Outer Banks?

But there were no decisions made yet, and so I held my words. Jericho was struggling. He didn't know if he would stay or go with me. Torn was the word he'd used. He felt torn. I stared at my feet, shampoo bubbles racing to the drain, a few tears shed to join them. It wasn't fair of me to have made Jericho feel that way. It wasn't fair of me to have asked him to uproot his life and follow me to Philadelphia. I was torn too.

Probably deservedly so. I began to rinse my hair, tugging hard enough to feel it in my scalp. My eyelids closed, ears filled with the noise of water gushing, I thought of the letters, the invitations, and most of all, I thought of the word guilty written on them. Guilt can feel like a hot stone sitting in your gut. That's what I was feeling. Guilt was gnawing at me. It had been what I dreamt about the other night. But the guilt wasn't about the case, not about Charlie Robson or Bernadette Pare. The hot stone was inside me, my guilt for having pushed such a massive decision on Jericho. It was my decision to make. Not his.

Unlike the dirt and grime of the day behind, guilt doesn't wash away with soap and water. Despite that, I tucked the hard feelings away as best I could and went about the motions of the morning. The routines. The toweling and drying my hair, the dressing and then retrieving my gun and badge. It was routine that forced me to put away thoughts of Jericho and the move north so I could concentrate on the case about the sunflower girls. That's what they called themselves. The sunflower girls. It wasn't anything official, nothing established by their school. Just a name they'd come up with and used. And now two of them were dead. Shot to death with what we believed to be arrows, their lives taken in a sunflower field. But why? What were they guilty of?

We stayed east this morning for a meeting in the conference room of my station—my soon-to-be ex-station. The nightshift was over, the queue of evening troubles put to bed early to clear the station's front benches. Alice, our station manager, looked happy, offering me a wave while I opened the short wooden gate that separated our cubicles from the rest of the station. While the benches were clear of perps, a few reporters hung out, their microphones and cameras in hand, gazing into the void with a hungry look like seagulls waiting for food.

"Guys," I said politely, carefully keeping eye contact with the station manager. I didn't have time for questions. Nor did I have any statements.

"Detective?!" one of the reporters asked, rushing through the gate. "Any comments on Charlie Robson's murder?"

"No comment," I said with a flutter in my belly. Charlie's name hadn't been made public yet. Not in these parts anyway. Or had it?

When I paused, a stout man with a camera approached behind the gate, joining the reporter who pushed a fluffy microphone closer to my face. "Any comment about Emanuel Wilson's relation to the victim?"

It was best to play it cool. Nothing else. "Again, no comment." Emanuel had been a celebrity in a previous life. Connecting his name to Charlie's wasn't more than an online search. I waved my hand across my front, the reporters gaze retreating to the floor. He looked to the gate next, and then his shoes. "That's right, you're in the forbidden zone."

"That means off limits to you and yours," Alice said gruffly, our station manager nabbing the reporter's arm to guide him back to front. "Sorry about that, Detective."

"No harm, Alice," I said, and made my way to the conference room.

Tracy and Nichelle were already packed and free of any hourly work obligations, joining me to work the case. They loved Emanuel too and would do anything to find his cousin's killer. The room smelled of coffee and pastry. Our appetites were gluttonous, our excuse the days of boxing and taping and stacking the contents of our homes.

"I don't care what this thing says today," Tracy exclaimed, holding up her hand to show her smart watch. "If I'm going to sit all day, then that's what I'm going to do."

"Right there with you," Nichelle commented, placing two laptops side-by-side, the second issued from the FBI, approvals given by her manager.

"You'll thank her for me?" I asked, tilting my chin.

She slipped her FBI identification badge into the side of the laptop, saying, "I will."

"And hopefully, we won't need it." I tapped my keyboard, sharing my screen on the display at the front of the room. Benjamin Palto's mug shot showed. Tapping again, a picture from the trial appeared next to it. "I say hopefully since Mr. Palto is our leading suspect."

"That's my cue," Tracy said, sitting up, arms crossed, elbows perched on the table, she clicked her mouse, her screen displayed on a conference room monitor. "Benjamin Palto, fifty-five years old. He grew up in California where he also attended UCLA."

"That's him," Nichelle said in a voice without impression.

"Expecting a monster?" I asked, understanding. Benjamin Palto's appearance wasn't the monster expected. He had straight brown hair covering a high forehead. His eyes were small and his nose narrow. He could have been anyone. A street worker. Your delivery man. The guy selling insurance at three a.m. in an infomercial. Nichelle raised a brow, remaining unimpressed. "Monsters come in all shapes and sizes."

"Hmm, suppose they do," Nichelle commented, her chair rolling toward the table, fingers dancing above a keyboard.

"The plain packaging aside, the kids in the school loved him," I said. Nichelle's hands stopped midair and Tracy's face froze, her mouth stuck crooked. "Don't forget, the yearbook was published before his arrest. There are also the prior yearbooks, years of them. Looks aren't everything. Over and over, I read the same thing about Palto's humor and his being that one teacher who was most liked."

"Really?" Nichelle said, brow furrowed deep as yearbook pages flashed onto her screen. "I'll catch up."

"Fast forward," Tracy said, the front monitor updating with a picture of the university campus. "After college, he stayed at UCLA, enrolling, he went to grad school for a graduate degree in education. He never finished."

"Does it say why?" Tracy searched her profile while I moved to the conference room window, the mid-morning sunlight inviting. She shook her head. "What year did he start teaching?"

Tracy lifted her face, answering, "That's why." She changed the picture to show the high school, the home of the sunflower girls' archery team. "He was married the same year he started teaching."

"Wife is... scratch that, was, Linda Palto. She changed her name back to Linda Smith," Nichelle said, filling in the blanks for us. Keyboard rattling. "From her LinkedIn profile, she'd also been a teacher and had gone to UCLA, which tells us how they met. Her family is from North Carolina, where she currently resides."

"Young couple meet at UCLA, they're in the same classes, and then move to North Carolina to teach," I summarized, facing the window, the street empty save for a local I recognized from the sandwich shop a block away. "Was their divorce before or after Benjamin Palto was arrested?"

Their heads ducked closer to their keyboards, glances back and forth as they raced to find the answer. Nichelle had the experience, her technical skills impressive. However, she'd taught Tracy a lot, including many of her tricks. Tracy finished first, sitting up as Nichelle blurted, "It was after!"

"Damn," Tracy said.

"You hesitated," Nichelle told her. She looked at me then, confirming, "Linda Smith filed for divorce a week after the arrest."

"That's interesting. The timing of it." It wasn't the divorce that surprised me. It was when Benjamin Palto's wife filed for it. "To file for a divorce that soon would mean she'd already secured a lawyer?"

"I don't know if that's fast or not," Tracy said, focus jumping between Nichelle's screen and hers. "Never been divorced."

Pressing my back to the wall, wringing the tightness from packing, I reluctantly commented, "I guess I'm the only one here that has." I didn't want to open that can of worms, but one day I would have to tell Tracy more about her father. Tell her about the year after her disappearance and what that had done to our lives. But that wasn't today. "It was a long time ago. I guess finding and retaining a lawyer can happen that quick."

"We'll note it for review?" Tracy asked. With her question, I relaxed, touched with relief that she didn't dig into my divorce.

"Yes, let's move on." I went to the front of the room, dust shimmering in the projector's light, the picture of the sunflower girls taking up half the wall. "We can revisit the timing of the divorce if we find a need."

When I tapped the wall, Nichelle answered, "Deanne Somer."

"Do we know where she is?" I asked, believing all the girls on the team were targets.

"Deanne Somer lives near Virginia Beach," Tracy answered. "She was the first to come forward about Benjamin Palto."

"Stayed on the coast," I said, turning to face the window again, raising it to let a short gust of warm air spill into the room. It carried the smell of the ocean, faint since there wasn't much of a breeze today, the Outer Banks sand dunes keeping the ocean to themselves. But I caught enough of it to think of Jericho and staying here with him. My throat felt thick with the decision I'd have to make. An impossible decision. Wasn't it?

"Casey?" Tracy asked. I shook my head, attention snapping back. "Are you okay?"

"Long night is all," I answered, lying to them, shaking my hands as I went to the table to focus on the case. "Sorry, where were we?"

"Casey?" Nichelle said, dipping her chin with a frown, her eyes leveling with mine. "What's going on?"

I bit my lip, wanting to talk about it, but answered, "For another time." I held up two fingers, adding, "I promise."

"Promise, promise?" Nichelle asked, tilting her head to the side.

"Make it a double promise!" Tracy added excitedly. "A talk over lunch."

"A double promise," I answered hesitantly, having no idea what that even meant. It was probably something they cooked up, a thing only they knew and shared the way couples often do. "Lunch, later."

"Deanne Somer," Nichelle said, recentering the conversation and freeing me of any immediate obligation to explain. "Unlike the two victims, she did not go to the same school."

"That's something," I said, our having believed the connection could have started there. "And the other girls?"

Shaking their heads, trading glances at the screen. "None," they said together.

"That's one more thing to help Jacob Wright's appeal." Thinking of his case and the evidence that would clear his name, freeing him from prison. I displayed a copy of the note, Tracy following with the note Jacob Wright had supposedly written. With one on each screen, the word guilty written in fancy cursive, I considered a study of the cursive slants, the spacing between the letters, their heights and heaviness. Were there any peculiarities or exaggerations, any unusual letter formations such as embellishments, which we could find useful? Reluctant to ask Nichelle for the favor, I thought to frame it in a question. "What are your thoughts on having a handwriting analysis performed?"

"For a comparison? It's clear to me they're written by the same person," Nichelle commented, tapping her keyboard. She pushed a hand across her hair, the top of it bouncing. "If you think it'd help, I could submit it to the FBI for a review."

"Let's do that. The writing looks the same to me too, but I'm not a handwriting expert." Tracy switched photographs, showing the back of the first invitation, the map coordinates, a different set of numbers on them. "Why the GPS coordinates? The latitude and longitude?"

Shaking her head, Nichelle asked, "Why wouldn't they use the farm's street address?"

I raised my brow, seeing an image of the farmer on her patio, along with her family, lights from the patrol cars flashing red and blue across their faces. The field next to their home was a giant sea of green and yellow and brown, the size of it possibly being the reason for the GPS coordinates. "What if he didn't want the victims knocking on the door?" To confirm, I opened one side of a map, centering on the location of Charlie's murder, the coordinates on the screen pivoting, turning solid as I moved my mouse closer to the farmhouse. "She was found here, beyond the road. The farmhouse is a few hundred yards away."

"And the trees," Tracy added. I clicked to zoom onto the farm's property edge, the line of trees in view. "The coordinates were important."

"The coordinates were used to make sure the victims entered the field in the right location." I switched the screen to the small crop circle formation, Charlie's body in the middle. "That way the victim could be lured to the kill point."

"What else can we cover?" Tracy asked, changing the screen to show the high school picture of the sunflower girls.

"You found their yearbook online?" I asked, and began

reading the names. "Deanne Somer we already talked about. That leaves Jessie Smith and Patti Lymone."

"Patti Lymone still lives close to the school," Nichelle answered. "Single, a receptionist for a dentist a few miles from her home... let's see, what else—"

"An FBI profile?" I asked but saw that she was using her personal laptop.

"Nope," she answered flatly. "Just people posting everything about themselves online."

"How about Jessie Smith?"

Tracy took a turn, answering, "Not much here. Had to jump over to a small business site to find anything. Hey, look at that, she is the owner of a shop in Duck, an ice-cream shop."

"An Outer Banks resident and business owner," I said, having an idea of where we'd go for lunch. "And saving the best for last of who we want to review, where is Benjamin Palto these days?"

"Benjamin Palto was the easy one," Tracy answered, swiping her hand like a magician, the front screen showing his mug shot. "Since he's on parole and a registered sex offender, we've got everything needed to track him."

"We'll need his whereabouts on the days of the victims' murders, which means questioning him." I went to the front of the room where the picture of his face spanned the wall. He was the obvious suspect, with an obvious motive, revenge. Sometimes the obvious wasn't the clearest, though, and if that was true here, then who else would have wanted these girls dead? "What do you guys think about Benjamin Palto being the murderer?"

Chair wheels squeaked as they stood, Tracy answering first, "He'd be the first one to suspect."

"Revenge for putting him away?" Nichelle said, asking. "What if the girls lied? What if they made up the whole thing and got him convicted?"

"And there's the archery, and the sunflower fields," Tracy added. "That reminds me, I'm still looking into the types of arrows."

"Keep at it," I said, feeling unconvinced. The obviousness of Palto as a suspect felt suspiciously like a trap. I sensed we needed a break and closed my laptop. They closed their laptops too and yanked cables, rolling them up into balls, the ends dancing across the glass top. They were hungry, eager to go to lunch. I wrapped my knuckles on the tabletop, asking, "Who else had the most to lose?"

"Come again?" Nichelle questioned, confusion on her face. "Lose what?"

I shrugged, raising my hands. "Anything... everything."

"When Benjamin Palto went to prison?" Tracy asked, seeking clarification.

"Exactly." I joined them in collecting our things. Another team in the station were beginning to pace outside the conference room. We were already five minutes past their scheduled time and getting hard looks filled with annoyance. "Something to think about. With Benjamin Palto in prison, who else had everything to lose?"

THIRTEEN

The spiders had labored throughout the evening, stringing their webs from plant to plant, the silk shining against the sunrise, turning them lightning-white, cut sharply by the red and blue emergency lights. The sunflower field had been left untouched until the morning haze had burned off and a body discovered by an officer on patrol. Jessie Smith's Toyota Corolla was located parked alongside the road, the officer finding it abandoned. When she radioed the vehicle plates, there had been a report made by her brother, Jonathon Smith, stating his sister was missing, that she'd never arrived at her place of business.

The scarecrow was visible from the road, a half dozen of its nemeses perched above our heads, talons clutching the telephone wire as if mocking us with their presence. While the scarecrow and its stitched eyes and mouth were a fright, reminding me of the nightmare I'd had, it was the abandoned trailer that pulled my attention, a direction for the investigation of the scene. Tracy and Nichelle joined me, the three of us standing on the road, the sun beating on our heads while patrol vehicles blocked the north and south access.

The crime scene was extended to include the sunflower

field where Jessie Smith's body was discovered, the adjacent road with her vehicle on it, and, per my insistence, the abandoned trailer. Doctor Foster arrived with her assistant, their faces sharing the same expression while we assessed the scene.

"Gloving up," I told them, slipping the booties onto my shoes. The box of gloves was brought out, carried in one hand, a jumpsuit in the other. I looked to the field and then to Doctor Foster, asking, "Full wear?"

She pinched her waist, leaning back with a stretch, face grimacing as she shook her head. "Hands and feet are fine, but there's going to be some chiggers in there so change and shower later."

"I hate those things," Tracy said, and made like she was scratching. "Nastiest bites."

"Is that what those were?" Nichelle asked with alarm, taking a can of bug repellent from Doctor Foster. Tracy gave her a slow nod. "Those bites itched for a month."

"Wash up when we're done," the doctor warned again. She motioned to the trailer, adding, "Sunflower field might be fine, but that long grass by the trailer."

"That's where we think the killer was positioned." I was first to enter the sunflower field, carefully moving a tall stalk aside, the brown and yellow bloom standing a foot above my head. "These are bigger."

Tracy's gaze rose and stayed fixed on the tops of the plants. "They are," she said, the plants motionless, the air still. She sniffed with a frown. "I can smell the blood."

Doctor Foster smelled the air and lifted one of the leafy greens which was covered in dry blood. "If this is like the last one, the victim bled out."

"Jessie Smith," I said, taking to a knee next to the victim's body. "Murder occurring some time in the last eighteen hours."

And it was like the last one. A small crop circle had been created, the kill zone obvious with a clear path to the abandoned trailer. Jessie Smith's body sat squat on the ground, her hind quarters upright, her chest and face planted like the sunflowers surrounding us. There were puncture wounds across her legs and torso, and an entry and exit wound on her arm. Above her ankle, the Achilles tendon had been severed, but we'd no idea when that might have occurred. She wore a candy-striped blouse and skin-tight capri styled jeans, with white tennis shoes, the canvas blood-soaked. Her head was crooked like the scarecrow, strands of long blonde hair spilling around it and stained like her shoes. There was a significant injury to the side of her neck, which looked like an exit wound.

Doctor Foster noticed the concentration of blood on the ground around the victim's head, saying, "If you're right about the arrows, the one that passed through the neck looks to have struck a jugular vein." Her assistant held his hand for the doctor while she lowered herself for a closer look. "If an internal jugular was severed, she only lived another couple of minutes."

The flattened sunflowers crunched beneath our feet, Nichelle and Tracy actively working the bloody trail made by Jessie Smith. I stood to assess the distance, Nichelle standing where the first arrow struck, blood spatter dotting the petals of a sunflower. I opened the measurement tool on my phone, selecting the victim's final position. "This is where she died," I said and began to retrace her steps, following the trail she spilled. When I reached Nichelle, the measurement app indicated a travel of fifty-three feet. "This is where she stood when the first arrow struck."

"How far is that?" Tracy asked, raising her voice. "Twenty yards?"

"Good eye," I answered, sending the measurements to her and Nichelle's phones. "It's fifty-three feet, short of twenty yards."

Nichelle searched around us, finding a hole in some of the

plants, a couple with nicks in their sides, bent over in a lean, stalks broken at mid height. "Not a single arrow."

"Frustrating, isn't it?" I said, glancing around, my search repeating hers. From her backpack, Nichelle brought out a laser pointer. "That will confirm the direction it came from."

She held her arms wide, saying, "That sunflower there, and this one here, line up the holes."

I moved to the one closest to me. "There's a divot in the ground where the arrow struck. The damage here is lowest."

"And this one, it's higher," she said, following along, tossing me the laser pointer. I turned it on, green beam invisible without something to reflect it, the end a thick dot on Nichelle's shirt. "Up and to the right."

"Just a little bit more," I said, moving to line it up with the damage. Tracy joined us with a field glass in hand. "The air is dust free, we'll need those to be able to see where it's landing."

"You guys have it lined up?" she asked, her eyes covered by the glass and facing the suspected area, the trailer. She shook her head, "Uh-uh, not seeing anything."

"Maybe a lower angle?" Nichelle asked, motioning with her fingers, thumb pointed down. "But then the holes in the plants won't line up."

"I just need to be close since he would have been on the roof of the trailer. We only need to confirm that was the location." I tilted the front of the laser a degree, hugging the bottom of the hole in Nichelle's plant, waiting for a response, Tracy shaking her head. When there was none, I ticked another half degree.

"Got it!" Tracy yelled, fist raised. "I see a green dot right at the roofline, directly in the center of the trailer."

I stood up, the muscles in my legs cramped. "Let's finish up here and then take a look at that trailer."

We returned to the body, Doctor Foster and her assistant working with the victim, Tracy jumping into it with the crime-scene camera. "Casey?" Tracy asked, pointing to the victim's back pocket, the top of a cell phone sticking out of it. "Is that what I think it is?"

"Certainly, appears to be," I said, pinching latex gloves, slipping the victim's phone from her pocket, an invitation joining it. It fluttered to the ground like a dying butterfly, the folded paper the same type, the victim's name penned on the front. I opened it enough to show the inside. Tracy photographed the coordinates and the word guilty written in a fancy cursive. My jaw was clenched. The killer was working through the team faster than we could solve his murders. "Nichelle, would you dial in a protection order for Patti Lymone and Deanne Somer?"

"On it," she said. Behind us, tires ground to a stop and a car door slammed. The sunflowers kept the road hidden from us, but the voices carried, an officer telling someone the road was closed. "Want me to go see—"

"I'll go," I said, Nichelle following as Tracy continued to work with Doctor Foster and her assistant. We walked through the sunflowers, reaching the road to see an officer arguing with a man in his late teens. He was lean and tall, his hair and skin touched by the sun, wearing torn jeans and a ripped T-shirt. He held his phone, showing it to the officer and pointing to the victim's car.

"Can we help you, sir?" I asked, slipping the gloves from my hand.

"You in charge?" he asked, turning his back on the officer, a thumb continuing to point toward the victim's car. "That's my sister's. I want to see her."

"Sir—" I began to say, but he already knew. His eyelids squeezed shut, cheeks turning wet as his hands dropped to his sides. He looked at the victim's car and then the medical examiner van. When I reached him, my arm extended, I coaxed him back to his car, to a place away from the crime scene. "You know the owner of the vehicle?"

"My sister," he was able to say, wiping his face.

"Jonathon?" I asked.

"Yeah," he answered, eyelids wide with surprise.

"You called in a missing persons report," I reminded him. This wasn't the time to ask him questions, but he'd arrived at the scene, to a place that he'd likely not arrive to on his own. "How did you know where your sister's car was?"

"It was that note," he answered, wiping again, voice choked. He showed me his phone and a picture of a map with the coordinates from the invitation. "She didn't know what they were. When I didn't hear anything from the cops, I came here. That's when I saw her car."

"I am sorry for your loss," I began, in no doubt that it was his sister in the sunflower field. "You retrieved the note?"

"It was in the mailbox at the ice-cream shop she owns... I mean owned," he said, holding back a cry. "I gotta tell my parents."

"Is there anyone you can think of who would want to see your sister harmed?" I asked, reverting to one of our staple questions, having my suspicions.

"There was that chem teacher she had, but he went away."

"Officer?" I asked, concerned for the boy's welfare. "Would you drive Mr. Smith home?"

Jonathon shook his head. "I can drive. I'm fine. I know you can't have me here."

"Would you be available later for more questions?" I asked. "You and your sister's employees."

"Yeah, sure. Stop by the shop." He jumped into his car then, tires kicking up stone.

"Nichelle, let's get some officers out to pick up Benjamin Palto."

"On it."

FOURTEEN

It wasn't long before Benjamin Palto was tracked down and brought in for questioning. He no longer lived on North Carolina's mainland. Since prison, he'd taken up residence in the Outer Banks, forty miles from the school he'd taught at, the school at which he'd committed his crimes. His parole officer, a nice gentleman, a cop who'd made a somewhat lateral career switch, gave us every detail we'd need.

With his help, we knew where Palto lived, where he worked, when he woke up, and when he called it a night. The parole officer made it a point to visit often and get to know his parolees, especially the predators. When asked about the times of the sunflower girl murders, the parole officer had an answer. Benjamin Palto was on shift at the Flower and Garden Depot, three miles from his apartment. While it put a wrinkle in the case, we'd hear it from Palto himself.

"It's warm in here." I waved a folder, fanning my face. The air was thick. There were workers wearing bright yellow vests that shined, and leather tool belts as thick as my hand. I'd seen two on the roof, another one inside, the building's heating and air-conditioning unit being replaced. "It's going to get warm."

"Already is warm," Tracy commented, fanning herself, her hair frizzing like mine.

The walls were made of cinderblock painted white and the room was windowless, its single feature the steel table in the center, which was unmoving, bolted to the floor. There were safety guards for restraints, the room also used when interviewing prisoners. But we wouldn't use them today. Palto wasn't in custody yet.

Jericho opened the door to let some air inside while we waited. Most of his career in law enforcement was at this station, including his years as the sheriff. From the mayor to the district attorney and the officers working the third shift, they still held Jericho in high regard and never questioned his presence. He wasn't here today to help with the case though. He joined us after getting word that Emanuel might visit the station. The last thing we needed was to have Emanuel throw any complications into the case like an assault on the suspect. I'd let our station manager know that this was a closed interview and had her post a guard outside the interview room. Nobody except the direct team and Jericho were allowed. "You think he'll show?"

"He's angry," Jericho answered, looking official, clean shaven and wearing dress slacks with a light-blue button-down shirt. His mouth twisted as if chewing on the words he wanted to say. "I think he might have been drinking."

"Emanuel?" I said, shocked to hear it. I saw what Emanuel looked like in my mind, the grimace he wore when he'd learned what Benjamin Palto had done to his cousin. "I don't think I've ever seen him have more than one or two drinks when we've been out."

Jericho shook his head, saying, "He is holding on to a lot of guilt." Jericho shook his head then, forehead wet, adding, "It's not just the murder. It's what happened at the school."

"The poor guy," Tracy said, looking small in the corner of

the room, her hair hanging limp. Her laptop wobbled as she typed. She'd volunteered to take notes during the interview. "I feel bad."

"I feel for him too, but we can't have him here." A sigh, my breath hot. The tension in the room was uncomfortable. It wasn't just the case and Emanuel. Jericho had never said a word about his job interview. We'd barely spoken since he had told me he wasn't sure about Philadelphia. "Let's get through—"

"Detective?" I never finished my words. A patrol officer entered the room, a man my height standing next to him. "Benjamin Palto."

"Thank you, officer," I said. I offered the bench seat to Palto, the one fixed to the floor, the one we'd use when interviewing those in custody.

He was short with graying hair, his face unimpressively normal. But plainness can't be a measure of the criminal thoughts and actions. In my career, I'd found they'd rarely ever had a sinister look, not like they do on television or in the movies. The reality of it was that they were as plain as anyone else, all shapes and sizes and colors, indistinguishable. "Mr. Palto."

"Ben," he said, pulling one of the fold-out chairs and sitting before I could say anything. He eyed the bench seat with a slight grin of achievement. "You can call me Ben."

"Ben," I said, moving to sit across from him. Jericho sat behind the suspect, taking a position of insurance, putting himself between Palto and the door. I dropped a folder onto the table, leaving the manilla cover closed. Inside were the crime-scene photographs, which I'd use if the temperature of the conversation warranted. "Do you know why you're here today?"

He shook his head, bangs swaying, his shoulders in a slouch. "Does it matter?"

"Does what matter?" I asked, curious to his question.

"It doesn't matter why I'm here." Palto perched his elbows

on the table and rubbed his hands together, saying nothing while he surveyed the room. The door remained opened, his gaze fixed on the empty space inside the frame, shifting to Jericho briefly before finding Tracy, where it stayed. Tracy continued typing until the silence had her looking up. At once, Palto looked away, continuing. "This isn't the first time I've been questioned."

"Is that so?" Jericho asked, his voice deep, commanding.

Palto raised one brow in Jericho's direction. "I'm on parole. I've got a parole officer checking up on me a couple times a week."

"I'd say he's doing his job," Jericho added.

Palto tightened his grip, knuckles white. There was anger, and annoyance, blood rising on his cheeks. "I am getting dragged in on every single report of a child touched or looked at suspiciously. I served my time—"

"You're on parole," I said, interrupting to correct him. "You are still serving your time."

He loosened the ball of knuckles, freeing them, hands open, fingers splayed, saying, "Yeah, whatever!"

"And now it's our turn to ask some questions," Jericho commented, moving his chair closer.

"Then get on with it," Palto said as he wiped his brow, the stiff air making him sweat. "I've got a shift later tonight, stocking the shelves."

"The sunflower girls." From the folder, I placed a picture of the team. The photocopy was crisp, catching air like a wing, gliding in front of him. "We have some questions."

With the mention of the team, the picture of them, Palto's demeanor changed. The agitation of being here, the confidence too, they drained from his face, and he shut his eyelids. "When was the last time you saw anyone from the team?"

"Years," he answered, eyelids remaining shut, squeezed tight like he was trying to hide from them. But the past was unescapable. The past will always be the past, following. "Not since the trial."

"No other correspondences?" Jericho questioned. "Anyone reach out to you while you were serving time?"

A hesitation, Palto's mouth twisting. "Just some family."

"Anyone else?" I asked, believing Jericho might have clued in on something. I reframed the question, "Who did you talk to while you were away?"

His eyelids snapped open, wide, the color in them dark like charcoal. They were bloodshot and weary, his voice like bark, "Nobody! Nobody would have anything to do with me."

"You said family?" Jericho asked. "That was a lie?"

He shrugged his shoulders, crossing his arms. "They won't talk to me anymore."

I leaned forward, moving the team picture, centering it before him. "Did you do it?"

Palto's head tilted back with a jerk as if slapped. "Got convicted, didn't I?" He shoved the picture away from in front of him, sliding it back in my direction. "Is that why I'm here? You want to ask about the trial?"

"What about Charlie Robson?" Jericho asked while he slid a chair back, scraping the legs against the floor. "Have you spoken with her?"

"I haven't seen or spoken to anyone," Palto answered, his left knee bouncing. He might not know why he was here, but he knew when cops were fishing, and it made him nervous. He opened his hands, sweeping them wide, palms showing, asking, "What's this about?"

"Charlie Robson was murdered." Jericho's voice was low with anger. Palto sensed it, leaning away, afraid.

"Are you a cop?" he asked Jericho, searching up and down with his eyes. "You dress the part, but I don't see a badge."

"I was the sheriff when you were arrested and put away." Jericho ignored the comment, ignored Palto trying to get under his skin. "And I still work investigations. With that cleared, tell us when you saw Charlie Robson."

Palto's gaze drifted to the table and to the picture of the girls. The hard look he held on to softened, his saying, "I'm sorry to hear about Charlie. Great athlete." He shook his head slowly, blinking fast as he continued. "But I haven't seen any of the girls since the trial. Even then, only a few of them testified."

"Bernadette Pare?" I asked.

"Yeah, she was one of them," he answered. Beads of sweat coated his upper lip, the humidity and temperature climbing. "I think she was the first one. Or might have been Jessie Smith."

"They're dead too," Tracy said without looking up.

"Shit!" Benjamin Palto didn't watch the news or read the paper. He understood instantly why we were asking him questions. "I had nothing to do with this. None of it."

"You mentioned you're getting home checks by your parole officer?" Jericho asked, his phone in hand. "Let's start with his number."

"Yeah, yeah, do that," he said, giving us the number. Palto rose in his chair briefly and sat back down, his nerves ratcheting like the temperature. "He visits at all hours, writes everything down on his phone."

"Your work schedule?" I asked, knowing he had a parole job, an hourly wage earned for an hourly work done. "Garden shop?"

"Yes, ma'am," he said with formality, his attitude changed with the context of our meeting revealed. "The Flower and Garden Depot in Kitty Hawk. My apartment is a few miles from there."

"How do you get to work?" Tracy asked, fingers typing fast, which had me think he didn't have a license or a vehicle. "Drive?"

"I walk, ma'am," he answered her. "Rain or shine. I walk to and from the depot."

"We'll confirm your shift hours," I assured him, the strength of his alibi having the potential of freeing him as our lead suspect.

"Wait, got this... maybe this will help," he said, digging into a front pocket. From it, he placed a crumpled ball onto the table, doing his best to flatten it, pressing into the steel to rid it of the wrinkles. "My check stub. They always include the days and hours worked."

The table of letters and numbers was small but showed which days he was at the Flower and Garden Depot, as well as the number hours. "It's a start," I told him, the times of the shift missing. "Can we hold on to this?"

"Sure, sure, yeah!" he answered as I handed it to Tracy. He faced Tracy, wiping his palms against his legs. He began pegging the air with a finger as if dialing a phone. "Call it in, they'll tell you the time I clocked in and out."

"Can you get us the week prior?" Jericho asked, his voice remaining low.

Palto spun in his seat, facing him. "I keep all of them. My parole officer told me to since he takes pictures of them."

Commotion outside the room stole our attention. There was the sound of feet shuffling against the tile, rubber soled shoes chirping, a thud against the adjacent wall with threats and hollering echoing down the hallway.

"What is that?" Tracy asked, voice breaking, a look of fright building as the yelling grew louder. "Casey?"

"The door!" Jericho jumped from his seat, blocking the opening, grabbing the handle to close the door. But it was too late, an arm and leg appearing, the door slamming back, striking Jericho's head and face.

"Hold the door!" I yelled. Instinctively, Palto went to the ground, his reaction a muscle memory from the afternoons he'd spent in the prison yard. I ran around the table, touching Palto's shoulder, telling him, "Stay down!"

"Okay," he muttered, wide-eyed, a look of fright draining his color, fingers woven together and covering the back of his head.

Emanuel's sweaty face appeared in the door, his nose bloodied, the arm of the patrol officer guarding the room trying desperately to hold him. "I just want to ask him some questions," he yelled, the words rambled, the smell of alcohol permeating the air.

"Emanuel, you can't be here," Jericho insisted, shoving his arms into Emanuel's chest, leaning his body into him. Jericho's face was bloodied, a cut above his eye making tears that swam to his chin. He looked into Emanuel's face, pleading, "This isn't how we do things."

Emanuel frowned, eyes piercing, his cheeks glistening in the light. "Who was there when your wife's body was found!? Who held you?!"

"I know you did," Jericho answered, voice cracking, the emotion tugging. Emanuel forced himself forward, his size more than a match for two men. Palto sized the situation, focus darting from the floor to the top of Emanuel's head. His eyelids were gone, eyeballs bulging from their sockets, his color a ghostly white. Jericho strained to hold Emanuel at the door. "Emanuel, please!"

"I just want a couple of minutes!" he demanded. I put myself in front of Palto, the interview room inescapably small. Tracy tucked herself into the corner, holding her laptop close to her chest. If Emanuel got to Palto, there was no knowing who was safe. "You know what he did to Charlie!"

"I served my time," Palto said, his voice insignificant like a mouse. I glared at him, lips tight, finger pressed across them, telling him to shut it.

"There you are!" Emanuel snapped, finding what he'd come for. Palto's reply enraged Emanuel more. I thought of the word guilty, the reckoning the girls had faced. Emanuel had come with his own reckoning in mind for Benjamin Palto. Innocent of murder, or not, Palto was guilty of a crime against Emanuel's cousin. Although the case wasn't solved, Emanuel was certain that if not for Benjamin Palto, if not for what happened to the team of the sunflower girls, his cousin would still be alive. "Come here!"

Both of his feet were nearly inside the room, his body turned toward Palto. Behind his large frame, I saw the officer's eyes level with Emanuel's shoulder, a ragged scratch across his forehead. "Tase," I mouthed to him, hating to do it, my fear growing for all of us. "Now!"

The officer disappeared, backing away, his release freeing Emanuel to overpower Jericho. I stepped back, shielding Palto as Emanuel lunged forward. Jericho's body flew into the room like he'd been pummeled by a linebacker. I braced, every muscle, tensing to stand my ground, hoping to lessen whatever punishment might come. Emanuel raised his arms over his head, eyes fixed on Palto. I didn't recognize Emanuel, didn't recognize the detective I'd known, the man I'd come to love like a brother. Rage had made him into someone else. I saw in his eyes how murder was born from vengeance.

Hidden in the grunts and shouts and cries, there was the sound of a taser gun firing. The officer shot in time to stop Emanuel's approach. At once his body straightened like a board, causing him to fall sideways. Emanuel collapsed onto the table, eyes rolling into his skull. I grabbed Palto's arm, squeezing as hard as I could, driving him away from the interview room. As I exited, I saw Jericho drop onto Emanuel, a pair of hand-cuffs in hand. We wouldn't arrest him though, not unless the officer guarding the door wanted to press charges. But we'd hold him, sober him up with water and coffee and try to talk some sense into him. I wasn't at all sure we'd get him to listen, get him back.

"Where we going!?" Palto asked, panting feverishly, covering his chest with a hand. When I reached the holding cells, I opened the door. He stopped at once, jerking his arm from mine. "I'm not going in there. Am I under arrest?"

I shook my head, answering, "It's for your protection." I looked down the hallway, shadows moving on the floor. "He can't get you in here."

With the shadows, shuffling feet and hollering, Jericho's and Emanuel's voices tangling, Palto flinched with understanding and eagerly entered the holding cell, grabbing the iron bars to close them behind him. "Please, keep him away from me!"

"We'll do our best," I said, lying a little, thinking some fright was deserved. With the holding cell secured, I went back to the interview room to tend to my friend.

"Emanuel—" I began, but when I got to the room, a third taser had already been discharged. It released a cloud of confetti that rained around Emanuel's body, the bits of paper in the cartridges made to identify which gun was used. But this wasn't a party or a disco. We'd put down our friend to save himself from harm, as well as the suspect, and most likely ourselves. I raised my hands to tell the officer to stop, his finger on the trigger, pumping electricity into Emanuel. The officer let go and Emanuel let out a crying breath.

"Casey?" he asked as I knelt next to him. He'd tucked himself into a ball, a fetal position, a puddle of blood on the floor, his nose still dripping. I wiped the sweat from his eyes and face, bracing his cheeks, his gaze bouncing wildly.

"Shh," I started to say, voice choked, heart aching for him. "You'll be okay."

"I'm sorry," he said, crying. "I didn't mean it."

"We've got you," Jericho said, hand on Emanuel's shoulder. Jericho was distraught, anguished and spent, the gash above his eye needing stitches. Emanuel grabbed Jericho's hand, peering up to see the damage, his expression softening with regret. Jericho forced a smile. "Don't worry about it. Another scar will only make me look tougher."

"Charlie is dead," Emanuel said, Jericho's smile dying. He heaved a long breath, Tracy joining us. Emanuel sobbed hard, chest collapsing as he strained to say, "She's never coming back. I should have known, should have been—"

"You couldn't," Tracy said, embracing him, the danger passed. She cried with Emanuel. We all did. We'd never seen him so broken.

Between the sobbing breaths, Emanuel continued to blame Palto. "I don't know if he did it, but if she'd never known him, she'd be alive."

"I know," I told him, feeling his pain, the same sentiment. There is no knowing what happens when people like Benjamin Palto enter our lives. "We'll catch the killer. I promise."

FIFTEEN

Jericho and Tracy tended to Emanuel while I consoled the officer who'd fired his taser. There was a graze on the officer's head, a scratch deep enough to have bled. He'd cleaned and bandaged the cut, its looking far less severe than it had. The patrol officer wasn't going to press charges against Emanuel. Benjamin Palto wouldn't either since he hadn't been harmed in the incident. We swept the confetti that had been discharged into the room. The colorful mess of paper was sprinkled across the table and chair and lying over the floor. We kept some of it, the pieces used in identifying the spent cartridge. Like any firearm, a taser is a weapon and it had been used. Any discharge of a weapon required the station manager and the sheriff to be involved. There was paperwork to do, part of the bureaucracy of reporting what had happened. A training exercise, the sheriff decided, expensing the cartridges, keeping Emanuel's name clear, with the agreement from the latter that he'd take a couple of weeks off.

As Jericho drove Emanuel back to his place, Nichelle, Tracy and I jumped onto Route 12 and headed north to Duck. Jonathon Smith had provided the address to the boardwalk shop on the edge of Currituck Sound, which lay on the bay side of the Outer Banks. It was Jessie Smith's ice-cream and waffle shop, which her brother had kept open. There were questions about the archery team that I hoped he could answer.

Sunsets in the Outer Banks are the highlights of many tourists' day and even of the locals and the transplants like me. The sky was nearly clear and the few clouds were like ribbons. The edge of Currituck Sound lapped softly against the boards, its surface blazing with ripples of white light. When I squinted, I could barely make out the mainland. The sun was a giant red ball sitting on it, the sky painted red and orange, turning to a lavender blend before the first stars were visible.

"Good crowd," Tracy said, standing next to me. She looked to our sides, the gathered crowd numbering twenty or more, another row behind us waiting to enter the ice-cream shop. Jessie Smith might have been a genius picking this shop with its location. She'd put her shop on the front row of the show to watch the sunsets, the stage set by the bay, the main actor dependable enough to set a watch by. Tracy turned back, shielding her eyes, saying, "A really good crowd."

"It is," I agreed, stomach growling at the smell of freshly cooked waffles coming from the ice-cream shop. Tracy saw me looking, heard my belly aching. "Yeah, I'm getting some just as soon as we're done."

The whites of her eyes flashed, dimples showing. "We're going to wait?" she asked, referring the crowd at the door.

"When it dies down, we'll go in," I told her. I was sure Jessie's brother was having a hard enough time. We had the evening to ask our questions and no reason to get in the way of their busiest time.

Tracy held up her phone. "Mind if I ask Nichelle to join us?"

"Sure," I said, the mention of her name reminding me she'd been doing some work this afternoon for her move to the FBI headquarters in Philadelphia. "She finished her training?"

The whites of Tracy's eyes flashed again as she shook her head. "Something like ten courses."

"She'll want the break," I commented and turned back. The sun's lower body was gone, tucked behind the earth and ready to sleep. There were sea birds in silhouette, an osprey hovering for a dive over the calm surface of the bay. In the serenity of the bay, I saw the lifestyle that was the Outer Banks. It was like no other place I'd ever been. "This is what it's about."

"Definitely not the city," Tracy said, her face showing concern as she shoved her fingers through her hair.

"You too?" I asked, thinking she might have reservations about the move to the city. While she'd lived her first years in Philadelphia, the majority of her life, her memories, were based here, on the Outer Banks. She knew nowhere else. "Having second thoughts?"

"Man am I," she answered, rolling her eyes. "I'm having seconds and thirds and fourths."

I took a breath, holding it as I braced the railing, uncertain of what to say. When I faced her, I saw the wet in her eyes, the sunlight bouncing off them. Gripping her arm, I asked, "What is it?" She shook her head, biting her lips as if fighting a terrible secret. With both hands, I held her. "You can tell me anything."

"This is home," she said with a shrug and forcing a smile. Her dimples vanished then as she held up her phone and showed Nichelle's name on the screen. "She'll be here in ten."

"But?" I asked, dipping my head to search her eyes. "This is home?"

"I love her, I do." Tracy stopped and faced the water where the sunset lights sparkled and put on a show. She had that same look that Jericho had. Torn. Wanting to leave but wanting to stay. "I don't know how to live anywhere else."

"I think I know," I said, heart aching for her pain. She was my daughter, but we'd lost out on the opportunities of building a bond. I knew we had our boundaries, but instincts had me moving, driving the fibers of my muscles, piloted by the natural instincts that are in each of us. I gently touched her back, shifting a step. Tracy leaned into me, saying nothing, her head resting against my shoulder. I breathed in the smell of her, reminded of the million times I'd held her as a baby, the scent beneath my nose that told me she was mine. I'd promised to share what was going on with me and told her, "If it helps you feel any better, Jericho is going through the same exact thing."

Tracy pulled away enough to see me, her brow rising. "He is? Is that what—"

I frowned, answering before she finished, "What is it about this place that's got such a hold on you two?"

She held out her hand to the bay like a model presenting a showcase. I saw a fish darting from the water, the osprey swooping to feed, diamonds dancing across the surface as the last of the sun dipped below the horizon. "Do you have to ask? I mean, that's just a tip of it. The lifestyle here is different."

"I get it," I said, having felt the change when I'd arrived in search of her. "Trust me. I do."

She let me wipe the tear streaks from her cheeks, dimples showing, her pupils big. "Jericho has been here forever."

"He has," I said, guilt weighing on my words. "Maybe I shouldn't have pushed it."

"That was my fault." Her voice rose as she spoke with her hands. "I got so excited... ya know!"

"You get that from your father," I said, smiling, seeing him in her mannerisms, the charisma. "He was always one to leap first and ask questions later."

"Yeah! That's exactly what I do!" Tracy spun around as a

car backfired. Her composure changed then, saying, "That's Nichelle."

"What? She doesn't know how you're feeling?" I faced the parking lot, but it was too far from the boardwalk. The line for the ice-cream shop had thinned, Nichelle's arriving in time to ask questions.

"Uh-uh," Tracy answered, drying her face. "Stays between us?"

"Of course it does," I said, seeing the top of Nichelle's hair. She wore it big today, the remains of the sunset turning her face golden along with her bright yellow sneakers with the thick soles. A backpack was slung from one shoulder. She waved and then saw the last of the customers entering the ice-cream shop. "Nichelle, you got here just in time."

"Hungry for sweets?" Tracy asked, brushing her hand across Nichelle's arm, pecking her cheek with a kiss. "You ate?"

Nichelle looked over Tracy's shoulder at me and put on a funny face. "Always looking out for me."

"She's a keeper," I said with a wink, switching gears, putting on my detective's face. It was one of the many I'd learned to wear, having worn it the most, and reminded them, "This is Jonathon Smith, the victim Jessie Smith's brother. He is in mourning, so let's keep that in mind as we ask questions."

We entered the ice-cream shop, refrigerators humming in the background noise of customer chatter. The outside of the shop was far larger than the indoors, the victim having kept an apartment above. A man and a woman with a child walked by us, their eyes crossing while they focused on their ice cream, tongues racing against the warm evening. "I'm getting one of those," I heard in front of me, Nichelle pointing at scoops of mint chocolate chip on a rainbow-colored waffle cone.

"Wow, some wild flavors," Tracy said, the three of us peering up at the menu.

"Two scoops each," I joked, playing the parent while

seeking out Jonathon Smith. The shop was big enough to hold twenty people standing. That is, if everyone held a deep breath. There were two counters, one across from the door, the other stretching opposite of it where they met in the corner. The refrigerators we had heard stood behind the glass counters, through which we could see the tubs of ice cream. There was every imaginable flavor. My mouth watered while I tried to pick one. "But which two is the question?"

"Help you?" Jonathon asked me, seeing us, but not seeing us. He'd given us a cursory look but didn't recognize who we were. Locks of blond hair sprouted from beneath a white paper cap, and the ripped T-shirt he'd worn to his sister's crime scene was covered by a drug-rug. The hippie, Mexican surfing hoodie sweater, which was common on colder nights, hung limp from his shoulders. "See anything you like?"

"Two scoops of coffee," I asked, adding, "One of those rainbow swirled cones."

"Live a little," Nichelle said, nudging my shoulder. "You always get coffee."

"My sister's favorite was a combination of coffee and banana-walnut," Jonathon said, his words fading when he recognized me. "You're not just here for the ice cream?"

I measured the crowd, another line forming now that the sun was gone, asking, "Do you have time?"

"Chrissy?" he asked, his voice loud enough to dull the crowd's chit-chat. "Karen?"

Two girls his age popped up from behind the other counter. "Sup?" one of them asked.

He held up his hand, fingers splayed. "I need to take five after I serve them." He turned back to me, adding, "All yours."

"I'll try your sister's favorite," I told him, his working a tub of coffee ice cream. Tracy and Nichelle added their orders while I put twenty dollars onto the counter.

"On the house," he said, motioning to the door. "There's a spot around the side we can talk."

I dropped the twenty into a small bucket marked with the word TIPS and followed him outside. "Your sister's apartment?" I asked, a sudden brain freeze making me wince.

"We keep the ice cream a few degrees below what's needed," he said, noticing, a smile forming. "Jessie insisted, even though it made it harder to scoop."

"Definitely colder," Nichelle said. "Does it last longer in the summer air?"

He wrinkled his nose. "It can't beat a hot night like this," he answered, shaking his head. "But Jessie thought if the customers took their time, they'd enjoy it longer and make for a lasting memory." His smile faded with a shrug. "That was just one of her ideas."

"I think she was onto something," Tracy told him while she carefully nipped at the cone. "And these waffles are amazing too."

"That was another one of her ideas. We made them to celebrate pride month in June." He dug into his front pocket and retrieved a key ring, two keys clanking as he handed it to me. "The customers like the colors so much, we kept making them."

"Her apartment?" I asked, closing my hand around the keys.

"One is for the shop and the other is her apartment." He pointed behind him, a staircase leading to a door above us. A frown formed, his gaze fixed on the landing. "I haven't gone in yet."

"Thank you," I told him, ice cream running down my knuckles.

"Good combination?" he asked, handing me some napkins. I nodded. The spark in his eyes showed how fond he was of his older sister. "Jessie loved it."

"Do we have your permission to remove items?" Jessie's

brother hesitated before answering. "We'd only take what might help in the investigation. And we'll inventory it for returning."

His eyes turned hard as he continued his stare at the apartment door. "If it means catching that guy, then take whatever you need."

"Benjamin Palto?" Nichelle asked.

"Who else would it be?" he asked, shifting, annoyed by the question. He crossed his arms tight, adding, "There's nobody in this world that ever had a problem with Jessie."

"Did she stay in touch with her teammates?" I asked, teeth aching, jaw trembling from the cold. "The ones who testified?"

"Nobody from varsity." He hung a thumb over his shoulder again, answering, "But she stayed friends with Karen and Chrissy."

"Karen and Chrissy?" Tracy asked, phone in hand, swiping through screen notes. "They were on the team too?"

"JV," he answered. "Palto coached both teams."

"Junior varsity?" I said, confirming. Our research had been limited to the varsity team. "How many girls were involved?"

Jonathon dipped his face, lowering it, disbelief in his eyes. "All of them," he answered, hands raised. "That's where it all started, JV team."

"None of the girls testified?" Nichelle asked, her brow furrowed. She joined Tracy, searching her phone. "I've only got testimony from the older girls."

"They were seniors, a few eighteen. JV is freshman and sophomore class." Jonathon checked the time on his watch. We had gone well past the five minutes. "They all gave statements though."

"Palto's plea bargain ended the trial, he pleaded guilty. If the trial had continued, the younger girls might have been called to testify." I shook the keys, motioning to the second floor, urging the girls to hurry and finish. "We won't be long. What time do you close?"

"Summer nights," he said with an eye roll. "At least eleven, maybe midnight."

"Karen and Chrissy?" Tracy asked. "Ask questions?"

"Possibly?" I answered, the count of Palto's victims doubling, possibly tripling. "Who knows how many more are in danger?"

SIXTEEN

The sun was gone for the day, the night sky a dark blue and turning gray. The shadow of bats flew in and out of the board-walk lights, feasting like the couples and families that exited the small ice-cream shop. We took to the wood staircase, eyes on the slim door above the shop, steps creaking as we ascended. A blanket of warm air gushed from the darkness of her apartment while I fumbled for a light switch.

"Cozy," Tracy said, scooting past me as I assessed first impressions. She waved to fan her face, adding, "But it's so warm."

"No wonder. Windows are free of air conditioning, and the refrigerators build heat below," Nichelle said while opening a window. She worked her hair into a bun, her large brown eyes drinking in the room. "This is cozy. I'd live here."

"What do we have?" I asked while carefully crossing the main room. There was a plush couch for two, a love seat, on one side of the wall, a bookshelf across from it. A plump green beanbag sat next to the door, light bulbs draped from a white wire in the corner, their filaments glowing bright. I went to the bookshelf, finding classic horror novels and newer thrillers. I pulled a hardback out, saying, "She's a reader."

Tracy joined me, sifting through the titles, tapping the spines. "Notice it?"

"What's that?" I asked, searching the shelves, finding what wasn't there. "Hmm. There's no tech. No eBook readers or tablets. Not even a television."

"There must be a laptop around here," Nichelle said with a frown, searching. "How else is she working payroll and taxes and all that goodness that comes with employing a small business?"

"I'll check the kitchen," Tracy said, working a counter that divided the room. There was a hotplate and sink, a countertop microwave and refrigerator. A few pots and pans hung from the walls, along with kitchen towels, and a pair of oven mitts. "Not much of a cook."

"Microwave dinners," I said, sifting through the trash and recycling. "I'd say Jessie Smith lived in her shop. She ate and slept here, did some reading in her downtime, but not much else."

"No computer or laptop," Nichelle said, poking her head out of the bedroom. "No tablet either."

Tracy returned to the victim's library and began to go through the books, pages ruffled as she fanned them open. "Can you run a business from a phone?" she asked. "I mean, if that's all you've got?"

"I could," Nichelle answered without hesitating.

"Sure, if that's all you've got." I joined Tracy, picking a book from the shelf, a newer Stephen King I'd had my eye on. I fanned the pages, feeling our time was wasting. I replaced the book, filling the empty space, saying, "Let's spend the time where Jessie Smith spent her time."

"Downstairs?" Nichelle asked.

"Talk to Karen and Chrissy?" Tracy added.

"Yes," I said, shooing them along, crowding around the door while I locked it behind us. "Do we have any pictures from the junior varsity squad?"

"Already loaded," Tracy answered, staircase creaking, the railing loose. "Karen Walter and Chrissy Jensen."

We reached the bottom, Nichelle staring back at the steps, offering, "I can get a profile started."

"If needed," I said, opening the door. The crowds were nearly gone. Coins clanked as one of the girls handed a young couple their change. She shut the cash register drawer. "Let's see if they know anything."

The couple exited behind us, Tracy holding the door for them. "Find anything?" Jonathon asked.

"Is it safe to assume that Jessie spent much of her time here?" I asked.

One of the girls let out a laugh, covering her mouth almost immediately. Jonathon smiled, telling her, "It's okay." He turned to us, adding, "Jessie had big dreams. All she did was this place."

"How about you?" I asked, curious of his position.

"I was only fifteen when our parents died," he began and picked up a broom. He pointed to a sign behind the counter, the JV girls following his lead to clean, the sign reading *When it's time to lean, it's time to clean.* "Jessie became my legal guardian. I suppose she's much more than just a sister to me."

"She took care of us," one of the girls said, her silver hair braided with beads. She had a tattoo on the side of her neck and piercings in her ears and nose. "She let me crash with her when I needed it."

"Chrissy?" I asked, phone in hand, the conversation opening to questions.

"I'm Chrissy," the other girl answered, arm stretching across the counter, wiping. She'd taken off her cap, red hair covering some of her face. Skin nearly white, made pale by the contrast of heavy makeup, inky black lining her eyes with thick mascara. "She's Karen."

Jonathon walked past us, flipping the sign on the front door. "We can close early."

"Karen," I said with a nod. "And Chrissy. How did you guys become friends with Jessie?"

The girls exchanged a brief look, Karen with a scowl, Chrissy a frown. "The coach," they both said at the same time. Chrissy straightened herself, adding, "None of us knew what was going on."

Karen shook her head, saying, "Not until Jessie said something."

"You mean she asked the team first?" Tracy questioned, the origins of the Benjamin Palto case not known.

Chrissy raised her hand. "She asked me. But only after she'd found me—" She stopped abruptly, hand covering her mouth, fingers trembling.

"It's okay, Chrissy," Karen told her. "It's over now."

"Jessie found me in the bathroom afterward," Chrissy continued. "I didn't know what to do. That's when she told me that it happened to her too."

"She'd thought she was the only one," Karen said, walking around the counter to join us on the other side. "He'd been at almost all of us."

"I'm sorry this happened to you," I said, seeing the pain, what Palto had done.

They didn't acknowledge the sentiment, their look hard. Chrissy scoffed, voice rising, "He's going to do it again!" She crossed her arms defensively, asking, "Who's watching him?"

"They should've disarmed him," Karen said, her voice short and incensed with rage.

"Disarmed?" I questioned, trying to think of the right words to use. Their concerns were valid. A high percentage of sex offenders repeat their crimes. "How so?"

Karen made like she was cutting paper, her fingers shaped like a pair of scissors. "Disarmed!" she repeated.

"If we'd had our way, we would have—" Chrissy began, but stopped abruptly.

I held up my hands, showing them my phone, and then tucked it into my back pocket. "We can speak freely," I assured them. Tracy and Nichelle did the same, putting away their phones.

"Revenge?" Nichelle asked, chancing what Chrissy was going to say. "Once you realized how many of you there were."

"Something like that," Karen answered for Chrissy. She cringed, disgusted by the memories we'd stirred. "He'd been at us. Some of us for more than two years."

"You wanted to kill him?" I asked, curious how far the girls had gone.

"Abso-fucking-lutely!" Karen said. She shook, as if bugs were crawling on her. "Every time his hands were on me."

"We all wanted him dead," Chrissy continued, speaking calmly, her words chilling. "We were going to make it look like an accident—"

"Chrissy!" Karen shouted, her eyes blazing.

"—we were going to make it look like an accident at practice," Chrissy finished, ignoring her friend's warning. Tracy and Nichelle stirred with the revelation. My heart thumped heavily with the unsolicited disclosure.

"They're cops!" Karen shook her head. "Why would you tell them that?"

Chrissy shrugged, answering, "Karen, Jessie is dead! So is Charlie. There is someone killing the team. Maybe coach found out! Maybe he started with Bernadette?"

"That's right, we think Bernadette was killed by the same person," I said, trying to join their discussion, hoping it'd open them to say more. "Someone is killing you guys."

"He wouldn't have the balls!" Karen exclaimed, unconvinced her coach would exact revenge.

"But someone does," Tracy said, challenging the comment. "And we don't know who it is."

Their eyes widened. "None?" Chrissy asked, her voice turning soft again. When we didn't answer, she covered her front defensively, and asked, "You've no idea?"

"Your old coach has been questioned and we've got him in a holding cell," I explained and shook my head. "But he was working—"

"The fucker has an alibi?" Karen interrupted, eyes fiery. She didn't wait for a reply, asking, "Like, can't you just kinda ignore it, make something up so he has to go back to prison for breaking his parole!?"

"We can't do that," Tracy answered, her tone flat, but the idea resonating. "Unfortunately, that's not how it works."

"Then why are you bothering us?" Karen said, taking a step between us and Chrissy. It was clear she was the leader of the two as Chrissy cowered in her friend's shadow. "Leave, if you can't do anything."

"We're doing what we can, which is why he is in a holding cell," Nichelle assured them.

"It was all of you who felt that way?" I asked, reaching back to the plans they'd made to murder their coach. "Both teams, the varsity and junior varsity squads?"

"Do they need a lawyer?" Jonathon asked and moved to stand with the girls.

I shook my head, answering, "I haven't heard anything that'd require it." I showed my phone again. Showed that it was turned off. "But they have the right to an attorney."

"Girls from both teams," Chrissy chirped from behind Jonathon and Karen. She appeared from the shadows and explained. "The girls he touched."

"How many of you?" Tracy asked, fingers to her lips, bothered by the idea of one man damaging so many. "Between the two teams, there were nine of you."

"It was eight of us," Karen answered, the fire in her eyes gone, replaced with a sadness I knew too well. It was the pain and hurt I'd seen in dozens of victims, maybe a hundred from the years in Philadelphia where I'd worked sex crimes. "He'd gotten to us all."

"Who else was there?" I asked, the math leaving one girl alone from the others. "There were nine on the team."

"That was Cara," Karen answered as she unpinned the cap from her head, freeing a wave of silver hair. She shook it out, adding, "She was on the junior varsity team with us. Real good too."

"How good?" Nichelle asked, phone returning to her hands. They noticed but didn't object.

"There was talk about the Olympics," Chrissy told us. "She was at the right age for the next one."

"And she'd already won states for her age group," Karen continued, picking at the tattoo on her neck. "If she went on to nationals, then who knows."

"Olympics?" I asked, the name of their teammate not registering. "What was her last name?"

"Palto," Chrissy answered, immediately telling me why there'd been eight conspiring to kill their coach.

"Cara Palto," Karen said, dumping the tip jar, coins clanking, a crumpled bill tumbling, a quarter rolling to the counter's edge. She slammed her hand to stop it and then looked at us. "Cara Palto was the coach's daughter."

"Whatever happened to her?" Nichelle asked, the phone's screen near her eyes. "There's no mention of her."

"She kinda disappeared." Chrissy joined Karen, the girls dividing the tips. "When we put her dad in prison, that like totally ended archery at the school. Probably for her too."

Jonathon rolled a mop and bucket past, eyeing the floor. He

looked to the door next and then his watch, asking us to leave, without asking it directly. "Thank you for the time," I said, backing toward the exit. "I know it was hard to talk about. I do."

"That's it?" Karen asked as if wanting to continue. When I opened the door, she made a pair of scissors with her fingers like she'd done earlier. "Remember what I said. Disarming him is the only way."

"Thank you again," I said, wanting to agree with her, but needing to stay in the role of authority, of being a detective.

When we were outside, the door closed, I spoke freely. "I'd hold his pair in the air and let them have at them if we could get away with it!"

"Casey!" Tracy said, shocked by my comment. She huffed a deep breath then and said, "Yeah, I'd help to hold him down. For sure, I would."

"Me too," Nichelle added. "He broke a lot of people, the prick."

"That includes his family," I said, thinking back to an earlier question. "Remember what I asked in the meeting?"

They traded a look the way they liked to do. I rolled my eyes, urging them, Nichelle saying, "Casey, you like to ask a lot of questions, which one?"

"The only one we need to concern ourselves with." When they didn't have an answer, I told them, "Cara Palto. Who else had everything to lose?"

SEVENTEEN

Cara Palto was now a suspect. But was she any more a suspect than the other girls? When we finished interviewing the teammates, Karen and Chrissy, it was decided that we'd interview Cara. I'd heard enough to want an all-points bulletin, an APB issued, but that was premature. With her father incarcerated, the high school discontinuing the archery teams, Cara may have had more to lose than the other girls on the team. But we lacked any physical evidence. With Cara, there was evidence of motive, which we could submit to the district attorney, its being admissible at a trial. However, proof of a motive is not proof of a crime. This slimmed our options to interviewing Cara Palto. Her father Benjamin remained our number one suspect, but his daughter was now a significant person of interest. One problem. Cara Palto was gone. She was nowhere to be found.

A beep. I woke with alarm to see Jericho's figure hunched over our gun-safe, fingertips punching in the code. There was a bang coming from the living room, the touch of glass striking glass, the clamor telling me the source was from the back door leading to the beach. What threatened to shatter was a decorative stained-glass window hanging I'd put there to catch the morning light. It bounced with another round, the ruckus leaving me breathless. The floor was cold beneath my bare feet, my toes turning hot from the fabric running against them, slipping my pants and shirt on, shaking a chill and fright. Jericho stood up, gun in hand, but I didn't think we'd need it. Burglars weren't apt to knock on the door and ask permission to come inside.

"Just in case," he said when the hallway light shone on my face, his seeing the concern.

"Keep it out—" I began to say, jumping to the sound of glass crashing. The suction cups I'd used for the window hanging broke free, the gift from Tracy falling to the floor. "Shit, I loved that piece."

"Casey," Jericho warned, calling after me as I left our bedroom, carelessly flipping on the light, anger fueling my step.

"Babe!? Come on out." Emanuel stood on the other side of the door, night bugs buzzing around his face and head. He swung at one, the motion stealing his balance enough for him to steady himself against the door. He had a bottle in his other hand, his face a twisted mess. I'd never been afraid of him, but the sight of his state made me think twice about letting him inside. Emanuel tipped the bottle to his mouth. "Jericho?!"

"I'll take this." Jericho touched my shoulder, urging me back, asking, "Some coffee?"

"Uh-huh," I answered, stepping behind the kitchen counter while Jericho cautiously approached the door. Glass crunched beneath his shoes, making me cringe while I hurried to fetch a dustpan and broom. "I'll clean that up."

"Thanks, I'll get that." I saw caution on Jericho's face, enough of it to warrant returning to the safety of the kitchen. I'd never known Emanuel to be dangerous. Then again, I'd never seen him in a state like this. The door opened slowly, hinges creaking, ocean waves breaking in the distance.

"Guys," Emanuel said with a heavy slur. The smell of the

beach reached me along with the stench of liquor. There was also the smell of sweat which had me thinking that Emanuel hadn't been home, that this was a bender. He nodded toward me then lifted a foot with glass crunching, words slurring, "Aw, Casey, I'm sorry it broke."

"It's late, Emanuel," Jericho told him, the coffee starting to percolate. Jericho took hold of the bottle, a fifth of whiskey. Emanuel's fingernails turned white with the tightness of his grip. Jericho shook his head and took hold of Emanuel's other arm. His voice firm, he said, "You're welcome to stay and drink some coffee with us, eat a little food. But not with this."

"Or?" Emanuel challenged, his tone putting me on edge. He eyed Jericho's hand, brow flattened.

Jericho lifted his hands free of Emanuel's arm and the bottle, opening the door and answering, "Or you can leave."

Emanuel glanced at me and then the coffee machine, a first cup already in the pot. For a long minute, he gazed at the bottle he didn't want to give up, and then handed it to Jericho. "Coffee does smell good."

"I think we have something sweet to go along with it," Jericho offered, leading Emanuel to a chair at the table.

"Drink this," I said, placing the fresh cup in front of Emanuel, steam rising. He sipped it straight, no sugar or cream, and made a face. His head glistened. The evening had been humid, the horizon warming with signs of an early sunrise. There was dirt on his shirt, scuff marks and a rip near the shoulder as though he'd been in a fight. His pants were filthy too like he'd rolled around in the street in a struggle. Concern for Benjamin was on the tip of my mind, thinking Emanuel went after him. But his knuckles were clean of any bruises, the back of his hands and arms without a single scratch. Could be he wandered the night away, falling over drunk, and then walked the beach until reaching our place. When he put the coffee cup down, I asked, "This isn't you. What's going on?"

"Shit," he snapped, spinning in his seat toward the kitchen, where Jericho poured the remains of his bottle, its glugging while it drained. "Thought you were just going to hold it for me."

"Drink your coffee." Jericho eyed the bottle a long second, his having battled similar, a struggle that happened before I knew him. With the faucet running, he rinsed the insides, killing the smell, surely a bad reminder of that time. He returned with a cheese and jelly pastry we'd bought at the market, one of his impulse buys we'd been afraid to eat. Jericho cut a sizable piece and plunked it onto a plate he put in front of Emanuel. "Eat it. The sugar will help."

"Thanks," Emanuel said, nipping at the corner and chewing slowly. He stopped, his jaw turning slack. He shook his head, one eye closing as he focused the other on me. He nodded toward the rear door, saying, "Casey, I am really sorry about that."

"Don't worry about it." I moved my seat closer to him, feeling less at risk, sensing he was calm. "Tell us what's going on?"

He dropped the pastry onto the plate and reached for his hip, my muscles tensing uncomfortably. I'd checked if he was armed but hadn't searched behind him where a holster could be tucked. From his pocket he held up his shield, his detective's badge, which was bright beneath the light, glinting silver and gold. The leather holder flipped open to also show his official identification from behind the protective plastic sleeve. "Couldn't bring myself to do it."

"Do what?" Jericho asked, our trading a look, our knowing exactly what he was going to do. Emanuel didn't answer, leaving us in an awkward silence. "How about you put that away, sober up and start fresh tomorrow?"

"Nah," he answered, shaking his head, mouth turned down. "Casey, I came to give you this."

Before I could say another word, the badge hit the table with a thud, his fingers pressing on it.

"Wait—" I began, but Emanuel pushed it in my direction.

"I can't be a cop anymore." He gulped his coffee, cringing again and then cleared his throat. "Not ever again."

"Look, Emanuel. I've been there," Jericho began, cupping his brow. From the stories he'd told me, Jericho had done the same when his wife was murdered. He'd become lost at the bottom of a bottle and given up his position as sheriff. He braced Emanuel's arm, rocking it. "I'll never forget how you helped me. Let us help you."

"I wanted to kill that man." A sip of coffee, Emanuel shaking his head. "That's not me. I'm done being a cop."

"I know it's a rough time," I said, trying to reason, and moved the badge in his direction. "Like Jericho said, we'll help—"

"You're not hearing me!" his voice boomed, eyes bulging with fierceness returning. I sat back in my chair, the anger in him deep. He swiped his face, the weepiness returning to his eyes. When he looked at me again, I saw the sorrow, the pain, the plea while he pegged his badge beneath his fingers and slid it in my direction. "Please, Casey. I'm asking you for a favor. Take this for me."

"Take it yourself," I challenged him, anger rising and hoping that maybe I could buy him time, rethink when he wasn't influenced by the drink. "You can resign, but you'll have to do it at your station. You don't work for me anymore."

"Really? Asking you to help me here," he scoffed, and finished the coffee. "I can't bring myself to go."

His look filled with anger, rage returning to his eyes. Jericho sensed I was afraid. He might have been as well. He stood up, cautiously, and moved close to me, asking, "How about taking a day?"

"Already took one," Emanuel blurted, getting up abruptly,

his chair falling backward onto one of the moving boxes. He saw it, adding, "What's it matter to you two anyway! You're already out of here."

"Please," I said, imploring him, hand raised, wanting him to sit.

"Just do it!" he yelled, eyes wet, lip quivering. He put his hands together like a beggar, his voice a rasp, asking again, "Please, Casey, just do this for me."

Before I could respond, his shoes were crunching the remains of the stained-glass window and the patio door was opening and closing. Our gaze followed him until Emanuel's figure was swallowed by the night. Left without words, Jericho put his arms around me, a shiver rising. Emanuel would never work for law enforcement again.

EIGHTEEN

I felt groggy, body zapped of energy. But more than that, I felt hurt by the events of the early morning. Emanuel wanted me to turn in his badge for him, so that he could cut all ties to the police force. Jericho suggested that we do nothing, that we sit on it while Emanuel came to terms with the murder of his cousin. It wasn't just the murder though. I think he wanted to end his career because of his reaction to Benjamin Palto. If we hadn't been there, I truly believed Emanuel would have murdered the man. That's why he couldn't bring himself to continue, to be a cop anymore. While we were law enforcement, we were human too. Somewhere during his career, he'd forgotten that being human was okay. Was it too late? As with most anything that required healing, time took time.

Our search for Cara Palto was dying a fast death. We didn't have much to go on, other than the name, her competition history, the tournaments she'd won, along with a few articles about her being an Olympic prospect. When her father was arrested and sentenced for his crimes, and then sent to prison, Cara disappeared. There were no more tournaments. No Olympics. There was nothing. She'd dropped out of the sport and moved away from the area with her mother. When I'd asked the team who else had everything to lose, we'd only had a passing thought of Benjamin Palto's family. When he went to prison, his daughter lost the Olympics. In the investigation to build a profile, there was one nugget of information we found interesting. Nichelle's online sleuthing recovered two driver's licenses issued to Cara Palto. While Benjamin Palto's family had relocated to northern Virginia during his trial, it was on his release from prison that Cara Palto returned to her hometown. It wasn't much, but it pointed the needle in a positive direction.

Wrights Bridge was empty of traffic, the midweek morning favoring our travels to give us a clear shot across it. Patti Lymone was a member of the sunflower girls, and according to Karen and Chrissy, she was considered one of the best on the varsity team. Only two girls remained from the varsity squad, including Deanne Somer. Patrol cars were parked outside their residences, including one for Deanne who'd moved to Virginia Beach, just over the border of the northernmost tip of the Outer Banks. It wasn't the safety of protective custody, but it was something, and the women were free to leave their homes if they chose to do so. There were four more girls to consider also: the junior varsity team. Available patrols for them were stretching thin. We were offering double-time to anyone volunteering the hours.

Tracy stood with me and gave the officer a nod. Patti Lymone's house was a small cottage-style home, the outside painted yellow, the wood porch floor painted a dark gray. It was a single floor house, the front door open along with every window, their insides showing thin curtains. If Patti was afraid of an attack it wasn't showing.

"Would you have locked yourself inside?" I asked, mumbling the question, thinking I'd stay away from any openings.

"Uh-huh," Tracy replied. She nudged my arm when a figure

appeared in the doorframe. "I would have boarded my doors and windows."

"Patti Lymone?" I asked. The woman was disheveled, her hair a tangle of wavy long curls which she'd wrapped mercilessly tight with scrunchies. Her face was cramped with fierce concentration as she rocked back and forth.

She waved in our direction, vying for our attention and clutched the door, Tracy commenting, "Yep, that's for us."

As we approached, the woman's eyes stayed wide, beaming, while she frantically searched around the front of her property. "Ma'am?" I asked, her demeanor making me nervous. "Can we speak inside?"

"Yes! Yes, do come in! Please!" She held the door with one arm, urging us inside with the other. We stood in a living room with a couch and television, a coffee table at the center stacked with books and magazines. A dining room set with full table and chairs was in the next room, eight placements laid out on the table with fine china and lacy doilies, as if Patti Lymone was expecting to hold a dinner party. Her home was tidy, a straight-through from the front to the rear. At the far end, there was the kitchen and a rear door with its chain dangling free.

The sting of chemicals itched my nose. "Cleaning?" I asked, gesturing to a pile of stained rags and bottles on the table, the smell explained.

"It's keeping me busy," she answered, wringing her hands. The screen door clapped shut behind us, Patti coming around and extending her hand. Gripped in her fingers, she held an invitation like we'd seen with the other victims. "You're here because I'm next! Isn't that right?"

"When did you receive this?" I asked, slipping on a pair of gloves.

Tracy worked on a pair of gloves too and opened an evidence bag, plastic rustling as she delicately took custody of the invitation to place it inside. She worked the invitation carefully, ensuring there was zero transfer from us as Patti watched, starry eyed, mesmerized by the motions of our forensics. "Ma'am?"

"It, it came the other day!? I think?" she answered, sounding unsure about the time. "But I don't always check the mail."

"Tracy, let's dust the mailbox—"

"I'll get on it right after this," Tracy said, words slowed while she carefully opened the invitation within the evidence bag so we could read the inside. She peered up at me, saying, "Casey, it's the same."

"That it is," I replied, looking at the set of numbers, the date and time. I held the evidence as Tracy worked her phone to take pictures. My chest thumped heavy, a new invitation, everything about it the same, including the word, guilty, and the penmanship used.

"For fingerprints?" Patti Lymone asked nervously. "Like on the TV?"

"That's right," I said. "Dusting for fingerprints. We'll rule out the mail carrier and your own as well."

Patti shook her head slowly, gaze drifting to an exercise bicycle on the other side of her dining table. "We were so close," she began, but then pursed her mouth to make a tsk-tsk sound.

"Close?" I asked, curious to learn more about the team.

"Competitive might be a better word." She palmed her forehead, rubbing her head. "I wasn't nice about it either. Especially to Charlie."

"Charlie Robson," Tracy said, clarifying the name.

"She was a year before me." Patti took to nibbling her fingertips, hand trembling. "She was getting better than me. Fast too."

"She quit when the coach was arrested?" I asked while plugging the coordinates into my phone.

"It was before. I remember the day too," Patti answered. "Just up and quit during a practice."

"During a practice?" Tracy asked, working the invitation with me.

"Sunflower girls," she answered, gaze drifting again. "That was her idea. She came up with the name. That was the last practice she attended. I think the coach got at her that day."

"Benjamin Palto," I said to clarify. A nod. "Charlie reported it?"

"I wish I'd been nicer to her. To Charlie." There was remorse in her words, a regret for a past that was impossible to change. "It was the beginning of the end after that."

"It was high school," Tracy said, seeing the guilt.

"Well, she's dead now," Patti said, clearing her voice and shifting to stand closer. "Coach got arrested a couple days after the yearbook picture. It was the last time we were all together, as a team I mean."

"You and the other girls testified together," I asked, reminding her. My words fell without a reply, Patti's attention returning to the invitation, her eyelids narrowing.

"This is what Charlie got? Isn't it?" Patti asked, fear returning, lower lip trembling. "The other girls got one too?"

"That information hasn't been released—" Tracy began to say, reciting a fixed response we'd sometimes use with press. Tracy gave me a look, asking if she could share. I nodded that it was okay. "Informally, they received the same."

"He's coming for me!" Patti cried, falling backward with a screech, her legs giving out. We jumped to get hold of her arms and directed her to a nearby chair. Her voice was a near shrill in my ear, the emergency of it making my muscles tense. "I'm next! Isn't that right?"

"Ma'am, you're safe as long as you remain inside." The house was empty as far as I could see. I looked at the open windows and saw the kitchen windows were open too. That's when I noticed the floor fan, its blades batting air with a steady whoosh-whoosh beat, forcing air to cool the living room. "But you have to stay clear of the windows."

"The windows," she repeated, fanning her sweaty face. "Okay."

Tracy held up the invitation, and then her phone, alerting to the time. "Casey, the invitation is for today. At noon." I turned the evidence bag around to see, to confirm while Tracy finished plotting the coordinates on a map. I still had Benjamin Palto in custody, his cooperation exemplary considering the assault by Emanuel. But our time to hold him was coming to an end. The allowance of hours given without an arrest meant we'd release him this afternoon. Tracy showed me her phone, the location mapped, a field of green filling the screen. "It's another farm."

"Ma'am, the windows. You'll have to stay inside," I asked, shaping my tone so the words sounded like a demand. "An officer will be outside, parked in the street."

"You're leaving?" she asked, the shrill in her voice returning. "You're leaving me alone!"

"Stay in your house," I commanded, lowering my voice, leveling my eyes with hers. I braced her shoulders and nodded until she nodded with me. "You'll be safe as long as you remain indoors."

"Indoors," she answered, drying her face, taking to a cushy chair, sitting in it, and placing her hands on her knees. She shook her head at me, adding, "I-I won't move."

"We'll return this afternoon, to ask some questions."

"I'll be here."

As we exited the front door and I went to close it behind me, I gave Patti a smile, offering some confidence I had in her safety. She returned it, forcing it a moment before fading as the door shut.

If I'd known what would happen next, I might have held back on the confidence, might have never left Patti Lymone alone.

～

There were crows. A lot of them. They wore their feathered overcoats and cawed at us while shifting impatiently. Sitting on power lines and the farmhouse, their beady eyes stared intently at the sunflower field. The plants had grown ripe with seed, their heads oversized and heavy, the green turning brown, the bright yellow petals wilting and dry. There were men and women and children working the farm, the job done by hand with tools and wagons, harvesting the rows, laboring to cut and carry the fully ripened heads for drying.

An hour. That's how long we gave it. At first, I'd parked a mile from the farm, far enough up the road to watch it safely. There was only the one way that gave us access, and if the killer was coming, we'd know. But when a cloud of road dust spiraled and the distant echo of farming reached our ears, I knew the killer wasn't coming today. I radioed to the patrol officers waiting a mile on the other side of the farm, putting an end to the stakeout.

As I drove past the farm, I saw a sign posted near the edge of the farmhouse that filled me with dread. On it, the farmer had invited the locals to help with the early harvest, offering money for every ripe sunflower, their harvester broken. The sign explained the arrival of extra cars, the parking alongside the road, and people dressed to cover themselves with long pants and sleeves. And it was the stains on the sign that told me we'd been setup, that this was a ploy, a diversion the killer had arranged, separating us from Patti Lymone. Rainwater had caused the cardboard to warp, the words inky and stained. It planted a sour thought that wouldn't go away, a nagging feeling I couldn't shake.

"You got quiet," Tracy said, her tone questioning. "What's the matter?"

"It's that sign," I answered, clutching the steering wheel,

turning it onto the street to where Patti Lymone lived. "When did it rain?"

"Rain?" Tracy asked, tapping the screen on her phone. "Wasn't it over the weekend?"

"Monday?" I answered, thoughts of the killer continuing to nag like a dull ache set deep in my bones. "It was raining when we drove to the mainland. I remember Wrights Bridge being wet."

"Yeah, Monday." Tracy looked confused and shook her head. "It rained. And?"

"The sign outside the farmer's house was hit by rain, a heavy rain." I reversed into a spot, parallel parking. "The sign has been there for days."

"Which means the field couldn't have been used by the killer," Tracy said, understanding with eyes widening. "But still, we have no idea how long Patti had the invitation though."

"It doesn't matter," I said, throwing the car in park, nudging my head toward the patrol car across from Patti's house. "The farmer had already set a date."

"Why would he do that?" Tracy asked, hurrying to catch up to me while I made my way to the patio and the first open window. Caution had me cradling my gun, the metal cold in my palm. Tracy saw it with alarm and whispered, "You think the killer did it on purpose?"

"Miss Lymone?" I called through the window, the breeze picking up the curtain like a veil, showing me the deadly secrets the killer left for us. Blood was splattered across the television and bookcase shelves, thick drops of it coating, drying where it had run down the screen.

"The door?" Tracy said, touching it just enough for the hinges to creak. It was partially open, a black void widening slowly to reveal Patti Lymone's body on her couch. "Oh my God! Casey!?"

"Officer!" I yelled. He startled behind the wheel, the car

door flying open. I pressed my hand against Tracy's chest, my gun drawn, telling her, "Wait by the car!"

"Okay," Tracy answered, hurrying out of the way, doing as I instructed while I entered the property. I held my firearm in position, training it on what was in front of me. My ears perked to blades paddling the air, triggering my limbs to spin and point at the floor fan stirring a thick smell of blood into the air.

"Jesus!" the patrol officer said, his voice raised. He followed my lead and drew his gun, the tip of it wavering while he covered his mouth and nose. "I-I was—"

But he couldn't speak. I raised my hand to have him follow me. We needed to clear the premises, having no idea if the killer was still inside. There were splashes of blood on the ceiling and floors, and on the walls and furniture, the scene far more a nightmare than what we'd encountered in the sunflower fields. Thoughts of booties and gloves, maybe crime-scene coveralls? These came to mind. They were required, but we had no idea what dangers waited for us and the house needed to be cleared.

My brain throbbed heatedly, brow beaded with sweat, heartbeat thrumming in my ears. I tried breath, my throat and tongue dry, the acrid stench threatening to make me gag. I tiptoed over a river of blood, Patti Lymone's attack beginning in the dining room and ending with her on the couch. There was an exercise bike behind the dining room table, the wall next to it showing more splatter. The fine china and lacy doilies dressing the table were dotted brown and red, stained in a way that had me thinking that that location was where the initial strike had taken place.

The dining room was clear, and I entered the kitchen area. The counter, sink and cabinets were also clear of the violence that decorated the other rooms. There was a dirtied dish and a glass in the sink, a half-eaten sandwich on the plate. I looked at the patrol officer as he cleared a closet and neared the rear door. The color in his face had disappeared, leaving behind a gray macabre look, his skin clammy, his jaw hanging slack. Like the front door, the rear was ajar, extending the crime scene to the back patio.

"Are you going to be sick?" I asked, kicking it open. He shook his head vigorously. "Take a break out back, circle around the front. Don't come back inside."

"I never heard a thing," he said, sipping at outdoor air.

"You weren't supposed to," I told him, knowing that nothing I said would help arrest the guilt he was feeling. "The killer played us with that invitation."

The officer slipped from sight, leaving quickly, his shoes shuffling across pavement while he gagged and choked. I went back the way I came, carefully matching my steps, which I'd mark later to remove myself from the crime scene. Tracy stood outside my car, midday sunlight turning the top of her head white. I saw that she was safe and the impatient worries that came with having my daughter on the job with me were rested. As I'd instructed, she stayed where I told her to.

"I called the medical examiner," she said, taking the initiative. "Is it bad?"

"Bring your gear," I said, the crime scene one of the worst I'd ever seen. Tracy had only glimpsed what happened to Patti Lymone, and I wasn't at all sure how she'd react once inside and working the scene. We'd worked some bad crime scenes before, but nothing like this. She opened the car's trunk as I held up two fingers. "Bring full body suits. We're going to be here a while."

NINETEEN

It was midday. Patrol vehicles were strewn along the sides of the short street of Patti Lymone's home. Crime-scene tape was strung up in the front and behind the property since we did not know where the crime began, or where it had ended. What we knew was that Patti Lymone had been killed indoors, dying on her couch, suffering greatly, the crime scene bloodied like none that I had ever seen. It remained a mystery as to how her murder could have taken place without notice, without the officer on guard seeing or hearing anything.

"Full body," Tracy said as she handed me the gear. She held up a mask, asking, "Masks or respirator?"

"Bodysuit is a must, that's certain. But the respirator?" I shook my head. "There are no hazardous materials. A mask is fine."

"Got it," she said under her breath, slipping a cap onto her head, turning enough for me to tuck her hair inside. She'd let it grow long, the time in the sun giving it natural highlights. The coveralls had a hood that helped. I unfurled it, the material crinkling. "I grabbed the bunny suits."

That's what we called the white coveralls, bunny suits. "It's good that you did, make sure there isn't any transference."

"Possible?" she asked, having seen some of what was inside.

I placed my hand on her shoulder. She faced me as I warned, "If you need to step out, you go. Okay?"

"Uh-huh," Tracy said, her focus on the front door. When it returned to me, she swallowed dryly, asking, "It's that bad?"

"Worse," I said, sleeving a leg into my bunny suit, the white material clean and bright in the daylight. "Booties, gloves, hood, a mask. All of them."

"Check," Tracy answered, approaching the front door. I closed the front of my suit and put on my hood, tightening it around my face. I followed Tracy, listening to her as she went through a checklist, voice nervous, "Batteries charged. Two packs. Two camera bodies. Wide-angle and macro lens, filters, and flash."

I got to the door, opening it, telling her, "And watch your step."

"Uh-huh," she answered, entering the main room, slowing when reaching the couch. She framed a picture and immediately went to work with the camera, training the lens on Patti Lymone's body. "No screams?"

"Nothing reported," I answered, cautiously stepping around blood until I reached the dining room. In the furthest corner, there was spatter on the walls, rising to the ceiling. Daylight from a nearby window beamed onto the wall, the blood shining like pearls. "The attack begins in that corner with the exercise bike."

"I'm going to start there and work my way to here, retain the sequence to what we suspect happened." Tracy passed me and knelt, the camera flash crisp, coming without a warning and creating green spots that floated in my eyes. "There's nothing in the kitchen?"

"Other than a plate and half-eaten sandwich in the sink.

The rear door was open, which is how I believe the killer entered." I went to the kitchen counter that separated the rooms, just as the medical examiner entered the front. She stopped immediately, her eyelids drawn back. "Doctor Foster."

"Detective," she returned, pinching her coveralls, adding, "thanks for the heads up."

"We're just getting started over here," I said as her assistant entered. He looked humongous in his bunny suit, his size reminding me of our assistant medical examiner in the Outer Banks. The assistant turned around to assess the crime scene, doing so without care, touching a wall with his bum unintentionally. It was a simple graze, but his white coveralls showed blood smeared on them. Doctor Foster saw it at once, tapping him on the shoulder to point it out. We needed our pictures to preserve the scene, to enter them as evidence, with nothing compromised that could give a clever defense attorney something to put doubt in a jury. The tight quarters and spread of blood would make this one of the hardest crime scenes to process.

"Sorry," the assistant said, palming his forehead. I didn't know the medical examiner's team like I knew our own. But my guess was that he wasn't seasoned like Derek was, didn't have the keen awareness of his surroundings like Derek. He faced Doctor Foster, asking, "They're just getting started, I can come back?"

"Right, that'd work." She moved to leave, saying, "Detective, when you've taken enough pictures—"

"Could you stay?" I asked her, interrupting. It would help to have her insight, and an extra voice to bounce questions. "I've got an issue that I'll want you to work with us."

"Yes, certainly," she answered, waving for her assistant to put the ME kit down. The screen door closed behind him, the dining room lighting up with Tracy's camera flashes, showing additional spatter I'd missed, a pattern that could be an exit wound. Doctor Foster saw it, her stare fixed. "Are you thinking that is the initial attack?"

"From here," I answered. I centered myself in the kitchen, along the corners where the rooms joined, and held my hands and arms up as if holding a bow. "The killer entered the residence from the rear, made it to this point with Patti Lymone over by the exercise bike."

"None of the neighbors saw anything?" she asked, her gaze fixed on the rear door. It had been the first thing I'd asked as well, a handful of patrols being tasked to take statements. We'd joined in briefly with the task, working from door to door, knocking on them, and then informing Patti Lymone's neighbor what had happened. None had heard anything though, or witnessed anything suspicious.

"Not a one, and we've questioned all the neighbors." Doctor Foster found a clear area of the wall and put her hand on it, leaning enough to rest her back. "The injuries are consistent with the injuries of the other victims."

"If arrows were used, like the other murders, that would explain the silence." She moved to the body, watching her feet as she did, a hard frown showing behind her mask and hood. It was clear the scene was bothering her as much as it bothered me. The human body is little more than a bag of blood and water, and Patti Lymone's injuries had spilled most of hers. Our paper masks weren't helping with the growing smell. "Bow and arrow. Those are not that easy to conceal, or are they?"

"If the killer is using a recurve bow, entering the property without notice is possible," I answered, having researched what was used in the tournaments. In the research I'd found targeting arrows, the types of bows, and what the competition rules required. When she inspected the puncture wounds around the face and neck, I explained, "The arrows have no barbs. They aren't like the kind used in hunting."

Doctor Foster straightened with a nod, her expression with

a look of understanding. "That helps to explain the injuries, including what we've found with the other victims."

"The killer retrieved the arrows easily and quietly," I commented, heavily bothered, the killer's movements like a ghost. A bright neon, almost fluorescent, scrap of paper caught my eye. It was tucked beneath the kitchen counter like a note that had been slipped beneath a door.

"You mean he pulled them out?" Tracy asked, moving to photograph the floor, a smeared trail where Patti Lymone tried to escape. "Plucked them from the body?"

"Plucked isn't the word I'd use," Doctor Foster said, motioning to the injuries on the face. "But it's accurate."

"I think I've got something over here." With the tip of a pen, I nudged the neon fluorescent paper. But it wasn't a piece of paper. It was stiff, almost like plastic, shaped in a form I recognized from my research. "Plucked is exactly what he does, leaving behind almost nothing for us."

"Almost?" Tracy asked. She joined me at the find, adding a ring light to the camera, taking pictures before we picked it up. "What is it?"

"Stabilizer feathers from an arrow," I answered, dropping it into an evidence bag. "We won't be able to get prints, but maybe there is something unique that we can use."

"Do you think that's what it is?" Tracy rolled the evidence bag over in her hand. "I think you're right. I can see the feathers."

"This is the first hard evidence we have to identify the murder weapon used."

"Tracy, could you take a picture of the victim?" Doctor Foster asked. "I want to move her head."

"Yes, ma'am," Tracy said, her camera shutter snapping in series. One of the victim's eyes were missing, an arrow puncturing it with such force there was little of it that was recognizable. Another injury was through the mouth, which might have broken the victim's jaw, the bottom part hanging loose with an unnatural offset. But the injury that Doctor Foster was interested in was closer to the top of the neck. "Can I help?"

"Yes, please," the doctor said, motioning to Tracy's free hand and the top of Patti Lymone's head. "Turn her face toward you."

"Okay," Tracy answered, making the motion, showing more injuries on the other side. "I need more photographs."

"Come around to my side," Doctor Foster told her. She mumbled then, words barely registering, "In all my years."

"What is it?" I asked.

"If these injuries are from arrows, then I believe one may have gone through her vocal cords." Doctor Foster showed an entry and exit wound on her neck. "I mean, the precision of this injury is uncanny."

"Or intentional," I said. "If this is from the first arrow, that explains why there were no screams, why the officer guarding outside heard nothing."

"Noting, the first arrow is through the neck," Tracy began, logging the information.

"Without a doubt, it silenced the victim completely." I stepped around a blood spill, focus shifting to the victim's hand. "From the exercise bike she tried to escape to the front since the killer was blocking the rear."

"Do you see something?" Foster asked, noticing my concentration around the left hand. It was closed, knuckles white. "Clenched fist. She grabbed something."

"Tracy?" I asked, wanting her to stand by with the camera. Rigor mortis hadn't set in, the time of death still early. But Patti Lymone's fingers were stiffening, lividity beginning, color draining as gravity took over for a heart that would never beat again. I could see it in her left arm, her hand slightly tucked beneath her as if she'd been trying to protect whatever was in her palm. One by one, I unfurled her fingers, knuckles cracking.

In her palm I saw crumpled flower petals. They were wilted, broken, and browned with age, carrying little of the summer yellow we'd seen in the fields. But even in their state, I could tell they were from the same plant that gave them the name of their team, the sunflower girls. Without an understanding to why they were there, I told Tracy, "Photographs."

"On it," she answered. A petal tumbled onto the blood-soaked cushions, looking bright against the stains, Tracy framing the picture. "Did the killer put these here?"

"If so, that'd be different," Foster answered. "Maybe the killer wanted us to know that her murder was connected."

"I don't think that's it," Tracy commented, daring to touch a petal. The tip of the leaf cracked beneath her gentle touch. "These are old. Really old."

Thinking of the killer, the possibility of his leaving us an odd clue, I asked the doctor, "Let's say the killer did place them in the victim's palm." I made a fist, mimicking a closed hand. "The killer would have held her fingers until rigor mortis set in. How long would it have taken?"

Her face brightened, answering immediately, "Too long. At least a couple of hours."

"The killer wouldn't have chanced it," I said, adding doubt. "Not with police outside and the possibility of our returning."

"And why so old?" Tracy commented as she continued with the photographs. "If not from the killer, then where did they come from?"

"See how they are flat?" I asked. "That's a clue too."

"The natural course for a plant is to shrivel after death." Doctor Foster eased onto one knee, shining a light onto the petals. "With the moisture gone, they dry out... unless you do something to prevent the shriveling."

"Like pressing them between the pages of a book?" I asked, searching the room, looking for an open book.

"Exactly!" Foster answered as I helped her return to her

feet. "That's how I used to preserve butterflies for my collection."

"You killed butterflies?" Tracy asked, alarmed.

"I'm sure they were already dead," I told her, defending the doctor, but seeing a slight eye roll. "Point is, these petals may have been pressed in a book."

"Question is, which book?" Foster asked, seeing them stacked in corners and on shelves. "Doubtful it's any that are already closed."

"Tracy," I began, shifting my mask which had become uncomfortably damp with my breath. Doctor Foster and Tracy looked at me, the doctor nudging her chin. "We've got some reading to do."

Beneath her mask, I could almost see her frown. She put her camera gear down and lifted the nearest book, fanning the pages, saying, "I knew you were going to say that."

TWENTY

The rains that had threatened all week came that afternoon. They moved in silently from the west, dark clouds lumbering over us, an unseasonably cold wind in their company. The air was heavy and wet, beading on every surface, a steady patter of plump drops falling from the surrounding trees. It was the afternoon of Charlie Robson's funeral. A hundred or more people had gathered closely around her grave. There were faces hidden beneath umbrellas, black veils that trembled as they cried quietly. There were family and friends of Charlie's. I noticed a few of them, just as they'd noticed me, our blending in with the attendees like damp brushstrokes in a sad mural.

The cemetery was familiar to me and Jericho, having been here before more times than I'd care to count. Some of those we helped to bury were friends, and some of them victims of crime, an unpleasant side effect for the career we'd picked. We stood opposite Charlie's family, a casket as white as snow between us. It was perched above an open grave and a mountain of flowers lay on top of it, their petals wet, their colors glowing bright in the gray light. I clutched Jericho's arm, the ground soft and threatening my balance. He held me too, his arm wrapped securely behind me.

Tracy and Nichelle were next to me, arm in arm and dressed in black, their expressions mirroring the sadness. The sight was mournful, and we'd come to pay our respects. But we'd also come to see who else was here, watching for anything that would warrant questions, anything oddly suspicious. It wouldn't be the first time a funeral stirred a clue or brought a murderer out into the open. Killers ofttimes felt compelled to observe their carnage like a craving that couldn't be denied.

Charlie's mother sat alongside her daughter's grave, dabbing her cheeks while Emanuel held her. It was the first time we'd seen Emanuel since he'd been to our place and forfeited his badge, asking me to turn it in for him. I kept a hope that it was the pain from their loss pushing him to quit, and that it would pass. He still had his service revolver, which he'd have to turn in at some point. Since he didn't give that to me, maybe my hope held some chance of becoming a reality and he'd change his mind.

"Tracy," I said, alarm stirring in my gut, a dark notion of the funeral services being interrupted terribly. There were tall trees edging the cemetery with an endless row of evergreens. Along them, brightly colored birds dove in and out, flitting from bush to bush. At the end of the hedges, fifty yards from the grave, a sycamore tree stood high above all others. Its trunk was scalloped, and the enormous branches were without leaves, bare arms that spanned a football field and looked like the bones of a skeleton. The tree was dead, but remained standing, its base the width of a car. "Look behind the tree."

"Nichelle," Tracy whispered, cautiously pointing in the direction of the tree where there was a man in a suit. He was dressed for the funeral, his hands clasped in front of him as if in prayer. "It's Benjamin Palto."

I squeezed Jericho's hand, bringing his attention to the same, saying, "I can't believe he'd risk being here."

"He doesn't see him," Jericho said with tension in his voice. We'd no idea what Emanuel would do if he saw that Palto was in our company.

A yell, "I know who you are!"

I glanced at the crowd, thinking it must have come from Charlie's mother. She was sitting up staring with a hard glare at the dead tree. But the tree wasn't the subject of her focus. It was Benjamin Palto. The suddenness of her voice created a rise, a murmur growing into a chatter and then a stir. Umbrellas were lowered with heads turned as attendees stood, some of them pointing, others looking away as though Palto were a hideous monster. And to many he was a monster. He was a vampire who suckled on the young, draining them of their innocence.

"This is going to get bad," Jericho said, shifting to take a step toward the tree.

"We all know who you are!" Charlie's mother screamed. Our eyes were on Emanuel who looked around confused, the green of a smaller sapling blocking his view. But when he stood to help his aunt who'd insisted on leaving her chair, his eyes bulged. He didn't react immediately but held his aunt's arms instead. She shook with a strain, her voice booming again, "You need to leave!"

"He sees him now," I said, Emanuel turning to face Benjamin Palto. Something needed to be done. I glimpsed the emptiness beneath Charlie's casket, the hole deep. My mind went into overdrive with wild thoughts. Emotions in the crowd were high and it wouldn't take much to bury Palto, to imprison him beneath a lowered casket. It would have been well deserved for what he'd done. I wouldn't have thought it would be in Emanuel to do, but after the other night, I didn't know that to be true.

"I'll take care of it," Jericho announced, a few men coming

forward to approach Palto. Jericho let go of my arm to raise his hands, his step hastened as he shuffled by the casket in a brisk walk to stay ahead of the victim's family. "I have this."

"Thank you," I heard someone say with a somber cry. There was appreciation on the face of Charlie's mother, but it was a far different look that I saw on her nephew's. Emanuel remained standing, his jaw clenched, breath shuddering, his hands fisted. When he turned, I could see the outline of his shoulder holster, his service revolver tucked against his ribs. The minister raised his voice to continue speaking, Bible in hand, wavering, as a voice continued with comments, "He shouldn't be here."

When Palto's face changed to show disappointment, it was clear that Jericho had conveyed the message. He shrugged and raised his arms, seeming to argue his right to be there. Necks craned to see the men, attention wrongfully stolen from why we had gathered. Jericho must have sensed it and blocked our view by guiding Palto behind the giant sycamore, taking him away from the funeral's sight.

"Should we go over there?" Tracy asked. She'd taken Jericho's place, lacing her arm with mine.

"I think he's leaving." I shook my head when seeing Palto exit the other side of the sycamore, the wind making its giant limbs rock up and down. Jericho reappeared, buttoning his suit jacket, and straightening it as the crowd watched his return.

"The guy has a pair," Jericho commented in a whisper, taking hold of my other arm. I wiped the rain from his face. He took my hand in his and held it to his chest, his eyes on Emanuel. "Would you believe he told me he loved Charlie."

"Loved her?" I asked, the thought of it sickening. Somewhere in his warped mind, in his sickness, he believed he did love the girls. "Still. Like you said, takes a pair to come here."

Voices came again when the minister said his final words and closed the Bible to give a blessing. I kept my eyes on the dead sycamore tree to see if Benjamin Palto returned. For his sake, he hadn't. Emanuel was watching too, jaw remaining clenched, hands fisted. The clouds had begun to part, the gray daylight warming, the sky finally emptying enough for the umbrellas to be closed. Those that had gathered to say goodbye began to leave the gravesite for a reception being held at Charlie's home, an invitation open to all.

"Did you see who else was here?" I asked Nichelle and Tracy, dipping my head in the direction of the girls from the ice-cream shop.

"That was nice of them to stop by," Nichelle commented.

"It was," I said, emotion in my voice as I watched the girl with the tattoos wipe tears from her face and touch the casket to say farewell to her teammate. In their grief, I saw fright, their knowing it could have been them perched above the empty grave. They filed by Charlie's mother and then Emanuel to pay their condolences.

"Shall we?" Tracy urged. We made our way around the groundskeepers who'd come from behind a tall mound of tarped earth, the loose dirt to bury Charlie Robson. Emanuel was first to come forward, taking Tracy into his arms, a grim smile of appreciation showing on his cramped face. Her voice muffled, I could hear her tearful words, "We love you, will do anything for you—"

After Nichelle and Jericho, I was next, the last of our group, and wiped the tears from Emanuel's face, the sight of him crying making me cry too. He shook his head, regret in his eyes. "Casey, you gotta know that wasn't me."

"I know," I assured him, pressing my hand against his chest. "It's the pain of it all."

"Tell me it goes away?" he said, asking, hope in his expression.

I bit my lips, unable to dodge the truth. "It'll always be with you. It just changes."

"Really glad you came today." He pulled me close, adding, "I wasn't sure you guys would."

"Of course, we would," I said, finding his jacket pocket and slipping his badge into it. He'd find it later and hopefully by then, his mind would have changed. My fingers pinched to the badge, the touch of cloth warm on my skin, I let go of it as he pulled away, sneaking it into place without his noticing. "Listen, we won't be at the reception."

"Patti Lymone's place?" he asked, having heard about the murder. He leaned over enough for me to kiss his cheek, his telling me, "I understand."

When we began to leave, the groundskeeper removed the tarp, the dirt beneath dry, a dusty cloud spinning above it briefly. Metal on metal clacked with a ratcheting sound, the casket descending. That's when Emanuel held up his hand and told the groundskeepers to halt. He held up his badge, having found it in his pocket and gave it a hard look. Without a word, he placed it on top of the casket, centering it amidst the bed of flowers that would accompany Charlie to the bottom of the grave. He waved his hands then, instructing the groundskeepers to continue. The casket jerked, the motion giving me a start as the clickity-clack broke the silent moment. With respect, we stood quietly and waited. We waited with Emanuel who stood over the grave to see his cousin lowered into the earth. With her lifeless body and the flowers, Emanuel buried his career.

TWENTY-ONE

After Charlie's funeral, we worked into the night processing the Patti Lymone crime scene, flipping through the pages of every book. Searching them for the source of the flower petals, the pages they'd been placed to dry and flatten. Whatever was on those pages was the clue we needed. Question, however, was whether it was a clue from the victim, or from the killer? I measured the passing hours by the color of daylight in the front windows. The rains had stopped earlier, clearing as the clouds drifted east. The grayness warmed the sky, brightening briefly with the sun's return which was then extinguished by the sunset. There was a full moon and stars, their company kept by a chorus of night bugs trilling and tree frogs singing.

We drove in the company of the medical van, escorting Doctor Foster and the victim, the roads wet with puddles to the sides, the traffic scant, the parking lot empty. The municipal building and morgue were both empty too, marking the late hour. An autopsy was planned for early the next morning, along with a team meeting, the latest press releases already circulating news about the case, the reporters having found the connection across the victims. They'd titled their headlines with bold print reading, *The Sunflower Murders*.

It was late when I got home, and I couldn't stomach a thing, preferring to stand beneath a cold shower and wash the day's heat and sweat from my skin, the coveralls filthy but saved to review for possible transfer. Lathered and rinsed, I could have sworn my shower had blood in the water, registering deep in my mind as though I had never left the crime scene. That happens sometimes when processing a crime scene that was beyond bad. The horror of it, the nightmare having a lasting impact like a bad dream that can't be shaken. And maybe I needed to hold on to it. Maybe I needed to continue seeing the crime scene, smelling it too as though we were still standing at the center of it all. Who knows, there could be an overlooked clue in one of those fleeting afterthoughts.

Sleep found me early once I'd rested my head on my pillow, its touch cool against my face. But the sleep didn't last long. The flower petals in Patti Lymone's hand wormed into my dreams, waking me with a memory of a previous case. It was the first case I'd worked when I had arrived in the Outer Banks. The victim had been a friend of Jericho's, and in his death, he'd intentionally taken hold of a dahlia flower, gripping it without the murderer knowing. It had given us the clue we needed to help break the case. Was that what Patti Lymone had done for us?

It was nearing two in the morning, and I kept my phone low to the mattress and pillow, shielding the blue light. I made a note to look at the books in Patti Lymone's home. We'd concentrated on the body, the floor where the stabilizer feathers were found, but could have looked past a clue. What was on the coffee table, or the top of the bookcase? An image of the exercise bike popped into my head, the spatter on the wall, the location of the first attack. Was there anything behind the bike?

I lowered my phone onto the nightstand, turning back to

face the ceiling, ocean waves breaking, their voices distant which told me it was low tide. Jericho didn't move, his soft snore continuing, our future together needling like the case, occupying my mind and weighing heavy on my heart. He stirred a little when I brushed my fingers across his bare shoulder, the sheet rising and staying still a moment before falling slowly. It had been a few days since our sunrise talk, his confession to me about staying in the Outer Banks. We hadn't talked about it since. I had to decide if I wanted to stay or follow Tracy to Philadelphia. It was my decision to make, and it wasn't fair that he didn't know that.

I slid my legs along his and pressed closer, skin touching and holding him. He stirred and then reached lazily, his fingers lacing with mine. "Hey," he said, groggy, eyelids shut.

"Hey," I replied, my sight adjusting to the dark enough that I could see him, see his hair and the tip of his ear. I leaned up until I could see the shape of his face, the whiskers along his jaw and chin, his dry lips, and the tip of his nose. I could smell the sea on him, its mixing with the shampoo he liked. He would always smell like the ocean to me, the salty air being a part of him. And there was something adorable about it, lovely in fact.

"Casey," he asked, his eyelids opening with a start, making me jump. "What are you doing?"

"Nothing," I told him. A touch. I gently brushed his face again, loving the rough feel of it. "Just watching you sleep."

"Oh," he replied, closing his eyelids. I held my stare, loving to watch him sleep, and thought of the different paths in our lives. There was mine with Tracy being kidnapped, disappearing from my life, destroying a marriage and setting me on a path which eventually took me to the Outer Banks. And then there was the one where Jericho's wife was murdered, his battling her murderer, nearly losing his own life and ending his career as a sheriff. These had been life-changing events, and yet, if not for them, we might not ever have met. It was almost ironic that so much tragedy could bring us together. "Casey?"

"Hmm?"

Jericho's eyelids were open again. I touched his lips, heart swelling.

"You're still staring," he said, brow furrowing. "It's kind of creeping me out."

I let out a laugh, touching my lips to his. "Can't sleep."

"What is it?" Jericho rolled onto his back, my moving with him effortlessly, resting a leg across his middle, my arm draped over his chest, and my head on his shoulder.

"It wasn't fair that I put the Philly decision on you." I swiped at my eyes, the topic painful.

He said nothing for a moment, his fingers in my hair, chest rising with a deep sigh. "It wasn't just mine or just yours," he said, words calm. "It was ours."

I tilted my head, resting my chin on his chest so I could see him. "Thank you," I said first, the guilt lifting. I hesitated then, picking my words carefully. "I don't know what I want to do."

"You want to do both." My eyes bulged. He saw my reaction, adding, "You want to live near Tracy, but you want to stay here."

"That's it," I agreed. I looked at him again, commenting about the move. "But I definitely would go back if you joined me."

He cocked his head and looked around the room, the boxes open, half full. "That's just it, I think I want both too. I want to be with you, but I'm still unsure about leaving the Outer Banks."

I rested my head again. "We didn't sign a lease yet."

"Nothing committed," he added. He nudged my back. I looked at him, a frown forming. "We also didn't resign the lease on this place."

"Shit," I said, having been so consumed with the case and

the possible move, that I had never thought about a contingency. "How much time do we have remaining?"

Jericho leaned over to grab an envelope from the nightstand. I recognized the outside envelope, the renewal agreement inside. He tapped my forehead, nodding, "We have a few weeks."

"A few weeks to sign the renewal or sign a new lease—"

"—in Philadelphia," he said, finishing for me, telling me in his way that he was still thinking about it.

It was my turn to sigh, feeling the pressure of a decision shrink a bit. It didn't disappear, but the weight of it lifted some. "Then we don't have to make a decision today."

"Casey," he asked, his tone having me sit up, my face near his. "Home is with you. I just need a little time."

"And home is with you," I returned, peppering his lips with kisses.

"I heard the Lymone situation was bad?" Jericho asked, shaking the sleep from his face and sitting up to talk about the case. "Like really bad."

"It was one of the worst crime scenes I have ever worked," I told him, thinking back to the sunflower petals, the shock of them being in the victim's hand. "I think the killer left us something but can't be sure."

"The flower petals?" Jericho asked. I raised my head, wondering how he knew. "Emanuel isn't back at work, but he heard it from the medical examiner."

I nodded, answering, "The flower petals."

"But you're not sure?"

"It had me thinking of your friend from my first case, the one with the dahlia flower in his hand."

"Robert Stewart," Jericho said, mentioning the name from the case. It felt like it was a hundred years ago. "You're thinking the victim held the flower petals to tell you something?"

"That's what I'm going to find out," I answered. Another visit to the crime scene was needed.

"Still can't get over Palto showing up at the funeral?"

"We had to release Benjamin Palto," I said with a sinking feeling that Emanuel would find him. "I couldn't hold him anymore. Patti Lymone was murdered while he was in our custody. For the sake of his career, I hope Emanuel leaves him alone."

"In my opinion, Palto deserves whatever is coming," Jericho commented, voice stiff.

"I know," I agreed. "That he does. But the law is the law."

TWENTY-TWO

The team meeting I had planned the next morning was abruptly canceled by an unexpected court hearing set to take place early that day. It had been a last-minute request from the district attorney, a judge had agreed, and the press were hounding the events from the courthouse steps. We would have almost missed it if not for Tracy staying close to the Jacob Wright case, the young man sitting in prison for the murder of the first sunflower girl, Bernadette Pare. I picked her up and we drove faster than we should have while I drank more coffee than I should have. But we reached the center of town, parking on the street across from the municipal building, along with a parade of news vans, broadcast antennas stretching into the sky, reporters gathered in the ready to air the court ruling live on television. The unofficial word was that Jacob Wright was going to be released. He was going to be a free man.

We hurried up the courtroom steps, shoes clopping loudly on stone, opening the brass and glass doors, hurrying. The hallway echoed our run until we reached a man in uniform, a tall figure standing outside the courtroom. He held the court-room doors shut, the mahogany wood nearly reaching the ceiling, intricate designs on their faces, soft chatter of court proceedings behind them. I showed my badge, giving him a nod, and was thankful that it was enough to get us entry.

The first three rows in the courtroom were full, an aisle splitting the benches. The judge sat highest in the room, her honors bench elevated, along with the witness stand, officers standing like statues, posted on each side. A woman sat at a table in front of the judge's stand, a stenographer machine in front of her, fingers in motion to record proceedings. The scene reminded me of a wedding with the groom's family on one side, the bride's on the other. Only, in the courtroom, it was Bernadette Pare's family to the left of us. And to the right, the family of the man who presumably killed her.

Jacob Wright sat at a long table in front of the gallery. He looked smaller than I expected and wore a Department of Corrections yellow jumpsuit, the letters DOC printed on his back. He didn't look at all like the college pictures we'd found online. Those showed a preppy man, skin tanned, his hair styled, clean shaven and wearing wireframe glasses. As a ward of the state, Jacob's complexion had turned pale with a breakout of acne around his chin, some of it hidden by a patch of dark whiskers that grew wildly. His head was shaved, revealing an old scar near the top, and he'd grown sideburns that extended below the lobes of his ears. A prison guard stood next to him, wearing a different uniform than the bailiffs. The guard's stare was fiery intense on his prisoner. But Jacob wasn't going anywhere. He wore handcuffs laced with a chain that ran across the table and to the floor, connecting restraints fastened around his ankles.

Two lawyers sat on the other side of Jacob, wearing suits made of fine materials that told me their hourly rate was more than I made in a week. Jacob Wright's family had done well in their fundraising, hiring the best. There'd been an appeal in the works, but considering the latest murders, the district attorney had bumped the date. It was the recent murders. The press biting into them, the stories gaining in clicks and page reads. People were talking about the sunflower girls, their murders, and they were talking about Jacob Wright. I was sure that's what had escalated this court hearing.

In the front row, sitting with Bernadette Pare's family as if to show solidarity, was Detective Tom Gardner. He had his eye on me and Tracy, nudging his chin, exchanging a respectful nod. It was a detective in his station who'd brought the charges against Jacob Wright, soliciting a signed confession. Just a boy at the time. I strongly suspected the confession was coerced, which was the source of his family's appeal.

"It's a good thing we moved fast," Tracy said, seeing Detective Tom Gardner, raising her hand to greet him, her politeness impulsive. She clutched my arm as though we were entering a funhouse, excited by the drama that was about to unfold. She leaned over and whispered, "We didn't miss it."

"The judge is already seated. I think we missed the opening formalities, but we're here in time to hear the DA's request," I said as we sat down in the first empty row, picking a spot that was close to the center. That's when I saw her, shock making me pause, a face in the crowd of faces that I would never have expected to see in the courtroom. It was Cara Palto, her jet-black hair unmistakable from the pictures we had seen. The previous driver's licenses hadn't been of help. But suddenly, we had Cara Palto in sight. She was heavier than she'd been in high school, her hollow cheeks round, her neck colored with a thick tattoo that was made up of strangely shaped glyphs I didn't recognize. Next to her were more girls, my thinking they may have been from the junior varsity team. "Look who's here and sitting behind Jacob Wright."

"How about that," Tracy said, opening her phone to take a picture. I breathed a sigh of relief, seeing the screen capture the image, completing it in silence. Not every courtroom allowed cellphones, citing security reasons. She snapped two more and included the seats next to Cara for us to review later. "Makes sense that she knew Bernadette Pare in high school, but I didn't figure on her knowing Jacob Wright?"

When the judge shifted, I covered Tracy's phone, saying, "Not sure we can do that here." The judge had broken from her statuesque form, bending in a lean in our direction. When satisfied with what she saw, the judge returned, sitting up, shuffling papers from one hand to the other. She had auburn-brown hair that was styled on the shorter side. She wore thinly framed glasses that were perched near the end of her nose, a safety chain draping from her ears. With the pleated black robe and lacy white collar, she looked a lot like Judge Judy. And if she was anything like the television judge, she'd throw us out in a heartbeat for disrespecting her court. I whispered, "The judge was watching us."

"Oh," Tracy mouthed with shock on her face. She tucked her phone away and held her hands on her lap, sitting still until certain the judge's attention didn't return.

I couldn't sense how much of the proceeding we'd missed. Were there opening statements? Instructions from the bailiff? All eyes were on the judge, the lawyers from each table waiting for her. The judge continued with the paperwork, scanning it like a speed-reader. The stack was high, but she was swift and, when ready, motioned to the table opposite of Jacob Wright. "Here we go."

A woman in a blue business suit stood up from the table, chair legs scraping with an echo that bounced against the high ceiling. Heads turned in her direction while she cleared her throat and held a document, the writing too small for me to read. From the page she read, "Your honor, in light of new evidence, the state requests all charges and the life-sentence for Jacob Wright be vacated."

A cry sounded from the family of Bernadette Pare, clashing

with a joyous chatter that rose behind Jacob Wright, his family's cheers growing loud, his lawyers patting his back.

"Order," the judge said with a sharp thwack, the gavel's sounding block bouncing from her strike. She wagged the gavel, threatening another strike, the courtroom quieting. "Before we proceed with the state's request, the court wants testimony regarding the new evidence."

"What's happening?" Tracy asked, whispers among the families growing. There was concern from the Wright family, and agreement in the voices from Bernadette Pare's family. "Casey?"

"I don't know—"

"Order," the judge repeated. "Does the state have a witness to provide testimony?"

The district attorney seemed caught off-guard as she searched the faces around the courtroom. "Your honor, we didn't prepare a witness—"

"Evidence is in the form of a new case?" the judge asked the district attorney, sitting up in her direction.

"Yes, your honor."

"Then is there an investigating officer present?" the judge asked.

I felt my body shrink, felt Tracy bump my elbow with hers.

"Your honor, this is highly unusual," the district attorney exclaimed, an objection in her tone. "There've been no subpoenas issued or—"

"Unusual or not," the judge said, interrupting, a frown joining the frustration in her voice. "Before vacating the conviction of a case involving murder, I want testimony entered regarding the new evidence. Let's not forget, this is my court."

"Your honor?" I said, standing, legs weak and feeling like jelly. Heads turning, finding where the voice came from. When the judge found me too, I continued. "My name is Detective Casey White."

"Casey, what are you doing?" Tracy asked, voice raspy.

"Detective," the judge said, waving me to come forward. "You can approach the bench."

"You're doing it now," Tracy mumbled, covering her mouth.

"The state would like to request a short recess to confer with this witness," the district attorney asked.

"That won't be necessary," the judge assured her. "A simple question about the case as evidence to vacate this conviction is all that is needed."

The district attorney stepped around the table, her shoes ticking against the stone floor. She was dressed for the court while I was dressed for investigating a murder. I looked down at my feet, my shoes worn along the sides, the soles of them worn even more. It felt like a million eyes were following my every step as I approached the judge. "Your honor," I said when reaching the bench.

"Detective, thank you for your service," she said, her words making me feel humble, especially in her presence. My muscles tensed with reverence. She motioned to the stand, saying, "Please."

A bailiff stepped forward before I was fully seated and had me place a hand on a Bible while raising the other. He was a shorter man with dark complexion, a mustache bouncing as he spoke. "Do you swear to tell the truth, the whole truth and nothing but the truth, so help you God?"

"I do," I said, my insides fluttering, my heart racing wildly. The crowd was bigger than I'd thought, the sight of them making me quake. The shakes were inside though, which was good, save for my fingers, which I clutched into fists.

"Let's proceed," the judge ordered, turning to face the court. Through the lake of faces, I found Tracy and saw a look of shock pasted flat on her face, her bright baby-blues fixed, unblinking. I looked at Jacob Wright next and cringed with a pang of remorse for what he'd been through. The unfairness of it. The tragedy of a second life nearly lost forever in the wake of his girlfriend's murder.

"Detective," the district attorney began, her gaze fixed on the judge. It shifted to the stenographer next, fingers perched above the keyboard, waiting for the next words. When the district attorney glanced back at me, she continued. "In your own words, please provide for the court a description of the case."

"Yes, your honor," I said. This wasn't the first time I'd been on the stand to provide testimony. As a detective, it came with the job. It was expected. However, this was the first time I'd ever done so without having prepared. I closed my eyelids slowly and took a deep breath, seeing every clue we'd collected, every detail from the first crime scene. When I opened them, I began, "The victim's name is Charlie Robson..."

I never glanced once at the clock, the minutes sweeping by quickly. My nerves settled while I described the details of the case as they related to what we knew about Bernadette Pare's murder, the likeness uncanny. Mine was only a supporting testimony to the evidence of a coerced confession which was also introduced.

The judge thanked me for the service again and excused me from the stand. During my time there, the nerves had faded, disappeared really, leaving me to do the job I was set to do. I spoke about Charlie Robson's death, answering a few questions, and gave the details that closely resembled Bernadette Pare's murder. And as I testified, I saw in the faces in the families the discontent, the hate coming from Bernadette's parents. They were there to see Jacob Wright remain in prison, but that wasn't going to happen. Not today. Not with the evidence we had.

I sat down without looking at the Pare family but felt the heat in their glare.

"That was amazing," Tracy said, greeting me. She bumped

my elbow again, her dimples showing that she was pleased by the performance. "I mean, really something."

"Thanks," I whispered, head turned toward her. "I think you're up next."

"What!?" she asked, face straightening, dimples disappearing.

"Kidding," I said, resting her fright.

"Oh, you," she replied, sitting up as the judge finished what she was working.

She addressed Jacob directly, shoving up her glasses, "Young man."

Jacob stood immediately, respecting the formalities of the courtroom and showing reverence for the law. "Your honor," he said in a low baritone.

"Mr. Wright, do you understand what is going to happen today?" the judged asked him, a smile appearing in the corner of her mouth.

He nodded and shifted from foot to foot, the judge's brow rising, wanting him to speak, to officially record his words in the court transcripts. "Yes... Yes, your honor."

"While I was not the judge presiding over your case, I want to say that your conviction was a tragedy, a young life terribly disrupted." While there was no mention of the coercion that solicited his confession, the judge was familiar with Jacob's case. But this hearing was in response to the latest murders. "And it will be investigated."

She paused then, waiting for a response, Jacob shifting again, anticipating the words he'd come to hear. "Yes, your honor."

The judge smiled, and added, "This court accepts the district attorney's request, vacating the conviction of Jacob Wright." Another cry from the Pare family, drowned by the cheers of Jacob's, including the girls sitting with Cara Palto. The judge sat up, removed her glasses from her face, saying, "Mr. Wright, you are a free man."

With a swing of the judge's gavel, the clap of the sounding block, Tracy flinching, it was over. Jacob Wright's shoulders rocked as he began to cry. They were tears of joy, of relief, of an end to a nightmare he had been forced to live. But it wasn't just Jacob's conviction that was vacated. It was the solving of Bernadette Pare's murder, her family's closure suddenly ripped apart. Those were the tears I saw falling. They fell for a daughter, for a sister, a cousin, a best friend. They fell for a murder without justice.

Cara Palto hugged her friends, cheeks wet, her relationship with Jacob Wright an unexpected surprise. She glanced to the back of the courtroom, finding me and Tracy, her gaze falling to my badge, and then shifting back to her friends. She didn't know who we were, or why we were there. She knew as much about us as we knew about her. What was she doing here? I needed to find out.

Within the hour we were outside, sunlight baking the tops of our heads, assistants to the reporters holding blinds to cast shadows on a podium where Jacob Wright and his family stood. Prison had not been kind to the man. A front tooth was missing and his weight had thinned. His complexion was sickly also, leading me to imagine the worst for his ordeal. He was dressed in a polo shirt and jeans, the coveralls gone, along with the shackles, freeing his ankles and wrists. He answered the questions asked, his gaze fixed on the girls from the JV team, particularly Cara Palto, their relationship a deepening mystery to us.

"Might have been mail correspondence," I said to Tracy, our standing behind the pack of reporters. Cameras stood on tripods and microphones were extended on long booms, hovering past heads and shoulders toward the podium.

"Like prison groupies?" Tracy asked, regarding the idea. "Could be. Which'd be good for him. Had to be a nightmare in there."

"Question is, when did the two of them happen?" I moved us to the side, catching a tone from one of the lawyers, the end of the press conference nearing. "Cara Palto knows Bernadette Pare from the archery team. The team disbands with the arrest and conviction of Cara's father. Bernadette goes off to college, meeting Jacob. She's murdered and then he goes to prison."

Jacob stepped around the podium and into the arms of Cara Palto, his family clapping with a cheer. Tracy finishing for me, "So when did Cara and Jacob strike up a relationship?"

The mob moved with the couple, the earlier thoughts of a wedding party leaving the ceremony returning, as the crowd parted in the middle, a parade forming behind them. When they reached us, I held my badge, pinching one of my business cards, asking loud enough to be heard, "Jacob Wright?!"

Sunlight glinted off the face of my badge, Jacob squinting. "Yes, I'm—" but he never finished.

"Fuck off," Cara Palto said, turning him away, his lawyers intervening with a step between us.

"Not again!" an older man yelled and rushed at us, his feet clapping against the pavement, reporters circling, cameras training on the commotion. The suddenness of it put me on alert, thinking he was going to attack. I stretched to guard Tracy. He raised his hand as if to strike, forcing me to lift my other hand, cradle my holster as my mind raced crazily with the surrealness of what was unfolding. "Haven't you people done enough! You took my boy and broke him!"

"Sir," I said, my voice drowning in his words which had been joined by a mob behind him, their fingers raised at me and my badge. In the older man's face I saw the resemblance to

Jacob Wright, saw that it was his father. A woman stood behind him, her gaze weepy and frozen on my badge, the hurt on her face showing me that the trust was beyond repair. "I'm sorry for what happened, but I'm here—"

"What do we do?" Tracy asked, more of the crowd coming behind us.

"Stay calm," I said to her, an arm around her middle. "Keep cool, don't show you're scared."

"But I am scared," she cracked. The crowd moved closer, threatening. "Casey?"

"—You just get out of here," the first man yelled and waved his hands, shooing at us. A courtroom officer intervened, his frame towering over the crowd, arms extending wide. He said nothing. He didn't have to. His presence was enough to put the distance between us, giving me and Tracy a path to leave safely. We turned around and headed to my car, Jacob's father yelling, "Go on now, get out of here."

"We'll have to try another way," I said, picking up my feet to move faster. Tracy didn't reply though as she moved faster. Her face was bright pink, her lips quivering, panting. I rested my hand on the lower part of her back, guiding her to follow. *Guarding* was a better word. I suddenly felt overly protective like Jacob's parents were being. I knew what it was like to lose a child, and then get them back. "Tracy, are you okay?"

"I don't think I am," she answered, jumping into the passenger side, and stringing the safety belt across her chest. I stayed at the door until the fastener clicked into place, metal clacking. She looked up at me with big eyes, saying, "That was frightening."

"It was, and I don't think we're going to get an interview with Jacob now." I glanced behind me, the crowd disbanding. "It's Cara we want to talk to. That's what's important."

"I think this will help," Tracy said, stealing my attention from the crowd. She held up her phone, handing it to me. On the screen, a log file I recognized as a visitation register for a prison. "I have her full history, visiting Jacob in prison."

"That means she was a prison groupie," I said, scrolling, the screen listing visits upon visits. Tracy opened her laptop, pixels coming alive, their dimness turning bright as she hastily typed. "I'd say she was his number one groupie."

"More than that!" Tracy turned her laptop for me to see her finding. "Husband and wife."

"They're married!"

TWENTY-THREE

Cara Wright. The name changed with Cara's marriage to Jacob Wright. It explained some of the black hole we'd found ourselves when sleuthing online municipal records. Nichelle immediately began work on the marriage, sharing in the shock and surprise of its discovery, the sudden link between the Palto family and Jacob Wright unexpectedly huge. She mentioned an approach of gaining access to the prison logs, sifting through them with a script that she was perfecting. That's what she called it, *perfecting*. I'd come to learn that really meant she was debugging it. As in, it wasn't working quite as expected. But I had no doubt she'd find perfection in whatever it was she was developing. Nichelle always produced.

The parameters for our searches were straightforward. And we were fortunate to have found that the prison had logged every minute of inmate activity. They'd electronic monitoring systems developed specifically for their correctional facility. This included outside correspondence and visits. We needed a profile of Cara Palto's relation to Jacob Wright. When did they meet? Who initiated it? Were there letters or phone calls? Was there computer access and email exchanges? When did they get married? Most important, who else visited with Jacob Wright? Prison groupies was a thing, and Jacob Wright was young and handsome, and his conviction contested from the moment he'd been found guilty. It was all the ingredients needed to make for a popular news piece and a hungry audience. I'd expected he would have groupies. A swarm of them. I did not expect Cara Palto.

Benjamin Palto

I texted Nichelle while Tracy helped me pull coveralls up around my shoulders. I'd added an extra layer of clothes, since after the last visit to Doctor Foster's frigid morgue it had taken hours to shake off the cold from my bones. Benjamin Palto's time behind bars was in the same prison. The sentences served at different times, but the same systems used.

Let's get a profile of Benjamin Palto while you're at it.

Copy

She texted back. She began typing, my screen showing the bouncing ellipses. A pause. From behind the rubber doors, a saw cut into bone, the autopsy of Patti Lymone underway. Nichelle's typing continued, the dots bouncing, reminding me of a trumpet player's fingers.

Looks like the system is newer. We'll only have Palto's last two years.

Something is better than nothing

I texted back, disappointed that Benjamin Palto's profile would omit his first years. An idea came to mind.

Contact the prison. They may have kept previous logs and digitized them.

An archive, she quickly texted. *I'm on it.*

"Need a hand," Tracy said, turning around, pointing to her coveralls. She was like me and had layered the clothes. I jerked the coveralls into place, spinning her to face me, and worked the front zipper, absently finishing like a momma sending her child to school on a cold day. Tracy took my fingers in her hand, searching my eyes, and said, "I can finish it from here."

"Sorry," I said, shaking my head and feeling silly.

She squeezed my hands, adding, "I think it's sweet." She let me finish with the zipper, a smile frozen on my face, my heart warming despite the cold we'd face. We had never been close, as I'd hoped, like most mothers and daughters. But there'd been glimpses. Moments like this one. And I saved them. Saved each one in a treasure box that I kept close to my soul. Tracy made herself busy too, ensuring my coveralls were fitted properly while Doctor Foster's muffled voice spoke from behind the resin doors. "Ready?"

"Ready," I said, entering the room, my breath frosty. A red light above the autopsy table indicated the recording was active, a microphone hanging between three large lights, the setup like a surgical room. That's what this was, a surgery, every part of the body dissected, weighed, and studied. The extent of the autopsy wouldn't include some of the more invasive procedures since cause of death was expected to be blood loss. But sitting on the tray next to Doctor Foster, there was the electric saw used to remove the skull, its half-moon shaped blade wet, glistening in the path of a surgical light. "That was unexpected."

Doctor Foster turned when hearing my voice and followed my gaze. She nodded with an understanding, and flipped a switch, the audio recording stopping with a click, the red light turning off. "The injuries to the face," she said, my going to the other side of the table. Tracy did her best to hide her reaction when she saw the victim's head, saw the face peeled back, the top of her skull on the tray and a brain exposed. "I usually wouldn't have included a study of the brain, not without cause."

"But there was cause?" I asked. The number of injuries around the neck and head was higher in Patti Lymone's case than in those of the other victims. Was it the closer distance? The killer becoming more malign, sickening? "A brain injury?"

She held up two fingers, saying, "There was one through the orbital bone, and a second near the base of the skull."

"She was shot from behind?" Tracy asked, the question helping us understand the path the victim took, aligning it to the blood patterns on the floor and wall. "The killer moved as the victim moved. When her back was turned, he fired."

I leaned forward to propose an angle, saying, "The victim may have already been falling toward the couch."

"That would explain the angle," the doctor replied. She shook her head then, adding, "This poor girl was blinded in one eye and struck repeatedly while she tried to escape. But thankfully, she may not have suffered as much due to the brain injuries."

"I think the hit in the back of the head was an accident." I moved to the wall with the X-rays, the black-and-white images illuminated, bone splintering behind the left eye, and the other injury jutting inward at the base of her skull. Next to me, there was an autopsy weight scale, the digital readout showing a measurement for whatever was inside the plastic bag. It wasn't the victim's brains, my recalling from past autopsies that everything was weighed. I pointed to it, asking, "Stomach?"

"Very good," Doctor Foster answered, continuing her work, metal on metal, her fingers deep inside the victim's chest. She handed the assistant her scalpel, handle first, and lifted Patti Lymone's heart.

"Were the contents made up of bread and lunchmeat?" I

asked, recalling the half-eaten sandwich in the victim's sink, the bread fresh, the glass still cold, sweating on the outside. Depending on the state of digestion, it'd help in establishing some of the timeline. "There was a plate—"

"The stomach was empty, as were her intestines. The victim hadn't ingested any food for days. There were signs of dehydration as well."

"Empty?" I asked, her answer unexpected. She gave me a nod, a question forming in her eyes. I thought of how nervous Patti Lymone appeared. It made sense that she was dehydrated and hadn't eaten. How could she eat or drink anything? She was beyond fright. She was terrified. "Tracy! We've got to go!"

Tracy looked alarmed, the concern I felt registering. "Go where?!"

I didn't answer, and directed my next question at Doctor Foster. "The crime-scene cleanup crew? What service do you use?"

Her eyes widened. "Gosh, I've no idea," she answered. She eyed the time on the wall clock, adding, "I know they were given the green light to start."

"When?" I asked, hand splayed against the door, my words firm.

"They might have started. Why?"

"The killer made a sandwich. They ate it after they murdered Patti Lymone."

Traffic wasn't an obstacle. Not in the middle of the day. Not the way I navigated, weaving between cars and trucks, crossing the bridge, stomping the gas as my heartbeat thrummed in my head. There was a bite mark in that sandwich, giving us a clue that could be used like a fingerprint. And what of DNA? Was it possible to extract from the saliva?

None of it was going to help us if the cleaning crew had reached the kitchen.

Tracy worked her phone and laptop, the computer sliding on her lap as we turned sharply from street to street. More than a few times, I caught a surprised look from her, startled by a fear of crashing. I assured her that we'd be fine. And we would, as long as everyone got out of my way.

"Casey?!" Tracy said, leaning sharp against the door, holding firmly to her laptop, tires squealing. "Could we get there in one piece?"

"We'll be fine," I said, voice straining, my breath held while in the turn. We straightened, Tracy sighing, her hand against her chest. "Any luck?"

"Plenty. There are a dozen companies certified for biohazard cleanup." Another turn, tires edging the road's rumble strip. Tracy gripped her laptop and leaned to the left, remaining there until we were on a forward path again. "It could be any of them."

"Well, it looks like it's Bright-Bio Services," I said, reading the side of a red van, the lettering colored yellow like the sunflower petals. There was another parked in front of it, their doors open, workers carrying cleaning machinery from the back. I punched my car's flashers, double parking in the street, exiting with a honk. I held my badge for them to see, and yelled, "Freeze!"

Looks were exchanged, two women smoking stood, their bio suits open in the front, wearing shirts with the same logo. "Can I help you?" one of them asked, sucking on the end of a cigarette. She waved to the men carrying the heavy gear, giving permission to return the equipment. She glanced at my badge, asking, "Inspection?"

"No, ma'am. We're investigating the crime scene," I answered. She took another drag, and stomped it dead, grinding it with the tip of her shoe. "How far into the job?"

She looked through the trees lining the street, sunshine breaking through, answering, "Got here this morning." My heart sank. The woman covered her feet with booties and pulled her hood back over her head, preparing to go inside and continue. She saw the disappointment, adding, "We got the call late yesterday. Paperwork filed this morning, clearing us to work the scene."

"The kitchen?" I asked. She snapped her fingers, the workers going into motion at once. "There was food in the sink."

"You're in luck," she answered, going to the back of the van. She stared a moment, sizing me from head to toe. And did the same with Tracy. She handed us suits, sealed in plastic, bright orange like hers, compete with booties, gloves, a hood and goggles. "It's bad in there."

"We know," Tracy commented. "We worked it."

From inside the house, hammering erupted, wood prying, nails whining. "Prying the floorboards," she said, her look hard. "Blood reached the subfloor, leaked between them."

"We'll stay out of your way and enter the rear." I held up the gear, appreciating the help, saying, "Thanks for these."

"Not a problem. If you think of it, put in a good word for us."

"Will do." I waved behind me as we made our way around the house, neighbors sitting on the steps and standing in their driveways. They'd been there when we first entered the scene. And then again when removing Patti Lymone's body. We dressed fast, helped each other, sliding our feet into the booties, zipping the side and tightening the hood. We could have gone inside, knowing the crime scene, the blood absent in the kitchen. The commotions told me we'd need them. I opened the rear door, finding five others dressed like us. "In and out."

"In and out," Tracy replied, repeating my words. Her eyes were big behind the goggles, curiosity in the work being done. The furnishings that had been touched with blood were already gone. There was no cleaning some things, no salvaging them, like the couch where Patti died. Hammering rang in our ears, floor nails whined, a man and woman working a pry bar in the center of the living room. They dumped the wood in a large container marked biohazard, leaving holes in the floor, leaving the footsteps of Patti's ghost. "The sink."

We were in luck. There were red biohazard bags in the kitchen, but nothing in the sink was touched. "Fingerprints on the dish?" I asked, thinking it possible, deciding to take it along with the sandwich.

"The glass too?"

"Anything that might be of help," I answered, carefully placing the sandwich in an evidence bag. I double wrapped it, the bread having become stale, which might help to preserve the bite pattern. "Grab the butter knife. It could have finger-prints on it."

"I think that's mustard and mayonnaise," Tracy said, jumping when a board snapped, the crime-scene cleanup sounding like a construction site. "Refrigerator?"

"The condiments," I answered, and opened the door, a cold breath rushing over me. From the shelf, Tracy took out jars, our suspicion that the killer could have touched them and given us an opportunity to lift a fingerprint. "We'll see what we see."

"Is that it?" Tracy asked, peering into the living room, watching the cleanup. "What else?"

"We still haven't found where the flower petals came from," I said and shoved a biohazard bag aside to enter the dining room.

"Books again?" Behind me, I heard Tracy groan. "We searched them all."

"The petals came from somewhere right?" I peered over my shoulder, staring until Tracy agreed. "And we know the victim did not leave this house."

"Then where?" she asked, pleading, as she joined me next to the dining room table.

"I don't know." The table hadn't been touched yet, the doilies flecked by spatter, which had dried black. The settings would be collected and bagged for biohazard disposal once the cleanup crew reached the table. In the corner where we suspected the attack began, the exercise bike was still there, the floor bare, save for the bloody path marking Patti's attempted escape. "Patti Lymone said that she was trying to stay busy. Remember?"

"Right, it smelled like a chemistry class in here." Tracy followed me to the exercise bike. "She'd been cleaning."

"Might have been exercising too," I said, nudging the bike. "I like to read when I'm on an exercise bike."

Tracy shook her head. "Headphones for me, or maybe solitaire on my phone."

When I pulled the handlebars, the bike stayed in place. "Grab that side and help me move it."

"What's this thing weigh?" Tracy asked, muscles straining. Grunting, we inched it away from the wall, adding enough space to search. I shone my light behind the front, plastic housing hiding the wall. "Anything?"

"I think there might be—" I began to say, sliding my hand where the window's daylight met the shadow, my fingertips brushing against paper. "The victim liked to read too when exercising."

"Really, there's a book back there?" Tracy asked, surprised. We moved it again, enough to fit my arm, knuckles scraping the wall. "Can you get it?"

I closed my fingers around the spine and lifted, the pages arriving in the light. "It's a copy of the yearbook. She must have been looking at the pictures when the attack occurred."

"There's more back there," Tracy said, shoulder deep, her arm buried behind the bike. She stood up, brow bouncing, goggles fogged by perspiration, she flipped open an evidence bag, dropping a handful of recovered flower petals. "You were right about the pages, pressing the petals like Foster did with the butterflies."

"They must have fallen out," I said, the yearbook open to the pictures of the junior and varsity team pictures. Between the pages were the remains of a sunflower petal, along with the outline of the others, years in the making. We only needed one to confirm, and it was there, buried in the crease, cinched in the binding, preserved the day the victim had placed them there.

Tracy turned the yearbook around to see the page it was on, and asked, "It's the team pictures with the coach. What do you think it means?"

"I think Patti Lymone suspected that the person killing them is one of their own. The killer is a sunflower girl."

TWENTY-FOUR

Friday morning at the station was quiet, save for the small wooden gate slipping through my fingers. It shut with a clap that made the station manager jump. I gave him a wave, apologizing, his stare fixed before retreating to his computer. The area in front of our offices and desks was reserved for the walkins and the patrol escorting folks who would be held for processing. It was empty now, but the weather was clear and, more importantly, it was warm. And it was also Friday. That meant paychecks and money in pockets where it'd surely burn a hole, finding its way across tavern bars, the intoxicated chaos spilling onto the streets of the Outer Banks. By midnight, the small holding area would be shoulder to shoulder.

Coffee filled the air beyond the gate, Tracy and Nichelle sitting outside my cubical, their feet up and trading paint swatches. Their big move to Philadelphia was coming up fast. Less than a couple of weeks, the thought of it making my insides hiccup. Not just because we were supposed to follow, but because it was the city and nothing at all like the Outer Banks where Tracy had lived much of her life. I wasn't as worried about Nichelle. She was one of those types that you knew would always be okay. No matter what the environment, she'd blossom and grow. And though I held a deep affection for Nichelle, I loved my daughter and felt the sting of worry that only a mother could carry.

"Morning," I said, docking my laptop, a royal blue swatch passing between them. As the monitors came alive, the heaviness of the move with Jericho gave me pause. Our plans had surely stalled, and nothing had been said about it, the packing at our apartment had stopped, leaving the open boxes and spools of tape unused strewn across the half-empty rooms. It wasn't just Jericho either. It was me. I didn't know what was next for us and not knowing had me feeling too paralyzed to do anything. "That's a pretty color."

"It's for an accent wall," Tracy said, holding it closer for me to see. "It's called Indigo Blue. I'm trying to convince Nichelle we should paint the front wall this color."

Nichelle shook her head. "But the front wall is the original brick. They restored it after the old plaster was removed." Tracy scrunched her face, a disagreement coming. "It's great as is. I say we leave the brick."

"Casey, what do you think?" Tracy asked, lifting the swatch higher. "Indigo Blue or faded brick red with gray mortar."

"Uh-uh," I said with a tsk-tsk and shook my head. "You guys need to decide on your own."

Nichelle frowned, and then lured me with a smile, brow rising. "We're just curious what you like."

"Yeah," Tracy urged. "Do you like natural brick, or painted?"

The gate clapped shut, eyes averted to draw our attention away from the paint swatch. There were footsteps arriving and I stretched onto my toes to find an older man wearing a shiny charcoal suit, a likeness to the color and shine of his hair. I recognized him from Jacob Wright's court hearing, the morning coming with a surprise, our request to speak to Jacob having been acknowledged. When he saw our small gathering, he acknowledged that he was here to see me. But it wasn't Jacob that followed behind the lawyer, a tuft of jet-black hair coming into view past the lawyer's shoulder.

"Natural," I said to the girls. Tracy frowned with a pout while Nichelle's smile brimmed with delight. I shrugged, adding, "I think it looks better when the brick is original, not when it's painted."

"Detective White?" the lawyer asked, greeting me with his hand extended. Face to face, he towered above us and smelled like an aftershave my father would have worn. "I have my client, Cara Palto. We understand you're requesting statements from the girls who'd been part of the junior and varsity teams?"

"Karen and Chrissy told me you were taking statements," Cara said before I could answer, her demeanor soft and not at all the reproachful manner we'd experienced after Jacob's hearing. She clasped her hands, knuckles white, and glanced at Tracy and Nichelle. She was nervous, which had me questioning. What did she have to be nervous about?

"Coffee, water?" I asked, arm extended toward our kitchenette. Both shook their heads, uninterested. "No? Follow me."

I grabbed my laptop, Tracy doing the same. Nichelle stayed back to continue working the prison logs for Benjamin Palto. They were incomplete, sparse by comparison to what we'd found with Jacob Wright. "Ma'am. Would it be possible to use that room?" Cara Palto stood outside the conference room, which was empty, the table cleared, the chairs tucked beneath. "I get claustrophobic in small places."

"I don't have any objections," I told her, budging the door open with my shoulder. Chair wheels squealed and their seatbacks groaned as we settled around the table. "Congratulations by the way."

"Congratulations?" Cara asked, a questioned look going to her lawyer. When he shrugged, she returned her gaze to me.

"On your marriage," I said as though reminding her. She gave me a look of acknowledgment and sat down, crossing her arms. I sat across from her, the conference room table wider than what I was used to when interviewing. But questioning wasn't about the where and how, it was about what was asked and answered. And I found myself wondering where to begin. I asked the most generic question anyone would ask when congratulating a marriage. "How did you two meet?"

She looked to her lawyer who gave the okay to answer. She cleared her throat and faced me, saying, "I knew he didn't do it and wanted to tell him." I kept still and showed no reaction, which helped to solicit more of a response. Cara lowered her head with a nod. "Bernadette's murder?"

"You were certain of Jacob's innocence?" Cara's brow bounced, agreeing. "Why?"

She sucked in air through her teeth, lips disappearing briefly. "I don't know." She relaxed then, finding a place of comfort in the answer. "I knew Bernadette and followed the story on the news."

"It was the questions raised about the signed confession?" Tracy asked, her laptop open to record the exchange.

"That was part of it, but it was in his eyes." With her lawyer's permission, Cara flipped through her phone until she had a picture of Jacob Wright on the screen, the image pixelated and skewed. "I took a picture of my television. It's from his trial. I dunno why, but when I saw it, I saw he was innocent."

I leaned forward and put my weight on my arms and asked directly. "Do you think whoever killed Bernadette is the same person killing your teammates?" Her lawyer shifted with that question. He recognized when questions were used like a chess game, one setting up the next five, the answers guided to trap the opponent into a loss. That wasn't what I was interested in doing though. Not like they'd done with Jacob Wright. My question was genuine. I shook my head, directing a comment to the lawyer, "I am interested in her opinion."

Cara's stare remained fixed on her lawyer, his company showing her apprehension, justifiably so given what had happened to Jacob. He allowed the question, her eyes returning to meet mine. "Of course. Don't you?"

She'd answered my question with a question, showing we were in agreement. But was it her? "That must have made you feel terrible?" Her hard stare turning soft with confusion. "When your father went to prison. When you learned what he'd done."

She didn't look at her lawyer this time, answering directly, "What do you think?!"

"What happened afterward?" I asked, curious what it must have been like in the school hallways, the lunchroom, her every day.

She slipped her hands from the table, hiding them in her lap, her head dipping with a scowl on her face. "Imagine the worst—" She looked up then, adding, "—and multiply it by a hundred."

"I'm sorry that happened to you," I said with sincerity, knowing how cruel school kids could be. Was there more there? I poked at the past, asking, "It must have made you angry? The things they said."

"Yeah." She scoffed and made a face. "But you get used to it."

"How?" Tracy followed up, having skipped grades and been on the painful side of schoolyard teasing before shifting to homeschooling.

Tracy's question connected, Cara looking at her, sharing a sentiment they could understand. She shrugged, answering, "Thick skin I guess, I dunno." Her gaze went back to her hands, fidgeting. "Maybe I never really got over it."

"Especially the Olympics." There was more pain there. An

opportunity to search deeper. Her father going to prison and the pain of being bullied must have preyed on her mind. "Losing the junior Olympics? Did that make you angry too?"

Her lawyer's ears perked up, his body language showing caution. "Really?" she asked, annoyed. Her frown turned into a grin, but it was to mock the question. "Might be that it did me a favor."

"How so?" Tracy asked, the chair's seat-back creaking. She spun her laptop around to show a newspaper article. On it there was a picture of Cara holding a bow and arrow, a banner headline reading FIRST PLACE, and another headline showing her path to the junior Olympics, its beginning when she was only eight years old. "Years of work. It seems that it was destined to happen?"

A faint scoff, shooing away what Tracy showed. "The Olympics?! That was my dad's dream. Not mine." She clutched her hands, her cuticles puffy and red as she picked at her fingers. A grin fading, she added, "He wanted it."

"Did you want those girls dead?" I asked, selecting my words carefully. Her lawyer abruptly sat up with an objection. I raised my hand, acknowledging, and then reframed the question. "Wanting something isn't doing it. You cannot be charged for wanting anything. Were you mad enough to want to see those girls dead?"

"Don't answer that," her lawyer warned. He looked at me, shaking his head. "Any answer could be used to help sway a jury's decision making. Next question, please."

Tensions rose. Her lawyer would argue against any question I asked that related to the victims. I needed a different approach. "Do you still practice?"

"What?" Her brow lifted. "You mean archery?"

"Yes, archery." Tracy followed my lead, her screen changing to show the hands of competitive archers, the fingers involved in repeatedly drawing the bowstring back until taut, and then releasing. A steady practice toughened them, creating thick calluses. There were pictures of what happened when you didn't improve the calluses, the blistering dramatic, the broken skin rubbed raw.

Cara glanced at her lawyer who looked surprised too. He mulled over the question a moment before giving her the okay to answer. With a slow shake, she answered, "Not since my dad went to prison." She cocked her head. "Actually, I haven't practiced since he was arrested."

"That's a long time," Tracy commented, flipping her screen back to the newspapers, showing it. "It was a big part of your life though."

"He was gone," she said, intonation gone, her body language flat. "Didn't see the use without his support."

"Not once?" I challenged, cueing Tracy to switch screens. When Cara saw the images, she leaned forward, her palms facing up for us. There was a time when hours were spent drawing the bowstring, aiming, and firing. She'd done that day in and day out for most of her young life. But I saw nothing. Without asking, I ran my fingers over the skin, which was scar free. It felt supple, without any blisters or calluses. "Your draw hand?"

"It is. See what I mean?" she answered, asking me to confirm. She looked at me direct, speaking to me and not through her lawyer. "If I'd so much as practiced once, you'd know."

When her lawyer touched her shoulder, she returned to her seat, Tracy changing pictures. "What about gloves like a baseball player wears when they're at bat?"

"We've all tried those, but they didn't work for me. My fingers still blistered, made them worse." Cara's hands retreated and she brushed her hair back. "We learned that the right way to do it was to grow the calluses."

She had no calluses. No wet blisters in bloom, or the rise of a welt, an abrasion that'd indicate there was use of a bow and arrow. "You could have waited for us to come to you. What brought you here today?" In my experience, a person hiding something doesn't offer themselves to an interview with the police.

There was no look to her attorney, no side glances, or moments of pause. "You asked if I wanted to see any of them dead."

Chair legs moved as the lawyer waved. "Let's move—"

"I want to!" Cara interrupted. They traded glances, the motion of his eyelids speaking for him.

"Go on," I insisted as she faced forward.

"It was him. My dad," she said. "I wanted him dead. But it isn't why you think."

"What would we think?" I asked, her comments confusing.

"He—" She looked hurt while struggling to find the words. "It's because he loved them."

It was jealousy. She was jealous. Cheated from having the father she deserved. It was abandonment or the sinister nature of his crimes. Adolescents, immature, victims, and the dangerous turns of infatuation. The *what if* questions began popping into my mind. "And what about your teammates?"

"A few of them loved him too," she answered, dipping her chin. "They still do."

TWENTY-FIVE

We weren't two steps out of the conference room when Nichelle's yelp alerted us. A hand in the air, swinging widely for our attention. She held her laptop in the other, the screen too small to read. Without a word, I handed my card to Cara Palto, nodding silently, her eyes finding mine. In them I saw the path of her life, the undeserving twists and turns brought on by the selfish acts of her father. I felt sorry for her and wondered who she would have become if she'd been afforded the opportunities deserved.

"Please," I began, pinching the card as she tugged on it. "If there is anything else you can share, don't hesitate to contact us."

"Yes, ma'am," she replied, her indifference to us returning as she turned and walked away.

"Nichelle?" I asked, Tracy already by her side, their eyes glowing bright with the image from the laptop's screen. "What is it?"

"I was able to get scans of Benjamin Palto's visitor logs." She shook her head, adding, "His visits were nothing like we saw with Jacob Wright."

"No groupies?" I ran my finger down the screen, a woman's name appeared over and over, the last name shared. "Sister or a mother?"

"Theresa Palto is his mother," Tracy answered, her laptop open with a fresh search. "Visits ended when she died a few years after his sentence began."

"What am I missing?" I asked Nichelle, not catching the source of her excitement.

"It's the mail too," Tracy answered for her. "Show her!"

On Nichelle's screen there were photocopies of mailing envelopes, dozens upon dozens sent to Benjamin Palto. The handwriting was distinct, and the return address was the same. "Who lives there?"

"*Lived* there, is the proper tense." Nichelle opened a map app, the view showing a small cottage-styled home. "It's the home of Chrissy Jensen's parents."

"One of the girls from the ice-cream shop?" I asked, recalling the oily red hair and pale skin. Tracy and Nichelle shared in the confusion, the girls being adamant about cutting off Benjamin Palto's manly parts. "I wouldn't have expected there'd be letters from her."

"Hate mail?" Tracy suggested.

Nichelle scrolled down the page, the correspondence seemingly endless. "That's a ton of hate mail."

"The writing," I said, the penmanship changing the further Nichelle scrolled. "Look at the progression of it. Are these sorted?"

"Yeah. They're sorted by date." With the pages, the writing style on the addresses changed, morphing into something fancy, something that matched the invitations the victims received. "I don't think this is hate mail."

"No, I don't either." Tracy opened a screen to show the driver's license for Chrissy Jensen, the address on it the same as her parents. "That was all an act in the ice-cream shop?"

"Only one way to find out." I gathered my things, Nichelle and Tracy doing the same. "We can call this a lunch break. I know a great little place in Currituck."

There was no line outside the ice-cream shop, and no warm smell of waffles baking like there was before. Jonathon Smith stood outside the shop with a padlock in hand, readying it with a pair of shiny keys. When he saw us, he nudged it, one eye closed in a squint from the sunlight, its reflection bouncing off the water.

"No ice cream today," he said, slapping the padlock in place, the latch giving back, leaving it open. He frowned with a curse and tried again. "Damn thing."

"I can help with that," Nichelle offered. She was like that, always eager to lend a hand. He made room for her, the padlock refusing to latch shut. "What gives?"

"Closing early?" I asked, my focus rising to the apartment above.

"They're not there," Jonathon answered, his gaze following mine. He shrugged, adding, "Wish I knew where they went."

"They quit?" Tracy asked, moving to help Nichelle. "Without notice?"

"I got notice!" He showed a text on his phone. Two words on the screen, typed in all caps:

WE QUIT.

He shook his head, angered. "They really left me hanging here. I have to close up until I can get help."

"Sorry for the troubles," I said, pitching a toe into the wood and biting my lip. "And they're not upstairs."

"Not since Jessie was killed." He smacked the padlock, the

chunk of metal swinging sideways. Nichelle and Tracy made room for him, his frustrations showing. The pressures mounting, his voice broken. "I can't even close this place."

"I hate to ask, but would you know where they've gone?"

Jonathon looked up, and snapped, "Like I care!"

"I understand," I said and began the retreat to the car.

"We're closed," Jonathon yelled. Behind us, a steady stream of patrons had started to arrive, a line forming. A low chatter rose, their asking what was said. "Closed. As in not open!"

Tracy was already looking at the line, and then to me and Nichelle, the idea to help finding a place in my head and heart. On my phone, a text message read, *Negative.*

It was from the patrol I'd sent to Chrissy Jensen's home address, her parents' place. It was still listed as her primary address, but she hadn't lived there in a long time. We had no address for Karen Walter either, which left us without a next step. "Jonathon?" I asked, my voice loud enough to be heard over the growing crowd.

"Huh?" he asked, looking up from the door handle and padlock, his distraught expression tugging at my heart. "I-I don't know where they are."

"It's not that," I said, taking the padlock from his hand. "We can help."

There was confusion first, and then surprise, which was followed by relief. "You know how to scoop?"

"Do we know how to scoop," Tracy laughed, catching on to the real intent. We could help him by scooping ice cream, and also help ourselves to search the place for any clues Chrissy or Karen might have left behind. It could be a tucked note with an address or name even. Anything to move the case forward.

Nichelle understood the intent as well, turning to face the crowd, saying, "Ten minutes, folks."

A cheer. Jonathon shook his head. "I don't have any money."

"Maybe you could help us with some questions about Chrissy?" I asked, confessing that my motives were not entirely unselfish and out of generosity. "We found something we don't really understand."

"Yeah, sure, whatever you want," he answered, wiping his eyes, and drying the sweat above his brow. "I've got plenty of waffles, had to close from yesterday, and a fresh shipment of ice cream. Tapped out every cent from the cash register."

"We'll fill it again," I told him, feeling the outline of a few dollars in my pocket. It was small, but anything would help.

Thankfully, our time to help was kept short. We donned the hats that Jessie Smith had picked out herself. Baseball caps with a brown lip and white mesh. We also wore the colorful aprons and helped Jonathon through the immediate rush, scooping ice cream into the funnel cake cones, pleasing parents and putting smiles on their children's faces. Within the hour, two of Jonathon's friends arrived. They'd driven from Virginia Beach, to reach the Outer Banks before the crush of sunset tourists crowded the shop. They'd also come with bags in tow and a promise to stay until replacements could be hired.

"That wasn't so bad," I said, Nichelle and Tracy grunting approval as they ate their earnings, two scoops each. I drank a cup of coffee with a need for the late afternoon pickup.

"Not a bad trade at all," Tracy said, cone appearing beneath my nose, offering a bite. "It's mint chocolate chip mixed with chocolate chunk."

"Delicious," I said, my mouth full, the cold on my teeth rocketing to my brain. From my pocket, I presented a crumpled piece of paper, handing it to Tracy. "While searching the place, I found this."

It was a sheet from an order tablet, the front blank, save for the faded green bars. But on the back, letters from the alphabet. Only, they were drawn similarly to the fancy writing on the invitations. "This could be the same."

"Lemme see," Nichelle said, holding her phone next to the paper, comparing it to an invitation.

"It's the same," I assured them. We piled into my car, seat belts clicking. "The question is, who drew it?"

"Where are we headed?" Nichelle asked, the top of her head filling the rearview mirror. "Back to your place?"

"Let's get some clarity around the prison logs and show that piece of paper." I turned right, spinning the wheel, gravel crunching beneath the tires as we jumped onto Route 12 to drive south. "I don't believe Benjamin Palto was being completely honest with us."

"This is where he lives?" Nichelle asked. The ice-cream cones were gone by the time I parked the car and draped my badge around my neck. The building was two floors and looked more like a seedy motel, the kind where patrons paid by the hour, paint peeling, iron railing tainted with rust.

"This is the place." The stairs were covered with bodies, beers in hand, one of them with a radio on his lap, a sweet song playing that had become popular this summer. Nearby, heat rose above a charcoal grill and made the air shimmer with what might have been chicken and ribs sizzling. Another man and woman had children helping around a picnic table, a checkerboard tablecloth snapped and spread across the surface. My badge caught a stare as we exited the car and began to search the numbers on the building doors. The men on the steps covered their beers and exited, making room for us while they regathered beneath the shade of a tree.

When we got to the apartment door, I rapped my knuckles

hard enough to hurt, making it impossible to be ignored. "Who is it?" Palto's voice answered, his voice wavering. "What do you want?"

"Detective Casey White!" I answered, lowering my voice, pressing my hand against the steel, feeling chips in the paint, seeing layers of past colors, the door's history revealed like the rings inside a tree. "Open the door, Benjamin."

"What?!" The door swung open, Benjamin Palto appearing in the light. He was disheveled, his shirt partly tucked, hair standing in a lean. Cautiously, I pressed against the door, opening it wider to get more light inside. His apartment was darkened by heavy shades. He squinted and replied, "I'm working nights this week, restocking."

"We need to discuss Chrissy Jensen," I demanded.

"What did they do?" he asked, moving aside to let us enter.

"They?" I asked, picking up on his words while I searched the small place. There was a corner kitchenette with hotplate and sink, an open case of water bottles on the counter. His bed was in the center of the room, pillow mussed, sheets shoved to the bottom. Next to it, a nightstand with his phone and a watch. Beneath the shaded window, clothes neatly folded and piled, cardboard boxes taped together to make a dresser. Benjamin ignored my question, passing through to the kitchen and flipped the top of a coffee maker. It was a four-cup Mr. Coffee, the same model I'd used during the years I'd lived in an apartment nearly identical to his—no amenities, just the essentials. "You said they. It was Karen too?"

"Yeah. Both of them." He cocked his head to the table, a single chair tucked, the tabletop covered with papers. There had to be years of bills and legal forms, an accumulation he'd no control of while he was incarcerated. He poured a bottle of water into the coffee maker, his hand shaking. There were days of growth on his face and his eyes bloodshot. It could have been the shift to working nights, but I suspected it was more. When he was done, he slammed the lid closed and said, "I told them *no*. A hundred times. No!"

"Told them no?" I asked.

He joined us at the table and lifted one of the bills, beneath it a stack of mail, a piece of twine wrapped around it. The handwriting on it was the same as the pictures Nichelle showed. These were the letters the prison had logged. Benjamin opened one and handed it to me. "But they kept sending them."

"From both of them?" I asked, seeing their names written along the bottom. I sifted through the contents, finding keywords proclaiming love and talk of a relationship and his freedom. "Not just Chrissy?"

"I never meant for any of it." His brow wrinkled and he braced the chair, explaining, "I never meant for it to get so out of hand."

"You love them?" I asked in a tone that sounded more like a declaration. He was playing the victim and it chewed up my insides. He didn't have the right. "You still love them, and they loved you back."

His eyelids closed and he shook his head. "I do love them. And I know I ruined them," he confessed, dropping into his chair, the room going silent, save for the coffee percolating. When his eyes appeared, he explained, "But I can't go back to prison. I can't ever go back to that place. If I'm seen with them, I'm gone!"

"But they think you rejected them?" Tracy asked, sifting through the mail, her phone in hand to reconcile with the prison logs. "They believed with your parole that you would finally be together."

"I had to reject them." He perched his elbows on the table, bracing his head. "If my parole officer saw them anywhere near me, he would have had me arrested on the spot."

"They blamed the other girls for the rejection?" Nichelle said, asking.

"You rejected them and that's when they went after their teammates," I said, my insides sour, sickened by the reach of his crimes. He had ruined them, and many other lives. Karen and Chrissy had a twisted interpretation of what love was, and that included murder. I raised my voice. "You realize that they are killing people. Yet you did nothing about it!"

He shook his head. "You can't pin that on me. I didn't know for sure." His cried into his palms, voice blubbering, "What could I do?"

"When was the last time they contacted you?" I demanded, believing no matter what he said, his rejecting them would continue to be ignored.

"I haven't seen them, but I will," he answered. From his back pocket he handed me an invitation, his name written across the front in the same fancy writing as the others. I opened the fold, the same thick stock, the numbers giving us coordinates, along with a time and the day set for tomorrow morning. And beneath it, the word *guilty*. Sadness lingered on his face as he continued. "It's my turn."

TWENTY-SIX

It was Benjamin Palto's turn to die. It was his turn to have the pointed end of sharp arrows driven into his body, his victims drawing the bowstrings and letting go. It was his turn to bleed out as his dying, wet breaths bubbled onto his lips and came in savage, desperate gasps. Karma had seeded my thoughts with this being the reckoning that was wanted. But we wouldn't let him die this morning. From his apartment, we confirmed the letters received in prison were from Chrissy Jensen and Karen Walter. Which one of the girls had written the letters remained unknown. What we did know was where one of the girls would be, and what time they'd be there.

He tried to reason, speak fondly of the letters, explaining to us that there was true love in them. My gut twisted when he spoke of love, the perversion of it he'd caused. They were girls, young women, impressionable, maybe even vulnerable to an unconditional trust that he'd broken. Distraught, even weepy, he confessed that things went too far, that their feelings for him were long-lasting and had turned to a sick obsession. That's when he knew he needed to end things.

The scrap of paper from the ice-cream shop confirmed that

Chrissy or Karen had also penned the invitations. But like the letters sent to Benjamin Palto, we still didn't know which one of them it was. What a show it was that the girls had put on for us in the ice-cream shop. They'd had us believing that Benjamin Palto was the devil, and that the only way to fix things was to cut off his man parts. It was all a show. Coordinated. Manipulating. An act. The girls were still in love with their high school teacher. And what they'd done wasn't just for love either. It was for revenge. It was born out of Palto's fear of going back to prison. Just the idea of it put terror on his face with a fear so striking that it had forced him to reject the girls. That's when the revenge had begun. And it was going to end with his murder.

The sunflower field selected for the attack was the largest of them, spanning acres. Our cars were parked along one of the dirt roads that led away from it. Trees lined the sides of the field, full enough to hide a killer. Two, as the case may be. The sunflower plants were ripe for harvest, bringing a hundred crows who sat on the branches in wait. In the morning light, their voices were like a rock concert, overpowering everything and making it near impossible to hear.

Sunshine was on the rise, the tall plants casting shadows that stretched across the road where they touched the other side. This was our only opportunity to find the girls. All other searches were coming up empty, the all-points bulletin broadcast across the state generating no hits. While this was a different field, the spiders had labored again during the night. They'd strung cobwebs from plant to plant, the evening chill creating dew drops, looking like a string of pearls when the sun struck them.

We read lips and motioned with our hands to communicate

over the noise, officers lining up. We'd thought to put one of the officers out front, have him dress like Benjamin Palto, his work hat borrowed, along with Palto's clothes. We'd even dressed him, the clothes fitting snug, tightly covering the protective gear beneath, making it impossible for an arrow to pierce. I decided against our dangling bait, decided against a stakeout. With the number of officers I was able to gather, we were all going in.

Bodies lined up along the row, my hand raised, balled into fists. Seven of us took to the front line, side-by-side and staying within an arm's length. We had our guns drawn and wore bulletproof vests that weighed heavy, our badges sitting in front. When I opened my hand, we entered, the ground soft and smelling sweet, arms brushing against the plants, our shadows moving in a field of shadows. When we passed the first row, we stopped and assessed. There was a morning haze that hugged our feet, hiding our shoes enough to trick our brains. It made me feel around, guarding against tripping. I opened my hand again to advance another row.

"Stay aware," I warned, mouthing the words. My ears were perked, trying to filter out the noisy crows. If there was someone else in this field, we were going to flush them out. I had two other teams setup the same as the first. They were coming in from the sides, the three lines forming a circle to meet at the center. "Keep an eye on those trees."

"We've got them too," the officer mouthed next to me. "If there is anyone up there, a hunter's perch, we'll have them."

"Good," I commented, breathing fast, a nervous sweat turning the back of my neck cold. It seemed impossible for there to be an attack. We had every inch of the field covered. But an arrow came, crows fleeing to the sky, drawing a black curtain above us with a winged rush. "Get down!"

"The tree—" the officer began, an arrow striking his leg, bouncing against the protective gear, making a loud thwack. A second arrow missed his head, disappearing behind us, a blur cutting through the sea of green.

"Up there!" I yelled, identifying the source, the rising sun bleeding into my eyes. The girls had the advantage, aiming down, sunlight blinding us. But I had officers beneath the trees, screams rising to put down their weapons. In the tree closest to us, I saw a hunter's tree stand, saw a pale face hidden in a veil of black clothing, a wisp of red hair flowing beneath a cap. It was Chrissy Jensen. "It's just the one."

"Drop your weapon!" Another warning. Chrissy lowered her arrow as I moved into position. When I was closer, she raised an arrow, sending it without warning, an officer firing their weapon in response, missing her. The head of a sunflower plant exploded, the arrow flying by me much faster in real life than they do in the movies. Chrissy fell to a knee, a bullet finding her. The officer yelling, "Drop the weapon!"

"Wait!" I screamed, the tops of the sunflowers shaking violently with the teams approaching the hunter's stand. She stayed upright, but hunched to one side as we completely surrounded her. I kept my gun on her form, the dark clothing making her look like a shadow in the dim light. "Chrissy, put it down—"

To my horror, Chrissy loaded her bow with another arrow, training the tip of it on me. I shook my head, my mind pleading while I sucked in a breath and aimed my gun. I didn't want to pull the trigger, finding I was suddenly in a horrible standoff with this young woman, this victim. Thinking through all the scenarios, I hated every possible outcome.

"Put down your weapon!" someone yelled. Her eyes were fixed on mine, but showed no remorse, no signs of listening to anyone. She drew the bowline back, the bow arching with a creak that reverberated through my bones. She was leaving me with no choice but to fire. When her thumb twitched, indicating a move, I pulled the trigger. White smoke launched from the tip of my gun, rising as her arrow was released at the same time, a puff of air whipping my hair around, the arrow passing by my head in a blur.

"Oomph!" she cried. Chrissy learned that bullets fly faster than arrows. It struck her in the middle, and she dropped her weapon at once. It fell from the hunter's perch first, an officer scrambling to secure it. Chrissy's lips puckered around a breath of air she couldn't have, the injury momentarily winding her. She tumbled forward, rolling over the edge of the perch, falling flat on her back with a thud. Four officers were on top of her a second later, securing her like they had secured her weapon.

"Shit!" an officer screamed, rearing up from Chrissy, an arrow sticking out the back of his leg. Three more appeared, blurs flying from the right side of the field, piercing the tops of sunflowers, two arrows striking the tree. Chrissy wasn't alone after all. I lowered myself from sight and scanned the field, facing the direction the arrows had come from. The air went still, the faint smell of blood in it, the feel of it electric. We were the hunters, but the tables had turned and now we were being hunted. When the field grew quiet again, there was only Chrissy's moans, her cries, the sounds giving me some relief that I hadn't killed her. Forty yards from the tree, there was the crunch of footsteps and the tops of the sunflower plants parting. It was Karen attempting to escape.

"I see her," I told the officers and took off in a run. I sprinted the first ten yards but had lost sight of Karen. She'd dressed in a camouflage jumpsuit, the browns and greens matching the stalky plants surrounding me. A twig broke beneath my shoe, triggering the release of an arrow which pierced my side. The force of it spun me around, another arrow flying over my head and nearly parting my scalp, its shaft grazing my head, cutting it open like a dull blade on a melon. The burning flesh made me scream, forcing me to cover my mouth and kneel as close to the ground as I could.

When it quieted, I tried to reason. "Karen, we can end this!" No answer. Blood ran down the side of my face, my scalp pulsing. The injury was only superficial, a cut that would heal in a week if I survived this pursuit. The other injury was worse, requiring a few stitches, but not severe enough to stop me. "What do you say, Karen? Can we end this?"

Footsteps resumed, coming directly ahead of me. While the sunlight beamed directly on me, I could make out the movement of sunflower plants. An officer's yells came from my left, his body slamming the ground, one of Karen's arrows finding him. Sunflower plants fell like dominoes as he hollered in pain.

Karen stopped after that, leading me to wonder if she'd used all her arrows. Twenty yards toward the end of the field, the head of a sunflower shimmered. It was slight, the golden-yellow flowers dancing, a sway showing when there was no breeze. I took off, changing my pursuit, Karen needing direct line of sight. She could see me, but I couldn't see her. I ran sideways, back and forth, my breath as hot as the sun, fright mixing with the adrenaline pumping through my body. My face had turned sticky, some of the blood drying, running into my eyes making them sting. I swiped errantly at it, annoyed, and pressed forward.

I fell hard to my knees when an arrow flew by my shoulder, Karen stopping to take a shot. She'd followed my pattern, forcing me to change it again. My legs were getting heavy, the running pursuit taking me out of the field, the two of us clear of the sunflowers, both of us in full view. We'd reached the end, the farm edged by a dirt road that was littered with farm equipment. Karen said nothing, remaining in the role of hunter, and drew her bow with an arrow aimed at me. She had me. My gun at my side, a moment behind her. It was checkmate. I was dead. One movement and she'd stick that arrow into my heart. A gunshot echoed against the far hill, the sharp clap making me jump. Karen dropped hard like a sack, the life in her body gone as she lay motionless, her reign of terror on the junior and varsity teams over.

"Jesus!" an officer said, her eyeballs bulging. She tugged on my sleeve, asking "Detective?"

"Yeah," I answered, panting, my chest aching, the muscles in my legs burning. Two officers were on top of Karen, securing the weapons, rolling her body to try and save her. There was no life to save though. From the way her body fell, her soul had jumped out before it landed on the ground.

"We've got paramedics coming," the officer told me, her voice distant like the rustling of leaves in the trees.

"Chrissy?" I asked, shutting my eyelids and forcing myself to breathe.

"Hold this," she instructed and patted my head with gauze. She removed my weapon from my hand and placed my fingers on top of the bandaging. "The other girl is alive."

"Thanks," I mumbled with a sigh and felt the sting of a cry, hating that I had had to fire my weapon at her, and hating that Karen had had to die. "It's over."

TWENTY-SEVEN

The case of the sunflower girls had been solved. There wasn't one killer. There were two. Both Chrissy Jensen and Karen Walter were involved in every murder, working together, their positions in the sunflower fields making for a brutal attack, impossible to survive. But only one of the killers would serve time. The gunshot that may have saved me, had ended Karen Walter's life. She had been dead by the time her body hit the ground.

A pang of sadness, perhaps guilt too, a young life senselessly lost. If only she'd lowered her bow. But raising it against us with intent to kill—that left us without options. The sadness of her dying lifted some when I learned from Doctor Foster that the bullet had entered Karen's side, had slipped between the soft tissue of her ribs and pierced her heart. According to the doctor, death was near instant, maybe fifteen seconds, the muscle shredded. Karen's death almost seemed unfair. It was fast. Too fast. And not at all like the tortuous death she'd delivered to the sunflower girls. I guess karma isn't always a player in the life and death of murder.

Although Karen was dead, we followed through with the

bite mark in the sandwich that had been collected as evidence from Patti Lymone's crime scene. A killer had made themselves a sandwich after Patti Lymone's murder, Doctor Foster confirming it was Karen. With Karen's body in the morgue, Chrissy Jensen wasn't shy about talking to us. She was a partner in crime and had sustained serious injuries. She'd lost a part of her spleen, the bullet inside her staying whole, which made for a non-threatening operation, as well as making for a good prognosis. It was her outgoingness that had me thinking Karen was the lead behind whatever twisted pact they'd committed. But her eagerness to talk also made me wary of what was truth and what was not.

Chrissy opened up to us immediately once she was well enough to speak. Her interview took place in the hospital recovery room where I had officers posted to guard the door. She wasn't in any shape to escape, but I also couldn't chance retribution from a victim's family member.

"This is the room," Tracy said, wrinkling her nose. The sting of antiseptic and cleaners was in the air, along with machines beeping and hallway announcements filling our ears.

"Officers," I said greeting the patrol, showing my badge.

"She's awake," one of them said, opening the door. "A nurse just left the room."

I sat next to Chrissy with Tracy taking a place across the bed where she held her phone to record a video. Nichelle lent a hand for us, arriving a moment later and taking a seat at the foot of the bed where she chipped away on her laptop. Before we started with the questions, we did things right and made sure Chrissy Jensen was properly mirandized.

"Shall we get started?" Chrissy's lawyer asked. He'd arrived before us, sitting motionless in the corner of the room, casting a shadow on the wall like a potted floor plant. If not for his words, I might have overlooked his being there.

"Your relationship with Benjamin Palto?" Tracy asked, a quick breath to expand on the question.

"We were in love with him," Chrissy answered abruptly, wasting no time, the hospital sheet in constant motion with her legs rocking back and forth beneath it. She rocked her head as liberally as her legs, adding, "He loved us too!"

"He approached you first?" I asked, watching fluids drip a second at a time, sixty in a minute, the cadence accurate enough to set a watch by. There were three bags of fluids, a large one and two smaller ones, clear tubes linking to the biggest, draped across the head of the bed, bubbles shimmering as gravity pushed medications into her body.

"Ouch—" Mouth twitching, her excitement to answer shortened with a short gasp, post-surgery pains making her heart rate jump. She cringed and looked at me as if I could help. I wanted to feel bad for her but struggled to do so, thoughts of karma returning and of how her partner had escaped punishment, her life fleetingly short once the bullet had found her. Perhaps this was some of the painful payback for what they'd done to the victims? Then again, perhaps it was just my wishful thinking.

"Breathe," I said, my nature taking over, having had my share of hospital stays, along with post-surgery pain. The court-appointed lawyer straightened, neck craning, seeing if we were soliciting responses while Chrissy was under duress. We weren't, but in light of the Jacob Wright case, I could appreciate the extra caution. Chrissy's eyes welled, tears spilling, her paled appearance flushed with redness. Our eyes square, I showed her how to breathe through it. She followed my lead, the pain dissipating. "In through your nose and out through your mouth."

"You're the one who shot me," she said with repulsion in her voice. She frowned with uncertainty and searched my face. "Aren't you?"

"You left me no choice," I answered blankly. I leaned

forward. "I mean, I had to. You were aiming an arrow at my chest?"

Her gaze quickly retreated to her hands. "I wasn't going to shoot you," she said with remorse.

"Benjamin Palto?" I asked, staying focused on the questions.

"Like I was saying, we loved him." Eyes shifting to her lawyer, hands busily moving, nervously pulling on her fingers. "Since that first time. He really did love us too."

"Both of you?" Tracy asked, confusion forming, challenging the statement.

"There wasn't any jealousy?" I added, curious about the arrangement.

"Oh gosh no!" Chrissy answered, sweeping her red hair behind an ear. Her color had returned to normal, looking better. "We were in love with one another. All of us."

"Karen and you. And Benjamin?" I asked, believing that may have been where the troubles began.

A nod, but her brow furrowed deep, the look on her face turning cross. "But the team ruined it!" Her voice frosty, the change in its tone making me shift, guarding. Chrissy's knuckles were white with her hands clenched, closing tightly into fists. "They ruined it all. With everything we'd done for him!"

"Bernadette?" I began to ask.

"She was the first," she answered, interrupting, nostrils flaring.

"Why the year?" Nichelle asked, looking over her laptop, sweeping her fingers across her keys.

When Chrissy frowned, unsure of what Nichelle meant, Tracy elaborated. "There was a year that had passed."

"It was Jacob Wright," she answered, seeking confirmation from her lawyer. When he made eye contact with me, I knew he was in the dark as well.

"Jacob Wright was involved?" I asked, needing clarification.

"No, he wasn't involved, but he got blamed for it. Bernadette was first because the coach loved her the most." Chrissy moved to sit up, a groan rising from deep inside her, a guttural sound.

"Breathe," I reminded her and held her shoulder, cupping her arm to offer leverage. There was surprise in her eyes that I'd help. I might have felt a bit surprised too but couldn't stand to see her suffering.

"Thanks," she said. Her forehead was damp with sweat, and I handed her a plastic jug with ice and water. She sipped at it, continuing. "When he got arrested and sentenced, we tried to get him released."

"You tried to help?" Nichelle asked.

The online fund-me page flashed in my mind. "It was you and Karen that were behind the online campaigns?"

"Uh-huh. But it didn't work. Nothing we tried worked."

"So you moved on to the rest of the team," I said, asking her to confirm. "Killing Charlie, and then Jessie and Patti too?"

"We had to!" Chrissy snapped, ice sloshing, arm swinging with the tubes following.

"Why?" I asked, standing to safely return the jug to the table.

"We were supposed to be together again. But he rejected us!" Chrissy cried, cheeks ruddy and wet. "They destroyed the love we had."

"That's why you did it?" Tracy asked. "You blamed them?"

She beat her chest, speaking in a breathy wheeze, "It broke our hearts." She wagged her hand then, continuing. "But it wasn't his fault. It was theirs. That's when Karen said we should kill them all. With them gone, maybe he'd love us again."

"You made the invitations?" I asked and nudged my chin toward the table next to her bed. On it, there was a pad and pencil, the letters of the alphabet drawn, upper and lower case, equally spaced, the style like the invitations. I placed an evidence bag on her lap, the scribblings styled similarly, the crumpled paper from the ice-cream shop.

"I did." Chrissy glanced at the tablet next, mouth twisting, "I like to practice."

"Practice?" Tracy asked, her phone above the pad and paper to take a picture.

"I wanted to be a graphic designer." Chrissy clutched the tablet, tubes following her hand. She flipped it over, saying, "Typography. You know what that is? I wanted to make fancy fonts and sell them."

"Would you be willing to write that down?" A part of me felt terribly sorry for Karen and Chrissy. Their ideas of love broken, horribly warped by what Benjamin Palto had done to them. They were now killers, but they had been victims too.

Her lawyer peered up to see the paper tablet and pen in hand. With her lawyer's nod, Chrissy took the pen and paper and began to write. She swiped at her face and then looked at us, asking, "What happens now?"

I didn't answer the question, leaving that one for her lawyer. But asked instead, "Would you be willing to write down everything that you've told us today?"

"Yes," she said, an image of a jail cell coming to mind. An image of her sitting at a steel table fastened to the wall, the chair a pedestal sprouting from the floor. She'd have plenty of time to design new fonts. I didn't ask any additional questions, having heard enough to understand the motive. I saw it in Tracy and Nichelle's eyes too. The relationships that Benjamin Palto started with the young women had turned into a love affair.

While it might not have been Palto's intention, the girls were more than infatuated with him, they believed they were in love with him. But it wasn't love. It was something they developed to cope with the inappropriateness of his behavior, the broken trust of it, which twisted into a sick compulsion.

At some point during his time in prison, he must have

touched on rehabilitation enough to see that what he'd done was wrong. On his release, he rejected the girls, staying true to a new path. But Chrissy Jensen and Karen Walter blamed the rejection on what put him in prison. They blamed their team-mates for destroying what they thought they had had, for putting him in prison. It was revenge they sought.

EPILOGUE

"Ready!?" Jericho asked, dropping his glasses onto his nose, throttling the motors while I gripped the console rail mercilessly.

"You bet!" I yelled over the roar, water spraying behind the boat as we launched, the bow rising until the boat leveled onto plane. I looked over my shoulder at the Marine Patrol station shrinking behind us, Jericho's old partner waving as he coiled a rope. We struck a boat's wake, the bump lifting me off my feet. "Whoa!"

"Traffic!" Jericho yelled, hair flattened by the wind, drops of water beading on his glasses and face. He pointed to the horizon, the sea flecked with boats and jet skis, lined by foam, their racing back and forth. We jumped another and then another, my stomach rising and falling. "It'll smooth soon."

"Busy day!" I said, seeing the traffic. The day was gorgeous, the season drawing to a close. I leaned into the next wake, the sea air rushing through my clothes enough to make me shiver. I could literally feel my blood pressure rising, the adrenaline pumping through my veins, the boat ride better than any roller-coaster. "How far?"

"Ten minutes," he yelled, voice a faint sound over the motors. He tapped the console, the GPS showing a trail that he'd saved from a previous trip.

The ride was soon quiet, the ups and downs gone as we reached a place where there was less traffic and the wind had eased, the ocean's surface turning tranquil. The sea looked like a giant mirror. And in it I saw the sunshine and giant clouds, its breaking off to the left with a family of dolphins. I let go of the bar, wringing my hands of the cramps and took to Jericho's side. I pulled back on the throttle, slowing us so he could lift his glasses and look at me. We said nothing, his gaze long and deep. I turned my engagement ring toward the sunlight, questions of us stirring deep. I felt it and sensed it in him too. When he turned back, bumping the throttle, I wrapped my arms around him, snuggling close enough to join in the drive.

"I love you," I said, shouting over the motors, his nod telling me he heard me, an *I love you too* soundless from his lips.

I recognized the GPS trail, a nowhere place to disappear to for the afternoon. Humps of rocky land were to my left, sunken islands that made up a barrier inlet with buoy markers around them to mark the shallow dangers. To the right was the Outer Banks, the last of the land before a large break with sea water, the beaches empty, save for a few abandoned houses, structures bare and leaning, a sad truth to rising sea levels.

In a minute, the land would be gone from sight, but we were still close enough that a cell signal reached my phone. I'd been given a watch that was paired to it, the text message flashing on the screen. It was from Tracy, a pair of hearts telling us to have a good time. She also mentioned that the arraignment for Chrissy Jensen had taken place without issue, and that her lawyer was working with the district attorney. There was blame on Benjamin Palto's shoulders in the murders as well. He'd broken Chrissy and Karen. He was the catalyst, his actions warping their idea of love and friendship. Murder was murder, but

Benjamin Palto complicated the case. Chrissy Jensen would serve time, a lot of time, but may have escaped the death penalty.

"Penny for your thoughts!?" Jericho yelled, his voice snapping me back from the case. I thought of Emanuel and his collapse, the end of his career. I thought of all the lives that had been irrevocably touched forever. What justice could be served? Put Chrissy behind bars forever? Put Benjamin Palto back in prison? "Casey?"

"I'm a little more expensive than a penny," I joked, but was overcome with thoughts of the case, the reaching impact it had had on lives far and close to us. The boat slowed, the motors cutting off, the wake chasing from behind with a tumble of white foam. We rose and fell with its passing as I grabbed Jericho hard and pulled him into me, clutching his shoulders, and held on as a wave of sadness came. "This case... Emanuel—"

"I know," he whispered, holding me, our swaying in rhythm to the sea. "Emanuel will find his way. He'll find a new place."

"But his job," I said, afraid for him, for his family.

"Nothing to worry there," Jericho said, pulling away. "They'll be fine. Emanuel wasn't just a great cop, he was a heck of an investor. If I had to guess, he'll probably coach teams and do his day-trader thing, or whatever it is they call it."

"Stock market?" I asked, having had no idea. With Jericho's nod, I could feel the worry lift. "That's good. I can't imagine him and his family doing without."

I jumped at a sudden splash, Jericho unrolling a rope, an anchor plunking through the surface. The sea was calm, the roiling from our arrival dissipated. "By the way, we're here."

"Here?" I asked, the ride feeling like it had only lasted seconds. I spun around to get my bearings and found the southernmost tip of the Outer Banks to my right. A smile crept onto my face, helping me shed the mood. "I remember this spot."

"Hungry?" he asked.

"Picnic," I said. One of our favorite things, complete with a large wicker basket. I curled my fingers around the handle while Jericho unrolled a pillowy mattress for comfort and whatever else might come to mind.

"It's your favorite spot," he said, the ocean a blue-green and tranquil, the weather cooperating. "Remember the first time we came out here?"

"Sure I do," I answered, seeing a distant storm hugging the horizon, its thunder clouds far enough they wouldn't be a concern. His smile was fixed while he reworked the anchor's rope, the water shallow enough to catch the bottom and slow our drift. I peered over the side of the boat, fingertips gliding across the surface, searching the watery scene to see fish swimming in schools.

"All alone too," he said, briefly shading his eyes. A salty breeze brushed his hair back and lifted the bottom of his shirt. I could see the shape of his muscles while he guided a second anchor toward the ocean's bottom. I knew he'd been working out, the time off from daily patrols giving back the hours in his days. He raised his arms. "Touchdown. That'll keep the boat from spinning us round and round like a top."

"Look at you," I teased, pinching his bicep. He flexed for me and made a playful grunt. "I'd say your working out is working out."

"It helps." He flexed again, picking me up with his good arm, cradling me with the other. He lowered me slowly, the jokes waning, replaced with a kiss that was genuine to who we were together. I ran my fingers along the ragged scars that had nearly taken his other arm. In my mind, I saw what it had been like when we'd first met. The injuries severe, the operations and recovery significant. He didn't shy from my touch. Not like he had when we first got together. "It's a lot better now. I barely notice the pain anymore."

"You still feel it?" I asked, saddened to hear that the pain had followed him, that he still felt it. I ran my finger along the longest of the scars like it was a map to the memories of his wife's murder and the attack that nearly took his life. I kissed it, wishing it could take the tragedy away. Tragedies were a part of us, a part of our past and a part of who we become. I looked into his eyes, sunlight rippling across his face. "I'm sorry you have to be reminded of what happened."

"I still think about it." He returned the kiss, adding, "But it's different now."

"Good," I said, my stomach growling, the sound making me blush.

He cocked his head, joking, "Please, I've heard a lot worse." I playfully shoved him. He lifted the top of the basket to show the spread of food he'd prepared. He held up a large jar, brown with a yellow label. He put on a face as he spoke, "I even found you some of that Marmite."

"That'll rest the demons," I said, rubbing my stomach.

We dove into the basket, the sea air making us ravenous. "This is so good," he commented moments later, his mouth full.

"A chef who likes his own cooking," I said playfully, food satisfying our appetites, my nerves rising about the conversation I knew we had to have. And it was the reason I believed Jericho suggested the picnic. I put my food aside, starting it off, "About Philadelphia—"

Jericho stopped chewing and let his fork slide on the plate. He put it down and wiped his mouth, the anticipation unbearable. "I wanted to talk to you about it."

"Me first," I said, speaking fast, wanting to get the words out before he said anything else. I shook away the sting of emotion, but it didn't go far. It stuck with me as I went to him, my hands on his leg, my heart swelling as I tried to explain, "I'm sorry. I shouldn't have put you on the spot like that. It wasn't fair."

"Casey!?" he began.

I pressed my finger to his lips, needing to finish. "I love you! And I love my daughter." He dried my face, his touch gentle. "But she's also a grown woman and in love with Nichelle, who is fantastic... they're fantastic."

"Uh-huh," he said, rubbing my hands as I spoke. I felt my words tumbling awkwardly, their having sounded much better in my head. "You love them."

"I do!" I answered, repeating myself. "Which is why I think they'll be fine. They're great together, with or without me."

"Us," he said, correcting me. "With or without us."

"Huh?" I asked, unsure of what he meant, but continued. "What I'm trying to say is that I want to be wherever you want to be!"

Jericho lowered his face, his eyes near mine, and said, "They're great with *us*. Casey, I took the job in Philadelphia."

My body went rubbery with the weight of surprise. "You took the job!?" There was a flood of shock and surprise and joy and relief. And I had no idea which came first. "We're going?"

"I think we'll have to now," Jericho answered with a wink. "How would it look if I was late on my first day."

He kissed me hard and held me tight enough that I could feel his heart beating against my chest. I shook at the thought I'd possibly ruined something wonderful. But I hadn't. This wasn't just a picnic on the water. He knew we were leaving the Outer Banks and wanted one more time on the water.

"We can always come back," I told him, believing nothing was forever. "It doesn't matter where we end up."

"It doesn't." He kissed me again then we turned to face the far-off storm clouds. They marched east with barely a sound, the lightning spreading. "As long as we're together—"

"—then we'll stay together," I finished for him.

"What is that?" he asked, stretching his neck, muscles in his arms becoming taut.

"What is what?" I asked, the moment over, his warm touch gone.

"That?" He went to the bow, a pair of binoculars in hand, the patrol boat lifting with a growing swell. I shaded my eyes and saw a distant speck drifting on the water, a leaf floating aimlessly in a pond. It rose opposite of us, a wall of seawater hiding it briefly before reappearing. "Casey, I think it's a dinghy."

"A dinghy?" I sensed his alarm and searched for a yacht or fishing boat that it would have come from. "Might be that it broke free?"

"Possibly," he replied, his attentions fully distracted, our afternoon ending. "Or not."

"Want to call it in?" I asked, but then heard an anchor line ripped from the water. Our picnic on the ocean was canceled.

"I'll radio it." Jericho might have resigned his position in the Marine Patrol, but that was only a formality. It was just a line item with names and descriptions and Human Resources codes that got buried in bureaucratic paperwork. Outside, where it mattered, Jericho was like me. He was a cop. He'd always be one. Jericho put on an apologetic look, saying, "We'll postpone."

"We will," I said with growing curiosity, the dinghy easier to see, its pale shape bobbing freely and without direction. With the anchors on board, and our picnic stowed, I took a place next to the console, the motors sputtering alive. "Can you see anyone?"

Jericho handed me the binoculars, its touch cool on my fingers. He yelled over the motoring, "Hold on!" The boat chewing on the ocean as it went onto plane, the bow rising, the wind driving me backward. The rushing air turned instantly cold, the binoculars pressing against my eyeballs. The chop was too rough, and I lowered the glasses, relying on the line-of-sight visual we'd established.

"A little closer." Jericho navigated the swells, running

between them until we were a few yards from the dinghy. Ten feet from bow to stern, it was slatted with a wooden bench in the middle. A blue canvas covered the rear compartment, a part of it hanging limp over the transom, bare of any motor, the dinghy having no propulsion beyond a pair of oars lying in the middle.

"Grab hold if you can," he yelled.

"Looks to have broken free." I grabbed hold of one of the oarlocks while Jericho tied it off, pairing the dinghy to the Marine Patrol boat.

"Grab that canvas," he asked, busily securing the other end. "We don't need that dragging beneath the water and hitting a prop."

The tarp was wet from spray, slippery, the shape of a head forming beneath it while I pulled. My heart skipped, blood rushing with a start. "Jericho!?"

"Easy," he said, joining me while we carefully removed the cover. A pair of eyes appeared, a wide stare and filled with fright, baby-blues glistening wet and shining in the daylight. It was a boy and girl, about seven or eight, bodies tightly laced together like fingers. Their pale arms and legs were knotted in a hold, indistinguishable as to whose was whose. They had light-colored hair, almost white, and were thinly dressed in a shirt and short pants. Jericho didn't reach into the dinghy, keeping his distance, asking, "Hi there?"

Lower lips quivered, a cry stirring. I knelt next to Jericho, perching my elbows, and asked, "My name is Casey. This is Jericho. What's your name?"

"Thomas," the boy said, his voice shaky, his lips cracked and peeling. The children were dehydrated but had used the tarp to protect themselves from the sun. A litter of empty plastic bottles surrounded their feet, a faint smell of urine mixing with sea air. "This is my little sister, Tabitha."

"Hi, Thomas," I said, handing him a bottle of water. The

bundle unfolded some, an arm appearing from the middle, bone-thin fingers stretching to retrieve it. "Hello, Tabitha."

Jericho worked the radio, calling in a report, background noise filling with a raspy squelch as he rattled off the coordinates. Tabitha said nothing, her eyes glued on Jericho. That's when I noticed her gaze was fixed, seeing through the world as though it were an empty space. Shock came to mind, the trembling lip a symptom as well.

"She won't say anything," Thomas told me.

"No? Why is that?" I asked, concerned. "Why won't Tabitha say anything?"

His chin quivered again. "Because we saw them kill Mommy and Dad."

A LETTER FROM B.R. SPANGLER

Thank you so much for reading *Their Resting Place*, Detective Casey White Book 8. I'm very grateful to have had the opportunity to write a new book in the series and to have included the Outer Banks as the main setting. I'm even more grateful to have readers who enjoy the tales spun up around such a fun and exciting cast of characters.

I hope you have enjoyed reading them as much as I have enjoyed writing them. If you did enjoy it, and want to keep up to date with all my latest releases, just sign up at the following link. Your email address will never be shared and you can unsubscribe at any time.

www.bookouture.com/br-spangler

Want to help with the Detective Casey White series and Book 8? I would be very grateful if you could write a review, and it also makes such a difference helping new readers to discover one of my books for the first time.

Do you have a question or comment? I'd be happy to answer. You can reach me on my Facebook page, through Twitter, or my website. I've included the links below.

Happy Reading,

B.R. Spangler

KEEP IN TOUCH WITH B.R. SPANGLER

www.brspangler.com

 facebook.com/authorbrianspangler
twitter.com/BR_Spangler

Printed in Great Britain
by Amazon

29867814R00135